WALKING THE WILDSIDE

"You aren't traveling in the mortal world now, Nyssa. Magic doesn't obey human rules. That bit of wood you have in your hand is a beacon. Any of us who walks in dreams can feel it when it moves. It's headed north, taking you to its owner." The man—if that's what he was—began walking toward her. His pace was slow, but it quickly ate up the distance between them. His shadowy cape was looking more and more like wings. "I'm here to take you sanctuary."

"Sanctuary?" Nyssa watched, fascinated and terrified, as he somehow managed to mount the stage with a single stride. She wanted to run but knew she wouldn't be able. Whatever this man was, he didn't belong to the race of Homo sapiens.

Two words came to her: Night demon.

STILL LIFE

MELANIE JACKSON

LOVE SPELL NEW YORK CITY

LOVE SPELL®

August 2004

Published by

Dorchester Publishing Co., Inc.
200 Madison Avenue
New York, NY 10016

ISBN 0-505-52608-5

Printed in the United States of America.

Visit us on the web at www.dorchesterpub.com.

For the goblin Malek—
I hope we're still friends.

STILL LIFE

Prologue

Nyssa leaned forward, staring intently, but not touching the case before her. The distressed monks of this monastery had once thought the skeleton resting inside was a holy relic: an angel miraculously fallen to earth and preserved in the trunk of a tree in their garden. But they were wrong—so wrong! True, the thing had had wings. But *El Angel de Sangre Cristo* was not cherubim or seraphim, or any angel at all. Anyone who knew the history of the Unseelie Court and their alliance with the goblins would have recognized it for what it was.

Nyssa inhaled slowly. An unpleasant ghost scent lingered in the air. The now absent body, the almost mummified flesh must have stunk, in spite of the herbs it had been packed in—as well it should. Legend said that tree hobgoblins were odoriferous from birth to death, and they grew worse thereafter. These particular winged hobgoblins, bred by the great Goblin King Gofimbel, were supposedly especially smell-laden when their flesh and muscle were stripped away.

Nyssa turned back to her parchment and made a

small note in her journal in a version of shorthand that she had developed. Though usually given to prolixity in her research notes, she kept all written references to her discovery brief and obscure—secretive even. They were a memory aid meant to trigger sequences of her thoughts and observations, nothing that would give anyone else a suggestion of what she was truly thinking or planning. Nothing that could get her committed to an institution for the insane if they were ever discovered.

She leaned over the ancient parchment and inhaled deeply. The ink smelled too. The whole monastery did, but the record rooms were especially dusty, filled with dry, desiccated, dead parchment—and living knowledge. She had come to love the scent of history. It smelled like the nearest thing to immortality that any human could know. It smelled like the answer to all her questions.

Looking up from her illuminated map, Nyssa caught sight of herself in a tarnished mirror whose rippled surface was slowly decaying. Even in the poor light she could plainly see the gray veil cast over her dark hair, shoulders, and hands. She smiled slightly at the indistinct image, not at all concerned that the filthy patina of the centuries had probably ruined her last good dress. Clothing was replaceable.

As she herself was?

Nyssa stopped smiling. Once again she felt it: the dangerous and crazy longing so profound that it cast a shadow over her soul. She hadn't managed to entirely silence the frightened voices pleading in the back of her mind. They went on murmuring, louder even than the blood rushing in her ears. One of them was her mother's. They all said to leave this matter be.

But was she really going to do that? How badly did she need the truth? How important was it to fill those holes in her memory? To remember her childhood? Considering where her research was taking her, wasn't she perhaps better off not knowing?

She laid her pen aside and began to walk, moving along the sagging shelves weighted down with the burdens of age and heavy books and small apothecary jars filled with things like nightshade, hellebore, and nux vomican that the ancient monks had used for healing. Staring at nothing in particular as she strolled, she tried to think clearly, unemotionally.

It was difficult to think at all. Prudence had long ago lost the struggle with curiosity; it couldn't survive if she was going to investigate the things she did. But the sight of this stolen skeleton's resting place had started renewed caution percolating through her nervous system. She wasn't dealing with speculation and myth anymore; not just dreams. This was real, the confirmation of the legend she had been chasing.

It was also potentially deadly. And, as they said about human existence: Life is short, death is very, very long. A wise woman would consider her goals and strategies carefully before rushing north to Nevada to ask those magical creatures, the fey, for help with this mystery. However, the same "they" who said comfortless things about death also believed that the enemy of one's enemy could be one's friend.

Of course, one had to always keep in mind that those sages had been talking about *human* relations. Who knew how the fey felt about such things? Their new parliament in Cadalach might think Nyssa as great a danger as the goblins. They didn't shoot spies there, but they probably did something with them. Seelie or unseelie, the fey had ways of dealing with intruders. And if they confirmed what Nyssa suspected, they probably would see her as a spy—which she was, even if she was spying for her own knowledge and not to help any lutin empire.

The air around her suddenly took on an electric charge and she began to hear a faint buzzing like a poorly tuned radio. The temperature also began falling and the air shimmered like a mirage.

"Damn."

The ghosts had found her again, the real ones. She could never escape them for long. Shadows began growing everywhere—even places where there was no light source to cast them. The darkness was beginning to pool, to take shape. It was time to go. She didn't need a spiritual entourage on this journey.

She returned to her journal and quickly put her notes away. She wished that she could use a PDA, but she had found that the mini-computers didn't work well around her. It wasn't intentional, but her extrasensory gifts tended to drain the energy out of batteries.

She needed more time! Just a few more hours here so that she could dreamwalk from this ancient building with its creaking, arthritic skeleton and basement full of untapped memories. It was the last place that the bones had rested, and the memory would be strongest here. But . . . no, she couldn't chance it. Time travel was a risky business even if the journey was made only with the mind. A persistent ghost

4

could confuse her, lead her astray in an effort to end its own misery. The danger was very real because of her selective amnesia. She didn't always know what was real and what was illusion, what was her memory or what was someone else's.

However, there *was* something she would need if she were to attempt a walk away from this monastery with any more answers. Nyssa looked about furtively, then got out a penknife. It took her only a moment to shave a sliver off the tree trunk that had held the winged hobgoblin. The wood vibrated in her hand, still alive, still distressed at the use to which it had been put, even two hundred years after being severed from its roots.

She would dreamwalk tomorrow night, after she was away from the monastery and the revenants of those dead brothers whose souls had gotten attached to the thing of power they had kept on their altar and then in their archives.

"You can go on now," she whispered to them, trying to be as kind to their gibbering souls as her mother would have been. "It's gone, and it won't be coming back. You're free. Depart."

It wasn't a lie. The thing they sought wouldn't be coming back here. The hobgoblin had gone somewhere. It had had centuries while captive here to decide where it wanted to go. One could speculate endlessly about the creature's plans, but one thing was certain: It wouldn't be coming back here, to its prison. Not voluntarily.

Chapter One

Jack Frost had a face that bore the burden of leadership well. Many were tempted to say that he was born to the role, and then they eventually realized that he actually *had* been born to it. He'd always been meant to lead The People. The change was that he was a death fey, and he was leading everyone while they were still alive. And he was doing his level best to keep them that way. It was a terrible burden. He had become a puppet-master, taking over the strings that once had been held by the Fates. And he was learning it was a full-time job not crossing the strands of his people's lives—especially when his people now included those of both the Seelie and Unseelie Courts. The realms of light and darkness had never mixed easily. They still didn't.

Io found Jack sitting under the restless oaks that guarded one of the lesser entrances to the tomhnafurach, Cadalach Fortress. He liked to listen to their leathery leaves rubbing against one another as their limbs danced in the moonlight when the moon was full.

"How is Zayn doing with the baby-sitting?" he asked his wife, smiling with pleasure at the way she looked in the silvery light.

"It's a good thing that he's a healer. I heard something that sounded distinctly like a cast-iron skillet hitting a rock-hard head."

"Wham-bam doesn't mean any harm, but she is a bit rough, a bit—"

"Yes, she certainly is." Io sat down beside her husband and took his hand. "But it's only a phase. Trolls have their terrible twos just like everyone else. And don't call her Wham-bam. You know Chloe doesn't like it."

Jack nodded. "I know. It's just that I can't think of the child as 'Clarissa.' "

"Yeah, I can see why. It's a strange choice of names. But at least Zayn talked her out of 'Judy.' "

Jack grunted. "She will probably grow out of looking like a capybara too. Eventually."

"I hope so. It would be better if she looked purely troll. At least they don't have beards."

"And how is our own offspring?"

"Mathias was eating like a pig and is now sleeping like a bear in deep winter."

"Both things for which to be profoundly thankful."

"Indeed." Io looked at Jack. "So, why are you hiding out here?"

"I'm not hiding. I'm thinking."

"Ah. And why are you thinking out here?"

"Because I don't like the things that the shian is

8

whispering to me, and Cyra and I thought I might consult the wind and stars for a change."

Io sobered. "What is it saying? It isn't anything about Roman, is it?"

Jack shook his head. "No, so far Roman doesn't show any signs of vampirism. The voices are talking about an escaped hobgoblin—"

"Another one?"

"Yes, a particularly nasty one called Qasim. He was Gofimbel's right arm, a real piece of work that the Unseelie queen finally captured and locked up about two centuries ago. And if that weren't enough, there are currently lutin spies in the area. That's just a nuisance to us right now, those spies, but there is also a useful but dangerous female who is headed our way with some sort of information we need." Jack looked up at the swaying oak branches. "I think I am going to send Abrial to intercept and escort her."

"Abrial? The Executioner?"

"He's not an executioner anymore. Queen Mabigon is dead. He hasn't killed anyone in years," Jack said mildly.

"Right, Mabigon is dead, so no one holds his leash anymore."

"He holds his own leash," Jack answered, voice still tranquil. "And he isn't hurting anyone. I'd know if he were. We answer to the same maker. Half of me is dark fey as well."

"Fair enough." Io exhaled slowly. "You think this female is a danger to us, then."

"Maybe. I know she's a potential danger to the goblins. And if H.U.G. finds out about her, they will probably want her too. Until we hear what she has to say, it behooves us to protect her."

"You're going to bring her *here*? Then you're sure that she's fey—or at least human. I've never heard of the shian acting this way unless it was warning of a goblin invasion."

"No, I suspect she isn't," Jack admitted slowly. "Or at least that she isn't *entirely* human or fey. But the shian is certain she needs to come here regardless."

"Then she must come, I suppose. Don't mind me. I'm just nervous with all the tension in the air these days. Maybe it's the approaching solstice that has the cosmos disturbed. Frankly, I am not certain that Seelie and Unseelie were ever meant to live and work together."

"I don't think we have a choice. Not now. Our numbers simply don't allow for the traditional separation. Anyway, you and I have dealt together very well."

"*Hmph.*" Io snorted. Then she did something very unusual and actually questioned her husband's judgment a second time. This told Jack that she was indeed very disturbed.

"Jack, I know that we have to work together and build trust and all that, but is it wise to send Abrial to deal with this? He hasn't dealt with the physical world much. He's also a bit cold and scary—not the best emissary to send to a woman on the run who is probably already very frightened."

"Yes, I know. I took that into consideration. But this woman is different, some sort of ghost-talker, and she does dreamwalking—into the past as well as the present."

"A dreamwalker to the past? She actually time travels?"

"Yes. Not in body, but in mind. And so, I think the son of a night demon who walks in dreams can probably handle her unique nature best. And he'll be of more help than anyone if she gets into trouble in her sleep."

"Trouble? You mean H.U.G. psychics."

"No. *Bigger* trouble."

Bigger trouble? He meant Qasim, the hobgoblin; and Io knew it. There had also been talk of the other goblins using psychics as mental bodyguards. It hadn't helped the hive in Sin City, but most goblin cities were hiring better talent these days. And it was only a matter of time before any defensive weapons of goblins became offensive ones.

"Is the hobgoblin near here? Maybe it's following her." Io's voice was troubled, and she was careful not to name the hobgoblin, since some names were invocations that carried power. She didn't say anything about Mathias, either, but Jack knew his wife was worried about their son and the other children being placed in danger.

"No. At least not as far as anyone here can tell. We don't see any patterns yet—and Thomas is keeping a close watch."

"I hope you're right," Io answered, and Jack had a sudden auditory flash of an Alice Cooper song from *Welcome To My Nightmare*. He and Io's telepathic conversations were rare these days, but they happened occasionally when she was upset.

"Me too. I'd hate to send a night demon after an entirely innocent woman."

Io was silent, but Jack knew that she was thinking it might be a bad idea to send this particular night demon after anyone. Abrial was beautiful, but he was very, very scary.

Chapter Two

Abrial's hair was long and black, a tone so dark that it seemed to filter the very light out of the air around him. It swallowed illumination like a black hole and made him appear to be always in shadow. His eyes were also dark and strongly resembled a lunar eclipse. The irises were stained the same black as the pupils, except at the edges, where they were rimmed in gleaming silver. On the rare occasion when he was amused, it sometimes looked like starbursts were exploding in his eyes. Only a fool would mistake him for human—but he had discovered that there were fools aplenty wandering in the physical world. And many of them were women. They believed his lies about contact lenses.

His body was long and trendily lean, while still being well-muscled. He was all gaunt angles and hard planes. Photographers drooled over him. Agents were always trying to sign him up as a client—model, actor, movie star; they were certain they could get him any work he wanted. Had he been interested in a day job, he might have taken them up on it. But he had other labors to amuse him, what he liked to think of as his continuing education.

It wasn't intentional, but since he looked like a fashion plate no matter what he wore, he indulged himself and dressed as he pleased. Most often he chose to wear black leather. Or nothing. Since he was going into the human world that morning, he had opted for leather—which, as a UV filter, you couldn't beat.

Abrial respected Jack Frost and understood the reasons for the death fey to forge an alliance among his race's traditional enemies. But even without that, he would have agreed to this assignment. It involved Nyssa.

Usually he preferred dealing with evil people, and he specialized in invading their sleep. Nothing was quite as much fun as messing with the wicked—human or fey—in their dreams before he executed them.

At the very least, if he had to go after sane and reasonable humans, he liked something with political ramifications—warning caesars of impending doom, giving Constantine visions and making him change religions, scaring Torquemada into a heart attack—just because he was The Executioner and could do so if he wanted. He liked to work on things cataclysmic, maybe to avert a holocaust or two. If only he'd been there when Eve was being tempted by the serpent, he could have laid some real Fear of God dreams on her. Now *that* would have been a genuine kick!

No, nice and probably human lady psychics just weren't his usual gig. But this woman, Nyssa Laszlo, was something different; she had intrigued him for a long time. For months he had shadowed her from a distance, tailing her through her dreamwalks whenever she stayed in the dream realms of the present. For some reason, he couldn't follow her into the past. He had tried, but had found himself shut out by an iron gate that stretched out and up into infinity.

It had irked him at first, that she could elude him this way, because no one should be beyond his reach in the kingdoms of dreams; and he had wondered for weeks what she was doing as she strolled into the past looking excited, then returned looking pleased. Finally, he had caught her coming home while carrying a forgotten mental prop from her journey. A music book, annotated by a Master. She must have been distracted that night, to make such a mistake, because it had never happened again. Maybe she had just seen Mozart die. In any event, Abrial's question about her forays was answered: She was taking piano lessons.

He was at once reluctantly charmed and disappointed. Humans! When someone with such a short life span was given the chance to see all of history, why would they choose to waste the opportunity and take music lessons? Unless that was just experimentation, early boot camp for more serious expeditions? Maybe she was like Prometheus, planning on snatching someone's divine fire, and she had put herself into training for the venture with more modest early goals.

That seemed like the most reasonable explanation, and since he enjoyed hearing her ritual meditational playing before she journeyed, he continued to follow her at night. He made every effort to show up early and hovered just outside the place where she staged her dream trance, so he could listen to her tickle the ivories before she went walking.

As the weeks went by, and as his attraction and frustration had grown equally, he thought more than once about approaching her. But he knew from past experience that unless he seduced them in a gentle dream, where his body remained hidden, most human women were more apt to be panicked than pleased when he spoke to them. Maybe it was the wings. Or maybe they sensed what he was: a bringer of death and punishment.

Anyway, there were other problems with the idea. Contact on any level had consequences, and on the metaphysical level of dreamwalking it encouraged telepathic lines of communication. Eventually two such dreamwalkers would become almost empathic— great for sex, but lousy for privacy. History had taught him that lovers eventually learned too much about him and could not handle who and what he was. There was also the fact that humans lived brutally short lives. He didn't need another loss. Losing a lover was somehow actually worse than losing a pet.

And yet, there was definitely something about Nyssa. He hadn't met anyone as interesting or driven since Joan of Arc. (A pity *that* hadn't worked out better, but the Fates had had it in for the French woman from the get-go.)

In a moment of resignation, he had finally decided that the choice about contacting Nyssa required some more thought and a better grasp of what she was up to with her noctambulations. He'd decided to consider the matter again when the moon was full and he was at the height of his powers.

Unfortunately, before he made up his mind about dropping in on her dreams for a get-acquainted chat, her pattern of behavior changed. There were no more happy jaunts to and from the past for music lessons. Nyssa had begun traveling later at night, and she no longer looked excited when she disappeared behind the iron gate into The Yesterdays. She was frightened—nervous going in and often grim when she came out. He could almost smell the fear clinging to her at times, but she kept going back. Her hobby or mission or whatever it was had become an obsession.

Human obsessions interested Abrial immensely. They almost always led to trouble, and to opportunity for such as he. Thus it really, really annoyed him that he couldn't follow her. But until he made a mental connection to her, The Yesterdays would remain closed off.

Abrial had started paying more attention then to her dreamwalking in the present, and he also began looking in on her normal dreams, though he never showed himself openly. He soon discovered that her current-day metaphysical journeys had branched out from visiting public and private libraries that specialized in folklore to dropping in on the Humans Under Ground *in spiritu* and ransacking their bookshelves and computer files with the help of a friendly poltergeist. It also seemed that she was questioning ghosts, in particular those shades who had been psychic. They maintained that power they'd had on earth, perhaps because they couldn't bring themselves to leave the earthly world behind.

Her normal dreams were even more interesting. They centered around a gloomy woodland that didn't look like anything in the human world, yet wasn't any place Abrial had ever seen in his journeys among the

17

fey lands. He couldn't swear to it, but he was fairly sure that it was something ancient and lutin. Sometimes he could hear a woman crying—and it was not Nyssa. It was some other woman, someone Nyssa knew and cared about. Someone who was lost or in prison.

Days had progressed, and the nights too. He'd grown impatient and yet ever more intrigued by Nyssa's mysterious activities, and by the woman herself. It was increasingly difficult to spy on her, because she was as nervy as a cat and on constant lookout for ghosts or other psychics; but he managed to catch the odd glimpse of the things she was investigating. Her search narrowed and the topic shocked and fascinated him—two things he almost never was.

Hard to credit it, but the little lady was after information about hobgoblins—tree goblins, specifically. These goblins had been imprisoned long ago by Queen Mabigon, with the consent of the goblin kings of old, because with Gofimbel dead, even other lutins were frightened by these creatures' powers and perversity.

The fact that one was rumored to have recently escaped from its prison and was again on the loose had to be connected to Nyssa's search.

Then, one night while in The Yesterdays, Abrial had sensed Nyssa found something that deeply agitated her. She had bolted back through the gates into the present with something clutched in her hands, and had suddenly turned her fevered eyes on Cadalach. She hadn't ventured close to that tomhna-furach on her dreamwalk, but Abrial had felt the moment when the shian became aware of her astral probing and marked her for observation.

18

It had also been the moment when the lutins somehow noticed her. They had reached out from behind their psychic gates and turned covetous eyes her way. Abrial had felt the ripples from both magical factions—the lutins and the feys—pass by, metaphysical queries and traps sent her way. Those traps Nyssa had so far avoided with the help of ghosts, but they were getting ever more deadly and devious. She wouldn't be able to avoid them forever. The lady needed help.

Thus, when Jack had approached him the next night with instructions to intercept this woman on her way back from Mexico, and to bring her to Cadalach, it hadn't come as any great surprise to Abrial. If the shian knew something, then Jack Frost and Cyra Delphin knew it too. And once they knew everything metaphysical they could glean from their fortress home, it would have been only a matter of minutes before Cyra's hacker husband, Thomas, found out everything there was to learn about Nyssa in cyberspace. He'd passed that information on.

Abrial was already acquainted with most of the enemies that the dreamwalking Nyssa Laszlo faced— and the list really was formidable. But just to make it interesting, Thomas had also discovered and relayed to him that the western headquarters of the FBI was looking for Nyssa. Who the puppet-master was behind this governmental search, Thomas did not yet know, but there were two top contenders—badasses both. Whether it was the leader of H.U.G. or King Carbon of the L.A. hive, the news wasn't good.

The situation was in fact fraught with deadly danger. That was perfect. Abrial did love a challenge, and he was quite looking forward to the assignment. He'd get Nyssa tonight, while she was busy ransacking whatever library next caught her eye.

He suspected that his interrupting her research into the arcane wouldn't endear him to her. It never did. Still, if he had to ruin somebody's night, he preferred that it be hers. Eventually she would figure out that he was saving her life, and she'd be grateful. Besides, it was past time for them to meet—face to face as well as in dreams. And she could start explaining just what she wanted to know about one of the nastiest creatures who had ever roamed the planet.

Abrial really, really wanted to know.

Chapter Three

Technology went awry around Nyssa often enough that she had come to dread the day that she might need major surgery. The problem was: when she slept, dreamwalked, or just got excited, she had a bad habit of sucking the power out of nearby things like batteries or even electrical outlets—often with explosive results. She had tried getting help at the Bracebridge Institute back in the days when she was freelancing as Margot Mimm, Psychic Business Consultant, and as Pandora Blaze, sometime tea-leaf reader at the Cosmic Conscience Tea House and Spa, where she made better tips and didn't arouse the wrath of the Better Business Bureau, as Margaret Mimm did. But Bracebridge could do nothing for her. Or *would* do nothing for her. And now that goblins had taken over, she could never go back.

At home, she had surge protection on all her major appliances and didn't use any more machines than absolutely necessary for daily life. She had no computer and hadn't worn a watch in years. She didn't fly. If a cell phone could take out a navigation system, there was no knowing what she might do if surprised with a bit of turbulence.

Now, safe in her dingy motel room, she prepared for her dreamwalk. It was important that she be back in her body before dawn or she'd be too fatigued to travel, so she worked swiftly, unplugging the old television and the bedside lamp. She couldn't do anything about the bulb in the bathroom, since it was mounted in the ceiling inside a wire cage, but she shut the door just in case it exploded. Lastly, she closed the drapes and pinned the gap closed, and then double-locked the door.

She sat down on the floor away from any furniture. Nyssa could dreamwalk while reclining but felt more in control—less vulnerable—if she sat up while putting herself under. The whole process was still a bit disconcerting, like working magic. One of her early mentors, a psychic who was a speed freak who dreaded sleeping and eventually overdosed in his efforts to keep awake, had explained it to her this way: There was a sort of underground river of the subconscious that flowed in the back of everyone's mind. Most people never knew it was there. But some—psychics and crazies, mainly—learned how to travel it.

What was she? Psychic? Crazy? Both? She had never heard of anyone like herself, no one who could travel to the past. No one who talked to ghosts.

She looked around the narrow room. Without the lights on, the only illumination came from outside, passing through the bars on the windows. Surely those bars were in violation of the fire code, but this night, Nyssa was glad of them. The broken streetlight gave the rented space a very film noir feel, changed it into a setting where you knew bad guys lurked waiting to get the girl. And though the film metaphor was somewhat unpleasantly suggestive of there being an audience, this was nothing new; the feeling that she was on stage had been there from the first time she discovered her talent for traveling the subconscious river against the natural flow of time. She just had to remind herself repeatedly that no one *was* actually watching. It was all in her head, little Freudian gremlins trying to vex her for their own neurotic pleasure.

It was a pity that her mother had died without explaining everything to her. The woman had told Nyssa about ghosts and how to ignore them—she'd had to, since they had apparently clustered about Nyssa's cradle and later her bed every time there was a storm; and finally they had started following her to school, a troop of invisible friends who got her in trouble with the teacher. But she had said nothing about her daughter inheriting the ability to dreamwalk. She'd said nothing about goblins, either. Or why Nyssa couldn't recall large parts of her childhood—like where she had lived before starting school, or even how old she really was when she'd finally begun attending kindergarten. She'd been more than five. A lot more, though she hadn't looked it.

Wherever Bysshe Laszlo had gone after her death, it wasn't to The Yesterdays; and she wasn't a ghost on the earthly plane whom Nyssa could summon for answers, either. Since no body had ever been found, just the remains of Bysshe's small boat near Catalina Island, Nyssa sometimes wondered if her mother was really dead. . . .

She shook herself. This wasn't the time to wander down this troublesome path. She needed to focus on more dangerous things.

Repelled by her stolen relic, but knowing it was necessary, she retrieved the sliver of wood she had shaved from the hobgoblin's prison. Taking it from her purse, she held it in her left hand, palm facing upward.

"Last chance to reconsider," her dream self said softly. This was dangerous: taking a walk while holding a thing or power without a ground to anchor her. *"Always swim with a buddy,"* her speed-addict mentor had said. But Nyssa saw what she was doing more as tightrope-walking without a net.

It was better with some safety precautions, of course, but there wasn't anyone who could be with her—there hadn't been for a long time. And she wouldn't have asked any of her old friends to risk themselves anyway. She would just have to rely on her mother's talisman ring to help her focus, and hope it was shield enough.

"I have to know about Qasim. Let's get started," she whispered to her dream self, finally naming the creature she was after. *Qasim.* She would have to be careful, once she was under, not to say his name or to even think it. She didn't want to call him to her. Not yet. Maybe not ever.

There were many ways to put oneself into a trance state; chanting, staring into a dish of still water, even the traditional swinging pocket watch. But she preferred to play Rachmaninoff's *Prelude* in C-sharp minor on an imaginary piano. The eerie, melancholy piece usually suited her mood when she went walking in The Yesterdays. In real life, she had difficulty mastering the music because she had small hands that couldn't span the keys properly. But in dreams she could lengthen her fingers and play the piece perfectly.

She started as she always did; envisioning and beginning her concert in a void where there was only herself and her red piano. Slowly, she allowed detail to creep in. A concert hall would form around her, red velvet drapes, a gilded ceiling dripping a crystal chandelier. The upright of her childhood home would be replaced with a black baby grand, and finally a white full-sized grand that gleamed with a metallic, automotive finish.

Rows of slightly worn seats, also in red velvet, would come into focus—all empty, of course. She didn't allow her imagination to invite any of the psychics she had come to know, although they were the only ones who might hear her metaphysical concert. No one knew that she played piano with such skill. How could she ever explain this gift when everyone knew that she had only taken up the instrument six months before? How could she confess to the few friends she still had that she had learned from the Masters, traveling back in time to witness those great ones' techniques, and sitting in on their lessons with long-dead pupils? Beethoven, Bach, Mozart—she had heard them all, seen them all. None of those other psychics could do that. Something about her was very different. Unique. Not quite human, she feared.

Finally, the piece was done. The echoes of the *Prelude* died away. Nyssa stood up slowly, pushing back the bench. She turned as she always did but this time did not walk down the left side aisle of the empty auditorium. She chose the right side. Probably it didn't matter. The gesture was symbolic. But this time all would be very different. She had no way of knowing what she would find beyond these new gates she would seek out, but the odds were that it would be something no living human had ever seen before. Tonight she was going to visit the goblin lands.

"What? No encore?"

Nyssa stopped in midstep and went into shock. Sitting in the front row of the auditorium was a man . . . a creature . . . a shadow. She stared at him in stupid disbelief as he slowly raised his hands—yes, hands, not talons; and only two of them, she was relieved to see—and began applauding.

"Excellently done," the deep voice said. "Rachmaninoff. I haven't heard that played as well since the Maestro himself died. You're improving."

"Who are you?" she whispered, looking quickly over her shoulder into the shadowy wings of the auditorium, wondering if she could escape that way if she needed a quick exit.

"My name is not something we will mention here." The man stood—unfolded himself, really. He was tall and lean and brought to mind some kind of raptor. Perhaps it was the leather cape he wore, which looked a lot like bat wings growing out of his back. "I do hate to spoil your plans for the evening, but I am afraid that I can't let you go outside. The goblins are on to you now, and the hobgoblin you seek has been warned in a vision that you are coming tonight. I couldn't get a clear look at him, but he seems to be in an unhealthy state of excitement. I'd normally predict a heart attack in his near future—but he doesn't really have a heart anymore. Queen Mabigon removed it before she shut him in his prison, and no one is certain just where the thing is."

"But that's impossible." Nyssa's voice was barely a whisper. "This is impossible."

"No, it's quite possible," the stranger replied. "She did it all the time—a little preventative measure to ensure against premature resurrection. They say it's hard to keep a good man down, but a bad man is even harder."

"I mean, how could he be warned? I'm going to The Yesterdays. The Past. It's the place of what already happened, and what I do or say doesn't change things, so he can't know." She said the words but knew they weren't true. Somehow, the impossible had occurred: She had been discovered. This man standing in her own mental construct proved it. And if she could travel to The Yesterdays, it was only reasonable to think that someone else might be able to as well.

The Yesterdays had ghosts too, and they liked to gossip. Could that be what this man was—not a living being who still walked the earth, but a spirit who went between the two worlds? It would explain how he had gotten close to her without raising any alarm.

"Yes, you go into the past. But like you, your enemies have found a way to bend the rules. All they have to do is warn your quarry in the past that you will be coming on this night. And he can take action any time he wants, now that he's free and knows where you will be."

"But how did they find me? How did *you* find me? I don't understand."

"You aren't traveling in the mortal world now.

Magic doesn't obey human rules. That bit of wood you have in your hand is a beacon. Any of us who walks in dreams can feel it when it moves. It's headed north, taking you to its owner." The man—if that's what he was—began walking toward her. His pace was slow but quickly ate up the distance between them. His shadowy cape was looking more and more like wings. "I'm here to take you to sanctuary."

"Sanctuary?" Nyssa watched, fascinated and terrified, as he somehow managed to mount the stage with a single stride. She wanted to run but knew she wouldn't be able. Whatever this man was, he didn't belong to the race of homo sapiens.

Two words came to her: Night demon.

"Yes, a place where you may be safe. For a time, at least."

"And if I don't want to go to sanctuary?" *With you.*

He smiled slightly, a twisting of lips that might have been meant to put her at ease but was completely comfortless. "Then I'll have to take you against your will. If you stay here, you will probably die. Or be imprisoned. Personally, I would hope for death rather than a stay in a goblin penal complex. They're positively medieval in their notions of proper treatment of prisoners."

Nyssa opened her mouth to reply, but then three things happened almost simultaneously: A heavy knock fell on the auditorium door. It was slow, like a death knell, and it shook the whole building with visible shock waves that distorted the air. Secondly, Nyssa finally saw the eyes on the man before her— black pits that looked as if they had swallowed whole universes—and they riveted her attention, even with

the pounding that filled the air. Lastly, and most terri-
fyingly, she felt a blinding pain in her left hand as
something stabbed through it.

Instantly she was back in her motel room, jerked
back to reality by pain and something else. Horror
held her transfixed as she watched the splinter of
wood she had clasped in her hand burrow into her
palm and start traveling toward her wrist, wriggling
like a snake beneath her skin. Unable to help herself,
Nyssa opened her mouth to scream.

Impossibly, a long tanned hand snaked out with inhuman speed and gripped her wrist like a tourniquet,
cutting off the wood's path. Another hand appeared,
its fingernails transformed into short claws. Before
Nyssa could protest or even gasp, the hooked nail of
the creature's index finger was cutting a line in her
flesh and those tanned digits were burrowing under
her skin. They withdrew an instant later, the bloodied
sliver pinched between thumb and forefinger. The
wood writhed like a centipede.

"A nasty bit of work. It was headed for your heart,
you know," the dark-voiced man said. "And that is
very interesting, very interesting indeed. Why would
a fragment of a hobgoblin's prison want to lodge in
your heart?"

Pain from her wound finally registered, and Nyssa
gave a small cry. She tried to pull back, but the long
hands had already put aside the miniature wooden
parasite and were enfolding the cut in her wrist, slowing the flow of blood. His claws, if they had ever actually been there, had retreated.

"Who are you?" she asked again.

"You are very lucky that Jack sent me," the man

said, not offering any sympathy with his tone and not answering her question.

"I don't *feel* lucky," she said. A wave of dizziness passed over her. She slumped against the wall, trying to see if the door was still locked. It appeared to be.

"I'm sure you don't. Why don't you go to sleep for a while? You need time to heal, and we need to move before the goblins and the FBI get here."

Both words, *goblins* and *FBI,* were things to which she needed to pay attention, but it was suddenly too much effort to focus. "I don't want to sleep," she tried to say, but her tongue was thickening and growing clumsy. She could feel something warm and velvety, but definitely foreign, wrapping itself around her brain stem, taking over control of her body and mind. "It isn't safe. I dream . . ."

"Too bad. I'll work faster if you're out of it for a bit and not asking a lot of questions. Don't worry. It won't be for long, and I'll watch over you."

"But you don't understand." Nyssa felt something, as if hands were gently strangling her thoughts, and then she fell into a void. It wasn't a scary place, being warm and feeling like living velvet, but she knew that she wasn't really in the void of normal sleep, just inside a dark place in this man's mind. She tried to claw her way back out. Impossible. The darkness swaddled her, not harming her but still implacable. She was down and would stay down until he let her up.

She made one last attempt to talk to the stranger, to warn him that violent things sometimes happened when she slept, but no words could rise out of the deep where he had sent her.

Chapter Four

When Nyssa next opened her eyes it was to find dawn light had filled the motel room. There was a brief moment when she flirted with the idea that everything had been a hallucination brought about by the dreamwalk. But if that were the case, then her hallucination was still with her. And it had bandaged her arm.

"Who are you?" she asked a third time as she struggled upright, hoping that the rules of magic would hold true and he would be compelled to finally answer her question.

It worked, or something did. This time the dark man replied, formally, as he continued packing her clothes: "I am called Abrial. I am the son of Ahriman—sometimes called Acain or Friar Rush. My father was rather well known to the Zoroastrians, Mayans, and medieval monks, though the Christian monks had him and his job description all wrong." The deep voice was reasonable, if it spoke obscurely. "It wasn't he who introduced death into the world. Nor did he compel anyone to sin or vice. It has always been about free will, and careless people attempting to escape responsibility for their actions." Nyssa's duffel was zipped up and set by the door; then her dark companion began wiping down the room with a dry washcloth.

"I don't have cooties," she said.

"That remains to be seen," he answered.

Nyssa looked at him carefully. He was wearing some biker's outfit made of black leather, but there didn't seem to be any bat wings hiding beneath. Maybe that part *had* been a hallucination. Heaven knew that she wasn't certain what she really remembered and what she had dreamed anymore.

"I recall the myth of Ahriman," she answered when her surprise and dizziness had faded a bit. "He and a female familiar, Az, used sex and drunkenness to weaken the intellect of the monks, and to sway people to lives of vice."

"So they say." Abrial's odd smile came again. "Good old Auntie Az. Nobody could sway like she did."

"Auntie Az?" Nyssa repeated.

"Not the sort of woman you want to spend summer vacations with, really, but fun in an awful sort of way. Did you use the phone?" he asked. "If you did, we'll have to take it with us. A bit of your breath might still be inside, and we can't risk them snatching it."

"No. Who would I call?" Nyssa glanced down at her bandaged arm. The pain was present but bearable. It sort of blended with her overall discomfort. Her skin felt as if it had been stretched tight over a drum instead of laid over muscles and bones. She also had what felt like a slight hangover. She was willing to bet it was a direct result of whatever this man, Abrial, had done to knock her out. When she had more energy and the world again made sense, she would probably be crabby about that.

Crabby, but not frightened, she realized with mild surprise. Something was still buffering her emotions.

"What are you doing?" she finally asked when she couldn't figure it out.

"Getting rid of your fingerprints, hair, and blood. We don't want to leave anything for goblin trackers to find."

"Oh." She digested this for a moment but found it too much to contemplate when she was so light-headed. She went back to Middle Eastern mythology. "It is also said that, when the stars were created, Ahriman flung himself into the sky like a snake, and in so doing brought all the baleful planets into alignment with the earth to create even greater wickedness. Ever after, the darkness of the universe was branded into his eyes."

"Yes, they say that."

It belatedly occurred to Nyssa that she might have been rude, discussing this man's father in so frank and unflattering a way. She forced herself to meet her captor's gaze, and she suddenly found herself wishing that he had completed his Hollywood villain look by wearing sunglasses. If one had to look into emotionless reflective surfaces, it was better that they be made of plastic.

"And you are thinking that the acorn doesn't fall far from the oak?" He shook his head and went back to cleaning. Then he paused a second time and looked back. His gaze remained black and still. "Believe me, my father's eyes were a lot scarier than mine."

"Yours will do," she muttered, and then stared transfixed as the silver at the edge of his irises blazed briefly and his deep voice boomed in a laugh. Both the eyes and the laughter were fascinating in a terrible sort of way.

"As you like. You had better get dressed. We have a hard day ahead of us. I hope you like motorcycles."

"I've never been on one. By the way, my name is Nyssa." She told the truth, giving her real name, not the one on her fake passport.

"I know. I've seen you in your dreams." Nothing about his dark gaze changed, but suddenly Nyssa found herself blushing. *I've seen you* sounded positively suggestive the way he said it.

"How do you know that the FBI is looking for me?" she asked, changing the subject to one slightly less disturbing.

"I have the sort of—let's call them friends—who know whenever our tax dollars are hard at work."

"You have useful friends then. But I still don't understand. Why would they be after me?"

"My best guess is because either H.U.G. or the goblins want them to be."

"Humans Under Ground?"

"Yes."

"But why?"

"Maybe one of your psychic playmates recognized your fingerprints. You've been visiting other people's files rather often of late, and many psychics work for pay."

34

"I don't think any of my playmates, as you call them, would work for Humans Under Ground."

"Perhaps not knowingly," he agreed.

"They'd know," Nyssa insisted, wanting it to be true. "It must be the goblins."

"Perhaps."

"That's a little frightening in its own right. I didn't think the goblins had that much to do with humans."

"Yes, it is frightening. But sometimes politics make for more than strange bedfellows." Abrial smiled grimly and gave her a shrug.

"Even if that's true, how could they have found me? I don't understand. I was careful—very careful," she said a shade defensively. "Not even the ghosts found me while I was dreamwalking."

"I found you," Abrial pointed out. "And what is more important, I found you first. You may live to see another day after all."

"I *may* live to see another day? You're not very good about allaying my fears," she complained.

"I'm not trying to allay them," he said flatly, tossing his cloth aside. "We'll live longer if you stay alert and frightened while we travel. And no more dreamwalking unless I'm along to play bodyguard. Last night was too close a call. It wasn't Opportunity who was knocking on that door."

"Fair enough," Nyssa said, getting to her feet. She had to use the wall for support, but she felt pleased that she managed without Abrial's assistance. "I'd just like to know one thing before I climb on a bike with you and go who knows where."

"Yes?" He looked interested.

"You're not an incubus, are you? I'm not sure I

35

want to be riding around with a sex demon. For one thing, my mother wouldn't approve."

That odd smile came again. "No, I'm not an incubus. That's not what I am."

Chapter Five

Nyssa was not sure how Abrial managed it—some kind of voice-boosting telepathy obviously—but they were able to carry on a conversation while speeding down the deserted highway in excess of all possible posted speed limits.

She didn't know anything about motorcycles but suspected that the engine on this black monster wasn't stock. For one thing, it was way too quiet. It took all the energy that should have gone into noise and turned that into speed. When she asked Abrial about it, he nodded his head, and then in a fit of what sounded almost like candor added: "Another one of my *friends* likes to work on cars and bikes. Jack has a real gift when it comes to machines."

"You mentioned Jack before. Are you speaking of Jack Frost?" she asked. She was surprised by Abrial's sudden revelatory chattiness. Her face was tucked into his back as she tried to avoid the hot wind whipped up from the melting asphalt. Abrial didn't seem to mind the wind and sun, but it was almost noon and Nyssa herself found the heat to be enervating. Even with the water he forced on her with monotonous regularity, she still felt as though she were slowly shriveling like a grape headed for a box of cereal.

"Yes. What do you know about Jack Frost?" The inquiry was mild but not random. She could feel his surprise in the sudden tensing of his muscles and the subtle shading of his voice. "He didn't mention that you were acquainted. Did you contact him before I got there last night?"

"No. We aren't acquainted. And I don't know much, except that he supposedly nips at your nose." Abrial waited patiently for her to go on. She tried waiting him out but found the charged silence unnerving enough to make her nerve endings tingle. Sighing, she added: "Also, he's the leader of the western fey and lives in a fairy mound called Cadalach. And he likes cars, I guess. He doesn't sound much like any fairy-tale character I ever heard about."

"Jack is . . . interesting." Abrial paused, as if deciding to say something else, then didn't.

"I bet he is." Nyssa thought of asking if they could make a pit stop, but since they were in the middle of nowhere without even a cactus in sight, she decided to suffer a while longer and hope for a town, or even a stand of waist-high bushes. She added idly: "Do you know, I've tried to run away from many things—my past, my family, my job, even lovers—but I've never run away from the law, I don't think. I'm not sure if I like it. It's kind of strange having a partner in crime too. I've been alone for a very long time."

Abrial nodded. "There's a first time for everything. You'll get used to it."

"Being on the run? Or having a partner?"

"Having a partner." That oddly suggestive inflection was back in his voice. "You need to open yourself up to the experience. Let whatever happens, happen. Believe me, it's less scary that way."

"Are you going to tell me that it's good to always try new things? That I need to expand my horizons?" she asked, wishing she could wipe away the sweat that was trickling down her back. How Abrial could stand being in head-to-toe leather she couldn't imagine. Added to that discomfort, he had his long hair tucked down inside his jacket.

"No, I wouldn't say that." He sounded serious. "I try not to make blanket generalizations. Especially these days. Rules are being reorganized regularly as the magical axis of power shifts. And I like to study things before leaping into the fray. Any wise person would do the same."

"Good. I like a man who thinks a lot." *Or else doesn't think at all.* Stupid men had their uses too.

"It isn't *always* bad to try something new, though. I can certainly think of worse things than being here with you."

"I should hope so! Many people think I'm very attractive."

"Do they?" He spoke absently.

"Yes." She made an effort not to sound annoyed.

"It wasn't difficult for you?" he asked abruptly. "Leaving everything behind? I haven't known many humans who could do that. Mostly they are creatures of habit, clinging to what they know, even as they are crushed beneath their lives' minutiae."

She thought back to the time she had almost

completely forgotten. It wasn't a place she visited voluntarily—and never with company—because all the gaps made her nervous, made her feel incomplete. But somehow, speeding along through the desert with her dark rescuer, it was okay to talk about what little she remembered, though even now she found it hard to explain.

Her first clear memory was that of watching scary shadows on a bed of beaten black earth. A dark tree trunk was somehow pulled in two by a group of hulking shadows, while its gray leaves shivered violently. There had been pain and also a terrible smell. That odor was a ghost that still haunted her. . . . Nyssa pushed the image aside. Even now, it had the power to frighten her. She'd have to start her tale somewhere else; this vision was too private. Even she was not allowed to see all of it.

"It was difficult at first—of course it was! But my mother was dead, and I needed quite desperately to know some things. After a while it got to be like that philosopher said: *'Loneliness becomes a lover and solitude a friend.'* "

"A darling sin. *'Solitude becomes a darling sin,'* " he corrected her. Then, perhaps feeling her discomfort, he changed the subject again: "I noticed that you don't use any makeup."

Nyssa shrugged, wondering where the catechism was leading. "No. I don't feel the need to paint someone else's face over my own anymore. I left my makeup behind when I left my old life. No more masks for me. If I look tired, I look tired. If I'm surprised, then I look surprised. It makes me be honest with myself. Anyway, if you wore makeup you'd understand the appeal of not doing it anymore. I think makeup and panty hose are the inventions of Satan."

"That is probably true." Amusement shaded Abrial's voice. "But I don't know about self-honesty. I think that Oscar Wilde may have had the right of that one. You know—about a little honesty being a dangerous thing, and a lot of it fatal."

"That was 'sincerity,'" Nyssa answered smugly, correcting *him* this time. "And you needn't worry. Though I am honest with myself, I am quite willing to lie to strangers. I won't tell you any uncomfortable truths you don't want to hear."

"How reassuring."

His voice was as dry as the desert around them, but she sensed he was still amused by their conversation. After a moment he asked, "So, would you say that you are an adventuresome person? Do you like surprise in your life?"

"Usually. Sometimes." Nyssa was beginning to grow wary of these seemingly random questions. It was almost as if she was being interviewed. "Not so much lately. There've been too many surprises and adventures, and they all seem to be damned dangerous and uncomfortable. But surprises are often wonderful."

"That feeling is rare. Most humans I know live their whole lives trying to avoid new experiences. They eat in fast-food restaurants, shop in local department stores, live in tract houses, listen every day to the same top-forty pop hits—"

"And never deal with goblins or run away from the FBI with total strangers." Nyssa shrugged, wondering why he had returned to the theme, and not liking it particularly. "It's all a trade-off. You have to compromise. You can't have everything, so you need to decide what you really want—what you really need. It isn't always easy giving up the old ways, but you have to be practical if you are going to survive."

She waited tensely for him to ask what it was she wanted or needed so badly that she was willing to face the goblins to get it. But he didn't. Maybe he knew that she wouldn't answer. Instead he said: "But you brought a pair of Prada sandals with you. Silly shoes with three-inch heels."

"Well, they're *Prada,*" she said defensively. "You just don't up and leave—what's wrong?"

Abrial's torso had stiffened under her hands.

"My intuition has once again been proven correct."

"What?"

"We've got company of a Federal sort. They're waiting up ahead. I see them."

"How do you know they're Feds?" she asked, trying to see around his shoulder.

"The sunglasses make sense for this landscape, but the button-up shirts and button-down collars? Come on, it's a hundred and fifteen degrees. Only one group is that style-fanatic."

"Ugly shoes too?"

"Big, black, and steel-tipped," Abrial answered. "Not Prada."

She sighed. "So what do we do now? Think up a good lie?"

"Time to see what this baby can do off-road. Hang on tight," he said. Then he laid the bike over on its side in a ninety-degree change of vector.

Nyssa opened her mouth to protest, but before she could say anything they were covered in a cloud of red dust and heading for a pile of house-sized stones carelessly and rather precariously stacked to the west of the highway. If they had been speeding before, they were going for a world record now.

"Oh, hell."

"We need some cruising tunes," Abrial said, and quite impossibly, her head seemed to fill with the raucous music of Bachman Turner Overdrive.

"You *are* a psychic!"

He said with a small laugh: "I guess this is your daily dose of surprise."

"I could have done without it." There probably wouldn't be any stopping off for the call of nature now. She hoped the ride wasn't too rocky. It would be mortally embarrassing if she wet herself before being arrested by the Feds. The thought mortified her, but the physical discomfort also kept her from being really afraid. Or maybe it was Abrial who kept fear away. "Do you have an actual plan? Or are we just going to explore the desert and hope for some shelter?"

"Yes, I have a plan—avoiding that roadblock back there. And the helicopter too." Abrial again laid the bike almost on its side and whipped around a large boulder. The wilderness wasn't designed for motorist safety, but he managed the trick as neatly as he would have on a paved surface. "There's supposed to be an old faerie road somewhere around here. If we can find it, we're sittin' pretty."

"Faerie road?" She gasped as the bike straightened. She was pretty sure that her stomach had popped out of her mouth and was lying somewhere back there on the desert floor.

"Yeah. You know—like *'you take the high road, and I'll take the low.'*" They were both shouting to be heard over the imaginary music in their heads. If the Feds were listening, they were probably wondering what the hell the pair was doing.

"But that refers to the road the dead travel, doesn't it?" Nyssa felt her stomach return, and sink into her toes.

"Yep. That's the one. Don't be scared, though. It's no worse than dreamwalking really. Or so they say."

"They *say?* Tell me you've done this before. You know what you're doing, right? Please, please say you've done this before."

"I have. More or less—just not on this road. It wasn't terribly popular. Here we are! Let's hope the password is still good!" Nyssa peeped around Abrial's shoulder and almost screamed. They were headed full-speed for a blank stone wall that had some large creature's bones embedded in its red striations.

Suddenly a helicopter appeared above them, sunlight glinting off its rotors and . . . machine guns?

"They've got guns," she shouted, disbelieving.

"I never doubted it."

Someone began barking at them, something about halting and surrendering their lutin empire documents.

"They wouldn't know lutin documents from extra-absorbent two-ply," Abrial muttered. "That's just an excuse."

"What?" Nyssa couldn't make out everything the Fed's amplified voice was shouting, but she understood the intent of the gunfire kicking up dust around them as Abrial didn't stop.

"Oh, Goddess!" she gasped, betraying her recent conversion to the old religion as the chopper's vibrations grew stronger and its shadow overtook them.

Abrial never slowed—and she was certain that he never considered doing so. He waited until they were almost on top of the mountain's face and then shouted something in a language she didn't know. Instantly a blank spot appeared in the wall, sundering the dead creature's ribs as the stone folded away like a curtain. They raced through the crack and then Abrial applied the brakes, spinning the bike in place with a scream of hot tires. They were turned around completely and facing the opening when the gap snapped shut behind them, closing them away from the hovering helicopter outside, almost lost in a red dust cloud, and into total darkness.

The motorcycle's engine died abruptly, and so did the conjured music. The sudden near silence was not relaxing, though, probably because it was not complete. Nyssa couldn't identify the tiny vibrations around them, but they sort of reminded her of the sound and feel of sand being crushed underfoot when one ran down the beach. It could also be the start of a landslide. Or worse.

An image from a bad horror movie popped into her head, and she thought of being swarmed by millions of stinging scorpions.

"Abrial?" she whispered, fear making her voice tight. "Can you turn on the headlight?"

"In a minute. You probably don't want to see this part. I don't much want to either. It gives me vertigo." His tone was relaxed, but she didn't like his words. "Just wait. It'll be over soon."

"Oh, Goddess," she said again, pulling up her legs and wrapping herself tight around Abrial's waist.

"Hey!" he protested. "Watch the heels on those boots."

"Don't let the scorpions get me."

"Scorpions?" Abrial started laughing. "No wonder I don't scare you much. Your imagination is absolutely lurid. Relax, dreamwalker. The cave's just moving us a little deeper into west Texas."

"Moving us?"

"Yeah. If I recall things correctly, we'll pop out somewhere near the New Mexico border. Or else in Utah. I never can keep these roads straight. I haven't had to use them until recently."

"It can really do that? We aren't going to some ghost land?" Nyssa was slightly relieved. Although she wasn't afraid of ghosts, as long as they didn't come in armies.

"Of course not. We're not dead, just passing through. We won't be crossing the Styx."

"Passing through what?"

"Passing through *where*. And damn quickly." He added: "At a high cost, though. I should have warned you. That's why we can't take faerie roads all the way back to Cadalach. Well, one of the reasons. Also, there could be traps. In the final days, a lot of pockets of survivors made last stands down in these caves. And the goblins have started using them too."

He was speaking of feys, not humans; humans hadn't had their Armageddon yet. At the time of The Drought, the explosions on the sun hadn't affected mortals. It had just killed off the creatures of air and light, and driven some of them insane.

"What do you mean, it's too expensive?" Nyssa asked, feeling foolish. She began to unwrap her legs, but Abrial folded a hand over her calf and held her in place. He stroked her through the leather, and she felt it much higher up.

"For you. For a lot of mixed-blood feys too."

"How so?" she asked, finding herself growing warm beneath his touch. The heat from his hand radiated out rather like a space heater. Of course, that might be part of Abrial's plan: distracting her so she wouldn't panic. She wouldn't put it past him.

"Don't you recall your fairy tales? What happens to those hapless humans who wander into a party at a faerie mound, or who join the wild hunt?"

"They age a hundred years in one night," she whispered, recalling her Celtic mythology. "And most of them go mad as well."

"Bingo. What most people don't know is that it can happen to certain feys too. A selkie would stand no better chance of coming out sane from a faerie journey than a human would. Especially on this road, since it belongs to the Unseelie Court. Or it once did."

"Enough with the honesty, okay? There is no need for details. I have plenty of other stuff to worry about. Like just what is this Unseelie detour costing me?" she asked. "We aren't going to pop into the next century, are we?"

"No, that isn't how the toll works on these roads. Do you have any fey blood? Any dark-elf or leprechaun?" Abrial asked.

For one wild moment, Nyssa wondered if he had discovered her secret. She reined in hard on her blossoming hysteria and hedged: "I don't know. Let's say I don't. How much of my life have I lost?"

He hesitated.

"You can be honest just once more," she told him. "I want to know."

"About a year. Maybe a little more."

"Will I be crazy?" she asked.

"We'll see. I don't think so, at least no more than you are already," he said frankly. "You couldn't see any of the stuff that would make you lose your mind. And neither did I. Anyway, you are used to astral travel with your mind, and even talking to ghosts. It shouldn't be *too* disorienting. I'm just being cautious."

"Oh." She swallowed and closed her eyes against the disquieting dark. She slowed her breathing. "So, this is an Unseelie road?"

"Yeah. Do you know the difference between the Seelie and Unseelie?"

She didn't think he was joking, so she didn't answer that seals were the ones without visible ear flaps. "Well, sort of. As much as one can without ever having visited either court's capitol. I couldn't dreamwalk before The Drought, and after that they were all dead and many places were closed off to me. I can only go into the parts of The Yesterdays when there is a connection—a living portal—in the human world."

"And that was why you were going to look for the hobgoblin. You found out he was alive and in the human world, and that he might give you a way into the Faerie past."

"Yes. More or less. I wasn't thinking about the

Seelie and Unseelie, though, and how different they could be."

"They are different and yet the same. The courts were not so much physical places as philosophies that brought certain geographical locales under the sway of different spheres of influence." Abrial didn't exactly shrug, but she had the feeling that he wanted to. "We, all of us feys, came from the same original source. You might just say we evolved along different lines."

"Sure, like good and evil."

"Those are human terms." He thought for a moment. "Think of it as light and darkness. Or energy. Magic is energy, just like everything else—including emotion—and energy is not inherently good or evil, it just *is*. We are in a place of dark, or Unseelie, energy now, but are about to be returned to the light. You feel better in the light because it is what you are used to, but that doesn't mean that this place is 'bad.' "

On cue, they were surrounded by an eerily powerful illumination. It reminded Nyssa of some of the otherworldly things she'd seen while dream walking, but her journeys were never accompanied by such an intense light. It was as if her head was filled with colored lasers, their high-impact shades foreign but not unnatural. A hot wind came washing over her, bringing with it a medley of smells that were at once familiar and yet not identifiable. It was all very strange, but not particularly frightening. Or not as frightening as waiting to find out if she had lost a year of her life and maybe her sanity.

Nyssa exhaled slowly, and Abrial finally let her leg

go. Around them the cave rumbled, and a sudden opening very like the one they had entered appeared before them. The eerie light dimmed abruptly.

"We're here. The road must like you. There was no delay while we were quizzed."

Still focused on Abrial's announcement that she had possibly lost a year of her life, and blinded by the afternoon sunlight that now looked odd to her, Nyssa lowered her legs to the ground. She again hid her face in Abrial's leather coat while she got her wits back. She liked the soft, buttery feel of the leather, though she couldn't identify what sort of hide it had been made from and hesitated to ask.

"Good news," Abrial said, attempting to restart the motorcycle. His raising up to kick start the bike dislodged her from her cocoon. "I know this place. It looks like we're almost to the Arizona border. They gave us an extra push at the end."

"Is that what that was? The wind and the light?"

"Yeah, that was a faerie travel equivalent of turbocharging." He kicked the starter again. "Damn. I wonder what's wrong with this thing. Maybe dust has gotten into it. Or maybe the traveling has ruined the gas, though that shouldn't be a factor until we exit the mound. You usually pay up after you leave."

"Is it an electronic ignition system?" she asked, her voice unhappy. "Something with a battery?"

"Yes. Why?"

"Check the battery. It's probably dead." She added honestly, "It's my fault. It's like I tried to tell you when you knocked me out before. I don't know how it happens, but when I get upset I suck the power out of machines. Watches, computers, dishwashers . . ."

Abrial half-turned to look at her. She couldn't see his expression through the tinted faceplate of his motorcycle helmet, but she didn't need to. "Are you serious? Did you drain my cell phone and PDA too?"

"If they weren't shielded, yes, probably."

"Well, damn. Can you put the juice back?"

"I don't know. I've never tried. Usually things explode when I drain them, so there isn't anything to put the juice back into."

He didn't say anything about failing to mention possibly blowing up his bike while she was panicking about scorpions, but he did suggest: "Well, this would be an excellent moment to give it a go. It's a long walk to the next town, and I don't fancy our odds if the Feds catch up with us while we're on foot. Depending on who is feeding them information, they may know where this road exits. They could be here shortly."

"Or the goblins could." Nyssa shivered, looking at the sun outside. It was much farther west than it had been when they entered the cavern, and thunderheads were beginning to form to the south. They had only a few more hours of daylight, and a storm was coming. That was bad. Facing goblins on the metaphysical plane was one thing; meeting up with them in the physical realm was another. She had no experience with physical battles, and she didn't look forward to any.

"Them too. But I don't think we need to worry about goblins until sundown."

"Why not?"

"Plasmolysis. It's a fancy word for dehydration. Most goblins don't do well in hot, dry climates. They shrivel up and blow away."

Nyssa looked at her chapped hands.

"Well, that's a relief," she said after a moment. And it was, a bit. "Okay, then. Any thoughts on how to do this?" she asked tensely, shoving her hands into her pockets. "I'm really not good with machines. They don't like me."

"Maybe. But let's get the bike out of this cave first. We don't want to spend any more time in here, and I mean that literally."

"Good thought, since it's my life we're spending," she agreed, as Abrial wheeled them into the light. She was hit with a small dose of vertigo as she passed out of the cavern's stone mouth, and wondered if that was what it felt like to age a year in an instant. Or to go insane.

"Okay. Give me your hand. Your right one."

Nyssa reluctantly took her roughened hand from her pocket and proffered it, leaning into Abrial's back as he guided her fingers down to the bike's engine. The metal was cool to the touch—apparently the bike had aged a year too. She wondered if her left arm was healed beneath her bandage. It didn't hurt anymore.

"Okay. I want you to concentrate on pushing power down into your right hand. I know you can do it. It isn't that different from dreamwalking. It's just shifting energy. Try to relax like you do before a walk, and get your mind focused."

"Do you mind if I play a little piano?" she asked. "It helps me concentrate."

"Go ahead. You know any Scott Joplin?"

"Yes."

"Then try it. We need something lively."

Somehow, Nyssa found herself smiling and she

started to calm down again. Maybe she had lost her mind, but if so, it wasn't an entirely bad thing.

"One 'Maple Leaf Rag' coming up."

Abrial didn't allow his frustration to show, but even Nyssa imagining and mimicking the motions of ragtime music wasn't getting the job done. He could feel the power in Nyssa dancing at her fingertips, and in her body where it rested along his back, but she just wasn't able to send a spark back into the battery and make the ignition catch; there was some internal block that prevented her from closing the circuit. She was unable to forget her fear of machines long enough to connect with the battery. He could feel the tension and frustration coiling in her body as the charge grew inside her. He knew of one way to direct it, one way to make her forget.

"Hold that thought," he finally whispered. "Don't let the energy go."

"Maybe if I went into a trance? I've never done anything like this while awake," she said. Nyssa was barely able to hide her emotions, and her voice showed her annoyance at being unable to start the engine.

"No. We don't know who might be waiting for you in the dream world, and what booby traps could already be in place." Abrial had lied about knowing that Qasim was waiting for Nyssa outside The Yesterdays, but that didn't mean the other goblins hadn't planned something just as nasty. He climbed quickly off the bike and remounted behind her. "Lean forward and put both hands on the engine—not the gas tank! Just—yes, that's perfect."

"Abrial, what are you doing?"

He glanced at her butt—it was the best he'd seen in centuries—and decided that it seemed wisest not to answer. She had, after all, requested that he not be honest any more today, and he preferred not to lie unless he absolutely had to.

He reached around her and removed her helmet. Combing his fingers through her sweat-damp hair, he caught her chin in his hand when she would have turned to look at him. It struck him as odd that her hair hadn't dried or grown longer when they came back into the human world. It should have been about six inches longer. He filed this peculiarity away for later investigation. Perhaps their mental connection had shielded her.

"Don't worry. I know what I'm doing. We just need to make the sparks fly a bit. I'm going to help you direct them outward." That wasn't a lie. He knew exactly what he was doing. What he didn't know was whether it would actually work. "What's the most sensuous piece of music you know? What makes you think of sex and flying?"

"Kraftwerk's 'Comet Medley,'" she answered promptly. "It's great with a nitrous-oxide chaser."

Abrial almost laughed. His little dreamwalker apparently had a colorful past, if it included having sex on laughing gas. They'd have to talk about that later.

"I don't know it. Can you play it on piano?" he asked.

"I don't think so. It's all synthesized." She sucked in her breath as he settled his hands on her ribs right at the flare of the waist. "I could try and imagine a synthesizer. It can't be that different than a piano."

"No, that's okay. I want you to relax. To do what comes natural. What's the sexiest piece of music you can play on piano?" he asked, leaning her over until she was lying forward on the bike. Yep—best ass he'd ever seen. Or felt. He didn't bother resisting the arousal that swelled through him; it would only help with what he needed to do.

"Pachelbel's *Canon* in D minor. It's always reminded me of the ocean and having sex in the waves."

"Play that," he said softly, and allowed his hands to start wandering over her body. He kept his touch light and nonthreatening—or as light and nonthreatening as he could manage. "And just relax. This will be wonderful, freeing."

"Um . . . Abrial?"

"Just play. And think of flying. Let me guide the power for you."

"Easy for you to say," she muttered. "You're on top."

Chapter Six

"Cyra, what is it?" Thomas Marrowbone asked his wife. "Is the mound talking to you?"

"I think Abrial and that woman are in some kind of trouble," Cyra answered.

"Bad trouble?"

"Is there any other kind?" Cyra paused. "And yet . . ."

"What?" Thomas asked again, fascinated to see a sudden blush crawl up through his wife's cheeks.

"Never mind. They can't be in that much danger if he has time for dallying."

"Dallying?" Thomas grinned, his gold eyes sparkling. "I wonder if Abrial knows that Cadalach is watching him."

"He may know about the mound. I don't think he knows about me getting reports—and I'd prefer it remain that way."

Nyssa looked over at the thunderclouds piling up in the south. They would bring rain, but also more trouble.

"Abrial?"

"Hush."

She wanted to. His hands were both relaxing and also exciting—more exciting than anything she had ever felt. And whatever power it was that shadowed her brain wanted her to enjoy herself.

It took an effort to say: "We really have to be away from here before that storm comes. If we can be. I'm sorry to bring it up, but things get weird when I'm near lightning."

His hands paused. "How weird?"

"It brings out ghosts. I think it's all the electricity in the air."

"There shouldn't be too many spirits around here. Nobody ever lived in this place." His hands slid lightly down her thighs.

"Not humans, no. But look at the rocks. Those are dinosaur bones. And who knows what's still inside the tunnel back there? The door hasn't closed yet."

For the first time, she sensed that Abrial was totally nonplussed. She wondered if his astonishment would prompt a degree of prudence. And if it did, whether she should be disappointed or grateful.

"Are you saying that this storm is going to bring out dinosaur ghosts?" he asked.

"I don't know. But once I was stuck in a storm in Texas and ended up surrounded by a whole herd of cattle that had died in a flood. It was terrible. They were so stupid! I didn't think I'd ever convince them to go away."

Abrial said a word that she didn't know but that she understood anyway.

"Sorry, I—" Nyssa was suddenly plucked off the bike and spun about in Abrial's arms. She swallowed, not sure if she was pleased or frightened by the show of strength. She was very strong—stronger than most people she knew—but between her and Abrial, there was no contest. It sometimes seemed as if nothing in her life was straightforward and easy.

"Enough," he said. "I would like to take my time with this because I dislike being rough and crude, but I need a spark from you. Give it to me."

"How?" Her voice was breathless.

"This way." And then he brought his mouth down over hers.

That velvety thing that had lain quiet and inactive at the base of her brain suddenly stirred to life and began flooding her body with strange sensations. Before she realized what she was doing, she had unzipped Abrial's jacket and pulled loose his hair. Once again, her legs wrapped themselves around his waist, pressing her tightly against him.

There was a wave of warm air, and then a light around them that looked like the Aurora Borealis even through her closed eyelids. She tried to remember what caused the phenomenon in nature but drew a blank. She couldn't think of anything except the man pressed against her.

Abrial allowed his head to be pulled forward, apparently enjoying first their kiss and then the tender cords of her neck, which he scraped gently with the edge of his teeth as he neared her collarbone. Nyssa shivered, half in fear of the unknown and half in longing. This stranger—whoever he was, whatever he was—was doing something to her. Something dark, something erotic, something overwhelming. And a part of her was aware that the teeth on her neck were weapons, and that the hands sliding down her back were sometimes armed with murderous claws. It said she needed to be cautious. The rest of her didn't care.

Her eyes slitted open, seeking some reassurance in Abrial's dark gaze that she would be safe if she gave herself over to him. But there was no comfort to be had there. His eyes were as endless as the universe, their darkness as vast as all space. They held the potential for creation and cataclysms—promises of unbearable excitement and adventure. But they were not warm. Not human.

Nyssa sighed and gave herself anyway. The compulsion was that strong. He could have her here, now, on the desert floor or on the back of the bike—she didn't care as long as he took her. And as long as she had him.

Abrial made a soft surprised sound and then returned to her lips. His first kiss had been just play; that was immediately obvious. This time he kissed her as though he meant it. It stole her ability to speak, to think, to even breathe.

"Now," he whispered, and something bright and hot flared inside her and then arced outside her body. Suddenly the motorcycle rumbled to life, its mechanized voice a soft purr beneath her.

Slowly, Abrial broke their kiss and backed off the motorcycle. Not immediately understanding, Nyssa tried to snuggle against him, but he reluctantly yet resolutely pushed her legs down and put her away from him, taking a full step back from her when she tried to hang on. The only part of them that still touched were her hands, which were threaded in his hair.

"Nyssa, stop. That's enough. We don't need anymore. At least not right now."

The velvety feeling in her mind subsided abruptly, and cold sanity returned in an unpleasantly chill rush. Nyssa felt herself blush from chest to hairline. Her eyes dropped as she tried to gather herself, tried to drain the arousal away.

"Don't," Abrial said, his voice harsh. "There is nothing to be ashamed of. It was . . . it was just something that had to be done. I just didn't know it would be so . . ."

Suddenly furious at herself for actually wanting him when she knew he had done something to her will, and still very frustrated, Nyssa let go of his hair, dusting it off as if it were dirty cobwebs. Then she swiped a hand across her lips as though wiping his kiss away too. The gesture was childish but made her feel better.

"Fine. It's done." Her voice was harsh. "Let's leave before the storm gets here."

"My sentiments exactly," Abrial agreed. His voice was calmer than hers and again rather dry. The fact that he could throw off his desire that quickly just made her more annoyed. *Emotionless beast!*

But then, maybe he hadn't actually felt anything. Maybe he didn't really want her at all. With that thing in her brain, who could tell? She didn't know whether to feel appalled or furious, grateful for having the bike back or wishing it had failed so that they would have had to continue.

"It's a conundrum," he said in reply. With a last unreadable look, Abrial remounted the bike.

"Not going to look at your PDA and cell phone?" she snapped. "I'm sure you got plenty of spark out of me for them too."

"Later. Now calm down before you make the bike overheat."

"What?"

"We've reversed the energy flow. You are pouring out power, not taking it in," he explained patiently, handing back her helmet. "Make an effort to control yourself before you pass out from exhaustion. You can be pissed at me later. Or not. It's really your choice how we deal with one another for the rest of this trip." He coiled up his hair with a few efficient swipes and tucked it back inside his jacket.

"I will definitely be pissed at you later," she said, but she made an effort to restore calm to her body. In her mind she began playing scales, endless repetitions up and down an imaginary keyboard.

"That's a pity," he said. "But as you like. Are you getting on?"

"Yes, in a minute." She pulled her purse off over her head and tossed it at him. "Some of us are human. I have to go to the bathroom."

"Fine." Abrial didn't turn his head, but there was sudden amusement in his voice. "Just don't go far. The scorpions might get you."

"Much you'd care if they did," she muttered, but there wasn't any heat in it. Fading lust made her able to partially appreciate Abrial's restraint. Though she was mad at him for stopping—or rather, for being able to stop when she'd been so lost in sensation that she would have done anything for him—she would have been far more mortified after the fact if he had actually taken her. She had been many things in her life, but not promiscuous. She didn't sleep with men who were virtual strangers, no matter how appealing they were.

And he *was* a stranger. Hell, she didn't even really know who or what Abrial was.

And he didn't know about her either. At least, she didn't think he did. That was another reason that she had left her last lover. Once she suspected what she was, Nyssa resolved not to get involved with anyone until she—and they—knew the truth.

Of course, maybe Abrial didn't like the idea of sleeping with her because he thought she was human—the bigot! Many fey were prejudiced against humankind.

"Are you all right?" he called.

"No scorpions so far," she answered, and then looked about to make sure that it was true. She played more scales while she squatted. It wasn't as satisfying as swearing, but it kept her calm and prevented her from thinking too much.

Abrial didn't look at her as she remounted the humming bike. Though she hadn't heard anything, the mountain was now closed, the portal through which they'd arrived vanished.

Nyssa exhaled and made an effort to be civil. It didn't go particularly well. "Look. I appreciate that you stopped us, okay? But just for the record, I'm not an STD, you know. Humans are just kind of different."

"It wouldn't matter if you *were* an STD," he answered practically. He didn't say anything about her being different. "Feys are immune to most human bacteria and viruses."

She stared at his back. Sometimes she didn't get him at all. In fact, most of the time she didn't. Then a new thought dawned. "What, are you protecting me? From you? Are you *infectious*—like a vampire or something?"

He shook his head and passed back a couple of small black boxes, which she stuck in her pocket. It was a sign of trust that he was giving her the cell phone and PDA. Or maybe he wanted her to be carrying them if they blew up. Her purse was gone, and she assumed he had put it inside the compartment where he kept the water.

"I'm habit-forming for humans maybe, but not because I actually alter people's DNA." He paused, gave her a pointed look, then added: "That isn't why I stopped us."

Nyssa mulled this over while Abrial put the bike in gear. He drove quickly but not crazily, and they soon reached a paved road.

"Okay, I'll bite," she said once they were again headed west. The bright sky wasn't as harsh now that the sun was lower and beginning to be lost in clouds. "Why *did* you stop then? Do you not like me because I'm *different*? Or because I'm a human."

"Don't be stupid. No one is more *different* than I am."

"I am not stupid. I am trying to understand," she said through her teeth. "And you could try being a little nice here. After all, I've been really good about blindly trusting you."

"Not stupid, eh? I'm not sure that that is the definition of intelligent behavior."

He was laughing at her. In spite of the scales her fingers steadily played, a spurt of anger slipped out, making the imaginary keys ring with disharmony. The motorcycle's engine coughed and then started to rev.

"Hey. Don't get mad. I'm just teasing. Look, I have three reasons for stopping us back there—all good ones, I think you'd agree." Nyssa snorted, but he went on: "One, I don't particularly want to be caught with my pants down if we are overrun by a herd of dinosaur ghosts when that storm arrives. I'm guessing you probably don't, either. I mean, maybe they're brighter than cattle, but I'm not banking on it."

"Okay, that's a pretty good reason," she admitted, feeling a little better. The engine began to run more smoothly. Thinking of their narrow escape from the missile-toting Feds, Nyssa added: "For that matter, I wouldn't want to be caught by anyone or anything."

"I agree. Two, as you are aware, our minds are wrapped up with each other now. They need to be, so I can guard you and your dreams. The thing is, I sort of have the upper hand in this relationship. That . . ." He hunted for a word that wouldn't be inflammatory. "That *kiss* wasn't your idea. I pulled that reaction out of you from deep in your subconscious. And it was a lot stronger than expected. Much too strong for casual sex, and you were in no state to be making rational decisions. In fact, the rational part of your brain wasn't working at all. Obviously, as I don't think it's rational for you to trust a fox that's guarding a hen house. And it's especially not rational to continue, not when what we were doing was exciting the power of the Faerie road that was also feeding your desire."

Nyssa blushed. She certainly hadn't been thinking much. "Okay—agreed. As long as we're clear that my *state* was your fault."

"It was. Completely." She couldn't tell if he sounded smug or not. The inability to see his face from her position was a real handicap.

"So what's three? There isn't a Missus Nightdemon waiting at home, is there?" she asked, suddenly uneasy with the idea.

"No." He seemed to sigh. "Three, is a little complicated. Let's just say that something is *different* between us, maybe because *we* are different. You don't feel like any human woman I've been with, and I have a suspicion that sex would forge ties that neither of us would ever be rid of—real *'til death do us part* stuff. It's something we both need to think about carefully. Maybe it was just the proximity to the Faerie road. But maybe not. Me? I don't think I'm ready to be making that sort of commitment on one day's acquaintance—even if your ass is spectacular."

Ignoring the compliment, she asked, "And any noose compared to mine is cheap?"

It was a paraphrase of Dryden's *Satire Against Women*. But inside she thought, *'Til death do us part*, and shivered. What would someone like Abrial do if they got into a relationship and he wanted out? Probably not hire an attorney and file for divorce. The last thought was enough to cool any remaining ardor. She wasn't afraid he'd kill her. At least, she was pretty sure he wouldn't, since he was going to a lot of trouble to keep her body safe. But there was no knowing what he might do to her mind. She didn't need any other holes in her memory.

And he didn't think she felt like a normal human woman. Because she probably wasn't. Was she ready for him to know this? If they had gone any further, would he have been able to see every thought in her brain? That was a scary proposition. Having him on the periphery of her thoughts was strange enough.

"Okay, fair enough. I'll bear it in mind." She would think about it too, and remember what a close call they had had. That should keep her from getting any dumb ideas if the attraction reared its ugly head again.

She didn't mention his comment about her ass, and he didn't either.

"Okay. Let's get up some speed before the Federal boys find us again. I'd prefer not to kill anyone if we can avoid it. I don't like going medieval during daylight hours if at all possible," he said, changing the subject. "It's like sending up a flare and announcing: We are here!"

"Sure. I'm not actually big on killing either," she said.

"Give it time," she thought she heard him mutter. "The idea gets more appealing the longer you deal with goblins."

By Abrial's own admission—and certainly everything she had seen led her to agree—the enemy they faced was evil, relentless and merciless. Yet Abrial didn't seem at all concerned that he couldn't handle them. There wasn't a weapon in sight, not here and not while they'd been dreamwalking, but he wasn't worried. Nyssa wondered if maybe she wasn't being a bit foolish for not being more concerned about the intentions of this man with whom she was traveling. Abrial was right. She really had been taking a lot for granted, just by assuming he wouldn't hurt her. That wasn't the brightest thing she'd ever done.

As if he heard her thoughts, he said: "You worry too much. Believe me, I will do everything I can to keep you alive. My life is yours until I get you to Cadalach." He ruined the declaration by adding: "Anyone this important to the goblins is too important to lose."

"Swell. You're mine 'til we're dead or to Cadalach. Then I guess everything's as rosy as a day at the beach, so I can quit worrying."

"Exactly. Sit back and enjoy the ride." Suddenly the Beach Boys' "Surfin' U.S.A." began playing in her head, drowning out her scales.

Nyssa considered banging harder on her mental piano, but Abrial was right: She was exhausting herself. Instead she forced her body to relax against him, and started humming the song. After a few minutes, she was even able to be amused at Abrial's inappropriately deep voice singing about waxing surfboards and catching waves.

She was even able to take some comfort in the fact that if she ended up facing some strange and violent death in the desert, at least she wouldn't be alone.

Chapter Seven

Their ride lasted until just after sunset, when some sort of missile came at them out of the dark and blew the motorcycle away. Fortunately, Abrial sensed danger at the last moment and was able to somehow jump off the bike, twist in midair, and pull Nyssa into the shelter of his arms before they returned to earth.

They hit the ground hard and rolling, but the impact was not as hard as it should have been because Abrial cushioned the fall, and he was able to get them into the shelter of some stacked rocks before their enemies fired again.

"Goblins?" Nyssa asked, her voice harsh but whispery as Abrial rolled off her.

"Nope. It's the G-men again." Abrial didn't ask her if she was hurt. He seemed to know that she was uninjured, and didn't want to waste time asking after her health.

His calm allowed her to also be matter of fact.

"This is a bit much. Where do they get off, acting like the IRS? I'm going to call my congressman and complain."

Abrial moved to a crouch and then pulled her more or less upright. She heard her clothes crunch oddly as she shifted—at least one of the black boxes had suffered damage.

"This way. We need to find a bolt-hole before they catch us. You can bet they have some sort of infrared or heat-seeking guidance systems. They won't be able to see me, but I'm not sure about you."

"Swell. How unusual to be so popular and yet so unloved. Not that I'm complaining," Nyssa called as Abrial started running toward a gap in the rocks, towing her along with him.

"It sounds like a warm-up to complaining," Abrial answered, his voice low. "It's something in the tone. I'm coming to know it all too well."

"I'm just being sensible. This is wild country. Aren't any roomy bolt-holes likely to be occupied?" She was still striving for calm, and was surprised when she achieved it.

"Not for long."

A bolt of lightning sheeted over the sky, followed almost immediately by a deafening percussion. Temporarily blinded, all Nyssa could do was stumble after Abrial, through the loose dirt and shale at the base of the rocks. She'd never had occasion to be grateful for her thick ankles but was pleased with them now. They were hard to sprain.

"Listen, I think your power is still tuned outward. If you can, reverse it—try to find that damned rocket launcher and drain it." Nyssa snorted at the seemingly glib suggestion. Abrial sounded exasperated as he added: "Well, just try. They are bound to use it again."

"Not if the lightning gets them." She knew her voice was suddenly and most unusually smug. It was also almost an octave lower than usual.

"Can you guide the lightning?" he asked curiously.

"I won't have to. It's headed right toward them," she answered, suddenly certain that this was true. As if to make her point, a second flash filled the air with painful brightness and an immediate ear-bashing noise. A second, smaller explosion followed. There was no way she could actually hear any screams, but she felt them in the charged air.

"Damn. This is it, I'm afraid. Not exactly five-star accommodations." Abrial pulled her into a sort of cave through a narrow gap. It was shallow but dry, and seemed unoccupied. He stopped right inside the entrance and listened carefully. There was only a moment of calm before the sky opened and a torrent of rain mixed with dark hail began to fall.

"Black hail?" Nyssa said with disbelief, as the temperature dropped around them. Her voice sounded more like her own.

"I don't like this," Abrial said.

"Well, who would? I assure you that I am not fond of either hail or being shot at." She wrapped her arms around herself, thinking about suggesting Abrial be a gentleman and lend her his coat.

"The storm isn't natural," Abrial explained. He added slowly: "I think it's the work of a weather goblin. It means that one has to be nearby. Or else someone very, very powerful is working from a distance—and I didn't think there were any powerful weather goblins left alive." He turned to stare at her. His voice was flat as he said: "And how conveniently timed. On the surface, one might draw the conclusion that the goblins are helping us. Now why would that be?"

"Why would you think that?" Nyssa asked, beginning to shiver in body and voice. "I don't see that bad weather is any help. Especially if there are ghosts nearby. It'll just make them stronger."

"One might think that the goblins were helping because you were absolutely right about where the storm was headed. That last lightning strike landed right on top of the Feds. And you weren't guiding it. I would have sensed it if you were."

Nyssa thought about that. "You're sure? I mean, that it hit the Feds?" she clarified, but knew he was right. She had felt it, herself.

"Yes."

"And it would be bad if the goblins were helping us?" she asked as complete darkness fell. She shouldn't have been able to make out Abrial's dusty clothes but had no trouble seeing him. Her night vision had always been very good, and it was getting better with every passing day. Many of her senses were sharpening, and others—ones she had no name for—were waking up.

"Well, there's bad and then there's *bad.*"

"And which is this? Bad or *bad?*" she asked. The rain stopped abruptly and heat rushed back into the cavern. The place warmed up fast, but Nyssa kept shivering. She didn't think that she had been in the presence of this sort of atmospheric magic before, but somehow she recognized what it was: not a weather goblin. A hobgoblin.

"This is unusual, and I don't like it." Abrial turned suddenly, freeing her from his gaze. "I wonder if we'll be hit by lightning if we try to leave this cave. I suppose a strike would answer the question about whether the goblins are helping us or simply turning back Federal trespassers because they are in an uncooperative mood."

"Do you really want to find out?" she asked. "Me? I don't have your faith that if it is goblins, their intentions are benign. The whole enemy-of-my-enemy-being-my-friend thing just doesn't work for me. I could stand to wait a few minutes."

"We might not have any choice. I think this may be an entrance to an old goblin hive. It has a certain smell . . ." Abrial inhaled. "It seems uninhabited, but not dead. These goblin holes have minds of their own. They're sort of like faerie mounds that way. Staying would not be wise."

"What do you mean a *goblin hole?*" The few bits of Nyssa's skin not already covered in bumps raised a fresh crop of gooseflesh. "That can't be. Goblins wouldn't live in the desert. Sin City was an aberration made possible only with human technology and piped-in water. This is in the middle of nowhere."

"This wasn't always a desert," he pointed out. "And goblins have changed in the last few centuries."

"Changed? How do you mean? The six arms?"

"Yes, among other things. *Phylum anthropoda,*" he told her as he began inspecting the cave's wall and floor. "That's science's answer."

"*Phylum what?* I'm afraid I'm not a devotee of the

Nature Channel." Nyssa turned to stare at the walls too, but she hadn't any idea what to look for. "Or is this top-secret Unseelie stuff?"

"The educational system in this country is abysmal."

"So you can write your congressman and complain too. In the meantime—*what are you talking about?*"

"Insects. You can read about them in those things humans call *textbooks*. They conceal a lot of this kind of information in places called libraries. You don't even have to pay for the books." Nyssa had a sudden flash of Abrial walking up to the desk and presenting a library card that said Abrial Nightdemon. Before she could ask if he actually had a library card, he added: "Or you could try the Net—ah, but then you have already been trying something better, haven't you? And in very creative, illegal ways. It's been fun watching you make like Nancy Drew on a bug hunt. There's no telling how far you might have gotten with a decent education."

Nyssa shocked herself and made a rude gesture, but Abrial just smiled his odd smile as he looked back.

"Sarcasm does not become you," she informed him. "And anyway, my method avoids a lot of spam."

"I'm not being sarcastic. About the insects."

"Insects?"

"Come on—open your mind. I know humans don't think about goblins much, but they should. *You* should. Look, here's what we're up against," he said impatiently. "There are over one-hundred-and-a-quarter-million species of bugs out there. Most people don't know the exact number, but they know that there are lots. Why should anyone feel surprised that some got big and smart? Look at lobsters and crabs. They moved into the ocean and increased their size a hundredfold. There's a nature special on about stuff like this every night of the week."

Common sense and barely controlled panic said that this wasn't the best moment for an intellectual discussion about goblin evolution, but Nyssa seized at it gratefully. Thinking logically always helped to calm her nerves, and it kept her from remembering anything that might betray her to Abrial. "I already thought of this: The insects increased their body size but not their brain capacity. But that answer is too easy, and you know it. Even Darwin would hesitate to say goblins are just big bugs. They are something more than just some freak of evolution—they're something magical. But not magickal with a *k*, if you know what I mean. They are unnatural magic—something dreamed up by a wizard. Not like the fey, who are just magick." He nodded, and she added: "It's like they were deliberately bred by someone or something."

"Give the lady a cigar. The thing is: I know this and you know this, but you'll never get human scientists to see it. They believe they descend from apes, and goblins bred with and descend from bugs. They believe there was no magic or planning involved. It's all very tidy, and lets humans feel superior. If only it explained goblin sensitivity to the sun and their need for water. Those aren't very buglike characteristics."

"Yes, all humans feel safely superior except H.U.G.—who I know prefer science to magic but . . ." She paused and then inhaled sharply as she remembered something she had seen on her last dreamwalk.

"Yes? What are you thinking?"

"I noticed something while I was going through their files. The H.U.G. people, they've been using GPR to map what I first thought were possible goblin caves. Of course, I thought they had it all wrong and were on a snipe hunt."

"GPR?"

"Ground Penetrating Radar. What struck me as odd is that they weren't just looking in known goblin habitation areas. I wouldn't have paid any attention, except I was trying to find out more about—"

"Hobgoblins?"

Nyssa hesitated, wondering if Abrial would know if she lied. "Yes. Where they might be buried. I'm just wondering now what H.U.G. was doing out here and in the other deserts around the world. I was thinking they were looking for fossil data on dinosaurs, since mostly that was what they were finding and making note of. But maybe not."

"No?" he asked.

"Well, *maybe* they were. But what if they were doing what I was, trying to find where the other hobgoblins were interred? Wouldn't the desert be a likely place for Queen Mabigon to put those things if she didn't want other goblins—or anyone else—coming around to dig them up again?"

"Yes, it would." He said slowly: "You think this was a sort of preemptive strike on H.U.G.'s part? A way to thwart any goblins who might be planning on resurrecting these hobgoblins?" Abrial looked thoughtful.

"Or they are looking for a weapon of their own." Though her voice remained calm, Nyssa's eyes were a little wide and her breathing a bit too fast as she considered the theory.

"A weapon?" Abrial repeated. His eyes flared. "You think they would actually try and use the hobgoblins to their own ends? But that's . . ." He trailed off.

"Dangerous? Crazy? Unreasonable? And what is H.U.G.?" She shrugged. "Maybe I'm being paranoid. Heaven knows that I'm not thinking as rationally as I once did. But look at it from the hobgoblins' point of view. If you had been imprisoned by someone and then left to rot for centuries, wouldn't you be willing to do anything to escape—even help a former enemy wipe out those who had put you in prison?"

Abrial mulled it over, then shook his head. "Maybe H.U.G. just wants to wipe them out before any goblins get to them and set them free. That would be more standard H.U.G. policy."

"But maybe not. I didn't see any plans for destroying anything. Just finding and excavating."

"That isn't conclusive . . . but I think I'd better call Jack. H.U.G. has done odd things before—and then there's always the possibility of rogue agents." Abrial looked up at the sky. There was darkness of a different kind tucked into those clouds, and it was hovering over them. "When we can. We won't get a signal here even if the storm moves on."

"Oh, damn." Nyssa looked stricken.

"Let me guess. You still have the PDA and cell phone, but the batteries are now drained."

"I'm afraid it's worse than that," she said. Reaching for her coat pocket, she pulled out the fractured cellular. "Sorry, but it's as broken as the third commandment. I landed on it when we came off the bike."

77

Abrial reviewed the Christian Top Ten list along with the phone. The third commandment involved taking the Lord's name in vain. "Personally, I think the seventh is more often violated," he answered.

"Not by me."

"Well, no. But you aren't married. The worst you could do is harlotry." He smiled a little.

"Will you be serious? If you think it's urgent, maybe I could do a dreamwalk and reach Cadalach and Jack—"

"No!" Abrial's response was swift. "Not here. Not when goblins are likely so close. They'd pinpoint your location immediately. You might even wake up whatever is sleeping in this cave."

She shuddered. "Then what do we do?"

"We leave. Find transport. Get to a phone or at least someplace that has a signal. I don't suppose that you can fly an airplane."

"Not really. I took the controls of my courtesy uncle's Fieseler Storch once, but what are the odds of us finding a World War Two airplane out here?"

"Slim."

She looked out at the empty desert. "What if there's more lightning when we leave?"

"We chance it. Do you really want to wait and see an army of ghosts rising up out of the cave floor if the storm gets closer?"

"No! Goddess, no!" Nyssa agreed. "Let's leave right now. I don't feel anything bad in the air at the moment. I think we'll be safe."

"I doubt that. But I don't think we'll be hit by lightning—not until that weather goblin has had a rest. A storm like this has to have tired him out."

"Makes sense," Nyssa answered, but a small voice down deep inside her disagreed. Whoever had been guiding the storm had stopped because they wanted to, not because they were exhausted.

"Abrial, can we stop back at the bike?"

"I don't think that would be wise. Why?"

"I have a notebook in my purse where I keep details of my dreamwalks. Maybe it has something useful in it about H.U.G. and their scavenger hunt."

"*Had.* Your purse and the bike have been reduced to charred molecules."

Chapter Eight

"Cyra?" Jack called softly to the kloka. Everyone at the table stopped eating. "What are you hearing?"

"Cadalach has found them again," she said softly, head cocked as she listened to the whispering fortress that the others could barely hear. "In Arizona. They were attacked—almost killed. But Abrial got them away."

"Where are they now?" Thomas asked, taking his wife's hand, trying to hear what she did.

"I don't know. They are out of the mound's range again. They're on foot. The FBI blew up their motorcycle."

"Well, damn," Jack said. "I liked that bike."

"Too bad. It's toast," Thomas answered.

Nyssa had a sharp pain below her sternum. Below, not above. The pulsing pain was in the location of the cross-shaped scar she had had since childhood, in the place where a goblin's heart would be.

Perhaps her organs as well as her psyche were in

disarray. That is, if she were human. If she were half goblin, maybe this was exactly what she was supposed to be feeling when she neared overexertion. She supposed she could ask a doctor if she really wanted to know, but she had never visited one, and the idea was alien to her. As long as her mother had been alive, she had needed no one else.

"How are you holding up?" Abrial asked as they jogged through the desert night. The temperatures were cooler on the mostly empty floor, but the pace was still grueling. Nyssa didn't know how long she could keep it up. Without her keen night vision, it would have been impossible to move at the speeds they were traveling. The disconcerting part of all of it was the certainty that Abrial could run a whole lot faster, that he was holding back for her sake.

"You have a destination in mind?" she asked, not bothering to complain about Abrial's insistence that they run as far and as fast from the goblin hole as they possibly could. She had sensed it too: that feeling that someone was listening in on them.

"Yes. There is a small mining town not too far from here. It's called Deadly. Population of twenty-three. A bus visits once a week, on Saturdays. I don't know if we'll be able to get a ride there, but at least I should be able to raise Jack on their radio."

"You can call Jack on a radio?"

"After a fashion. Thomas, Jack's right-hand man, has been able to adapt our PDAs to work with almost any kind of signal—even radio waves. Encryption is tricky because of using relays, so we have to use manual codes when doing this." His voice was smooth, and he sounded unwinded. "He won't be able to answer on radio waves, since the transmitter he'll use isn't set to broadcast to PDAs in unknown locations, but he can start mulling over the possibilities and also send some help."

Nyssa stared at Abrial's back. It was impossible to see through all that leather, but he didn't seem to be perspiring.

"Encryption? Why does that word sound so peculiar on your lips? And I want you to know that what you just said was pure gibberish to me. I'm not technologically competent." Her voice was not as smooth, and there was a definite gasp mid-sentence.

There came a soft noise that might have been a laugh. "Learning about this new world—your physical world—has been interesting. Now, stop talking and save your breath. We are almost to Deadly. I'd like to be in and out before sunrise."

A short time later, just outside the town, the purple chaparral and greasewood where Abrial and Nyssa knelt rustled stealthily until a careless buffet of wind made the dried plants shudder. The smell of torn and broken limbs was sharp in the air. The ground was also damp.

"The storm was here too. I wonder why. I mean, it is rather adding insult to injury to pummel this town, don't you think?"

"Behold me clueless," Nyssa muttered, exhausted after their run and beginning to feel in desperate need of water—gallons of it.

She understood what Abrial meant though. The town had been overshadowed by something. For some reason, the place made her think of Sleepy Hollow: closed up, wary, maybe haunted at night by something deadly. Clearly it was slipping into decay, and probably needed fumigation, if not actual exorcism. She would guess it was a place of unhappy ghosts—and maybe worse. Of course, what else could one expect from someplace called *Deadly*?

"What a perfectly ghastly noise," Abrial said. "I wonder if the wind blows like that all the time, or if this is something special laid on for us."

"It sounds like lost souls wailing at the gates of heaven."

His head turned. He smiled slightly. "That's my girl! Morbid to the end."

Nyssa grimaced and rubbed her temples. The barometric pressure was dropping again. It was probably just the heat and the eerie, hot wind that was keeping people indoors. But where were the lights, the sound of TVs? It wasn't *that* late. Someone should be stirring.

"Look!" She blinked, then blinked again, as a familiar and unwelcome form stepped out of a crooked doorway of the last house on the road. He turned to speak to others in the darkness of the tired old house.

"Well, well." It seemed a fairly mild reaction to seeing Humana Vox, the goblin front-man for the L.A. hive, but it was all Abrial said.

This modified lutin from the City of Angels had started his career as a lawyer who specialized in witness intimidation, and with Carbon's help had made a mockery of the federal witness protection program at regular intervals. Even the IRS had learned to leave the L.A. hive alone. Then, suddenly, Humana Vox had claimed to see the error of his ways and, taking a page from Father Lobineau in New Orleans, had recently changed careers. He'd married a supposed schoolteacher called Sharyanthia, and they now specialized in evangelical programming directed most particularly at children. The L.A. hive had a large television following among the human population, many of whom sent their children to Sharyanthia's school.

King Carbon, though a tyrant and unwilling to share power, hadn't lived in Tinsel Town for nothing. He was media savvy enough to encourage this public religious conversion—in fact, suspicious people believed that he had probably engineered it. Carbon himself converted to Christianity at a public revival meeting—an event that was aired on all the major networks. But the word was that he still ruled his hive with the same savagery as all the other goblin kings; it was just that he now had divine help. And Humana Vox was still rated as Dangerous Goblin #2 by H.U.G., having killed off everyone ahead of him in the chain.

Nyssa's skin began to creep, and her voice was a little breathless when she asked: "What's he doing here? Not the Stations of the Cross, that's for sure."

"Wearing SPF ten thousand sunblock and probably collecting pennies for the Damnation Army," Abrial joked. His voice wasn't given to great tonal variation, but she was certain that he was unhappy. Who could blame him? No powerful goblin was exactly moral, but King Carbon's front-man of Los Angeles had all the ethics of Jack the Ripper. Probably fewer, actually.

"He doesn't have a kettle and bell. No Santa suit either."

"No, his style involves more snake oil. And brass knuckles. And goons in suits. Always lots of goons."

"Oh, well, as long as he isn't after souls. Or finding more stray Sin City goblins to take home. L.A. is overpopulated with them already, since that hive was destroyed." She attempted a smile but failed. Things were getting worse by the minute, and for the first time she was beginning to seriously wonder if she would make it to Cadalach alive.

"Oh, he'd take souls. Collecting the human spirit is part of what you might call his church's long-term investment strategy," Abrial said, in his usual calm, dark voice.

Nyssa looked at him, hoping he was joking but knowing he wasn't. "What on earth would goblins do with souls?"

"Nothing. All they need to do is keep their owners from doing anything good. It's all about the balance of power. Evil is a lot stronger if good people are sidelined through greed or indifference—or blackmail. Humana's ministry is an excellent way to tie up their minds and resources. And the goblins can't kill all the humans they want. Not immediately."

Nyssa looked away from Abrial and swallowed. "I see. Would you say then that his presence isn't a good sign? That it might even be considered a bad omen— for us and for the good folks of Deadly?"

"It has the general outlines of one, yes." Abrial stood up. They were mostly screened by shrubbery, but Nyssa thought the action rash. Goblins had excellent night vision. Then Abrial said: "I think I may go have a chat with Mr. Vox, and find out why our goblin urbanite is visiting such an out-of-the-way place."

"What?" Shocked out of caution, Nyssa rose hastily and took Abrial's arm. It felt like stone beneath her palm until he relaxed the muscles. "Are you nuts? That creature's a psychopath and mass murderer. And you said yourself he never travels alone. He won't tell you anything."

"No, I am quite rational. And I am fairly certain that whatever his mental state, Mr. Vox will want to tell me things once the right pressure is applied."

"Yeah, and then he'll want to tell King Carbon about us—assuming we aren't dead in an hour and there is nothing left to tell. And I'm betting Carbon's answer will be to send more goblins. Lots more goblins."

"He'll want to tell King Carbon about us, but he won't get the opportunity."

"You'll kill him?" Nyssa asked, careful to keep all emotion from her voice. "And the others—what of them?"

"No, *I* won't kill him." Before she could answer this cold assurance, Abrial added: "He'll kill himself. I'll encourage him to. Much more confusing for the enemy that way. They won't know what happened. I'll only kill the others if I have to, if they get in our way."

"Great. That makes it all okay then."

"What would you do?" Abrial's voice wasn't impatient, just relentless. "He's a goblin and the enemy. Or do you imagine he is here looking out for people's health and well-being?"

"No, of course not."

"We need to move while we have the element of surprise."

"I suppose. I just don't want you near him." She squinted as the dry wind threw grit in her face, and then she shivered. She seemed to be doing that a lot lately, in spite of the heat. "Abrial, I have a real bad feeling. Would you believe me if I said I felt someone walking over my grave?"

"No. You haven't got a grave yet," he said heartlessly. "You just need some dinner. However, I will listen if you have another suggestion that is efficacious and will make you less nervous."

"Yes, I do have one. Let's steal a car and move along quietly like most people on the run."

"Won't work. Not unless we find and disable all the vehicles in the area. These goblins are likely here for you. They will give chase, and that could be dangerous on these roads, given that they are on a kamikaze mission. Even then, we are easily spotted if we stick to paved roads—and there aren't many in this barren region."

"We could take a faerie road," she suggested, a bit desperately.

"There are none nearby, and certainly none that could handle a car. Even if there were, there is no guarantee that the goblins couldn't use them as well. After all, some lutins were allies of the Unseelie Court. They may still have the passwords." Abrial freed his arm gently. His next words were a little more firm. "Go into that shack there and get out of the wind. I won't be long."

Nyssa glared at him. "And if I don't want to go into that nasty shack?"

"You'll go anyway," Abrial said evenly. He had a way of presenting a situation without any ambiguities.

"I don't want you facing Vox alone," she said, changing tactics and then feeling annoyed that she sounded so beseeching; but she was unable to calm the rising certainty that something was about to go very, very wrong. She considered suggesting something she would never before have dreamed of trying. "There's another way—a smarter way."

"Yes?" His head cocked.

"We go after him subconsciously—a sort of waking dream. We could do that. I can get you there, and you'll know how to ambush him."

"Assuming that we can figure out how to enter a wakeful mind, this still might be difficult. Vox is likely protected by psychic shields. Most goblin bigwigs have psychic bodyguards these days to keep H.U.G. away. And they will be looking for you."

"We can do it," she said stubbornly. "We won't use a direct assault. I'll create a mental diversion. Get him to chase me out into The Yesterdays—or somewhere a normal psychic can't easily go. I'm fast. And while he's distracted, you sneak up behind him and zap him in the brainbox—and then we give him the third degree."

"I suppose it's worth a try. But I can't get him if he actually somehow goes into The Yesterdays. I can't go there. Still, if I can get him outside the gates and question him . . . I can always kill him there if it doesn't work. And the psychics too, if there aren't too many around. But I don't want anyone living long enough to warn King Carbon—and one could escape if there are too many," Abrial admitted. He stared at her. "I want you indoors while we do this. You look pale and as if you are starting to dehydrate. I think the heat is also affecting your judgment, making you needlessly fearful. This is no time for mistakes."

"Anything you want," Nyssa agreed, not bothering to point out that it could be that, though jogging and a lack of water were definitely making her feel ill, they might also be affecting *him*.

She stepped cautiously into the shelter of the old shack, probably once used by miners. She looked quickly for spiders and snakes, but the place was forsaken. The old boards were like dry bones in the desert: fleshless and so long dead they were of no use to anything. Except her.

Abrial followed her inside and picked up the fallen door whose hinges were missing. He wedged it back into the opening, temporarily blocking out the wind's anguished voice. Thwarted, the wind switched direction and pushed rudely through the cracks in the walls and through the broken window. For an instant Nyssa thought she saw a sort of vision: a shadow made of moving air that peered in at them—fleet, brief, insubstantial, but real for all that.

"What is it?" Abrial spun about quickly, following the path of her eyes.

Nyssa blinked. The shadow was gone, and all that was left was a papery exhalation that sounded like it came from fossilized lungs. An image popped into her head of something huge and dark that breathed out dirt and desiccated leaves with its foul breath.

"I think someone is looking for me," she whispered before thinking.

"Vox?"

"No." *Qasim*. She was sure.

"Have they found you?"

She made her voice strong. "I don't know. And even if they have, it doesn't matter. We still need a car

90

and a phone if we're going to get out of here. We can't get those while Vox and his goons are in the way." Abrial raised a brow at her suddenly harsh tone, but she just said: "Where do we start?"

"Are you sure you're up to this? If someone is spying on you—"

"Yes, I'm sure." Nyssa exhaled slowly and then inhaled again. "Abrial, we need to move quickly. I don't know how long it will be before the storm ghosts find me. Once they're here, I won't be able to concentrate. Please hurry."

Abrial nodded, relieved. "I'd forgotten about those ghosts. That must be the oppression I feel in the air. Okay, sit down on the floor. Play the piano as you normally would, but this time I will arrange the setting. We aren't time traveling, we are just moving through space—so it won't require as much effort. Remember, this isn't like raiding computer files or libraries. Tapping into Vox's subconscious will feel alien and probably unpleasant because he's alive and because he's lutin. I'll keep you as far out of it as I can, and you don't have to stay there for long. Just pop up and throw a rock at him and a taunt or two, and then run. I'll take it from there."

"Okay." Nyssa sat on the floor, her legs folded in a yoga position. She looked up at Abrial, trying to see his face through the thick shadows and wondering what he was feeling. Even in this moment, he both baffled and intrigued her, but all she asked was: "Aren't you sitting down?"

"No. I'm going to keep watch while you play."

"You can be in both places at once?"

Abrial hesitated. "I don't know yet. But I'm going

to try. We can't forget that our bodies are in as much danger as our minds. In fact, it would help a lot if you could come out of your trance as quickly as possible and help guard the door."

Nyssa looked at Abrial, trying to decide if he truly wanted her help with keeping watch, or if he was just trying to spare her the sight of him questioning Vox. Finally, she decided that it didn't matter. Keeping watch was a good idea, especially if the goblins were about to cease being helpful; and it made sense that they would stop being helpful once she and Abrial attacked one of their leaders. Besides, she had no desire to see Abrial question Humana Vox about King Carbon's plans. She felt sick enough already.

"Okay," she said, and then closed her eyes. She began to play Rachmaninoff. She could feel Abrial with her, watching as she played, channeling her energy into strange pathways. It was very much like what he had done with the motorcycle, minus any erotic overtones. It was also a more insubstantial world they entered, like a slide show projected into a room with distant walls instead of onto a screen.

The world her piano formed looked very much like the world she had come from, except that the light was the refracted green of an old monochrome monitor. The view was also rather prismatic, sort of like looking through the eyes of an insect on some nature show.

Abrial spoke softly from the doorway, quoting Milton from *Paradise Lost* as he faced into the unhappy wind that swirled with new shadows: "'Of neither sea, nor shore, nor air, nor fire . . . In this wild abyss the wary fiend stood on the brink of hell and looked a while, pondering his voyage.'"

"I don't think this was ever Paradise," Nyssa said quietly, closing her piano and turning to look at Abrial's back. She could see both worlds—reality and her dream projection—and it was causing her mild vertigo. She tried to focus on the new world. "And Vox isn't grand enough to be Satan."

"I was not thinking of Vox," Abrial answered, his voice remote as he stared into the night.

"Well, I don't think *you* are quite grand enough either," she said lightly. "And if you are, it might be best not to tell me about it. I'm nervous enough, you know."

"Don't be. You're in my world. I will protect you from harm."

"Thanks. Do try to not get hurt, yourself. It would upset me."

"I'm not afraid of Vox. A lone goblin, or even a small army of them, cannot hurt me. Not in dreams. The danger is in betraying your presence to King Carbon, and him getting to you through me. I can't let that happen. You might want to close your eyes now. Don't let the physical world confuse you." He turned around to face her. "Last chance. I need to change. You needn't see this."

"I'm not afraid." That was only a half-lie.

"But perhaps you should be."

"Why? You won't hurt me." She hoped. "And you've said you won't let them hurt me either."

"I won't. But the loss of innocence will probably be painful."

"Probably."

Abrial's eyes held galaxies revolving slowly, suns flaring and dying and being born again. As Nyssa watched, his wings began to unfold, and talons descended from his hands. His skull shifted, elongated. And he grew—taller, wider, subtly monstrous. He turned back toward the door before the transformation was complete so she couldn't see his altered face.

"I am going to slip into the brush now and work around behind him. I need only a moment, and then you may call out to him." The voice was gravelly as he stepped outside. It too had changed. Nyssa followed, but she didn't get too close.

"Okay, I'm ready."

"Just get his attention and then go back into the shack." Abrial pointed. The miner's shack was still there, still the same as in the real world, but it had been reinforced and had a stout door with heavy locks. Its windows were also gone. It looked like the outside of a bank vault. Abrial was doing all he could to keep her mentally safe. "I won't be long."

Nyssa nodded and then watched Abrial step into the shadows. He disappeared, except for an odd leathery rustling that she was glad not to be witnessing up close.

Carefully she walked to the edge of the hill and looked down at the small house in Deadly where Vox stood. He was speaking into some sort of device—perhaps a walkie-talkie. The goblin looked very different, and Nyssa realized that she was seeing him as he was before the plastic surgery that had made him appear more human. Most people didn't think to hide their true natures on the astral plane. They didn't mask their minds and souls. Whatever his outward appearance, Vox was still all goblin on the inside.

He wasn't especially ugly as goblins went. He had

two recognizable scars across his cheekbones that looked a bit like miniature highway guardrails. Some people probably thought the look was the new fashion among the L.A. hive's goblin elite, since many in power wore it. But this look wasn't gained at a tattoo parlor. King Carbon had a habit of hitting his favorite people in the face with a lead-filled quirt when annoyed, and even when not. It left distinctive scars.

Nyssa blinked and realized that she had Abrial to thank for this tidbit of information about Carbon. Though he had raised shields around himself, she was still apparently connected to him by a slender psychic thread; and it allowed some information to pass to her.

Begin.

Vox returned the instrument to his pocket, and Nyssa stooped and picked up a couple of baseball-sized rocks. Not sure quite what to say under the circumstances, she opened their parlay by chucking one at him. Her aim was good, and not too hard. She didn't want to knock him out. The stone thumped off the front of his chest with a satisfying whap.

"Hey—tall, dark, and ghastly! I hear you're looking for me. Yeah, I mean you, greenie." Vox looked up, his expression at first baffled, and then when he saw her, shocked.

"How did you get here?" he demanded. He looked about quickly, probably wondering where his telepathic bodyguard was. Nyssa wondered if Abrial had taken care of the psychic, or if the bodyguard was just off taking a leak.

"Jeez, you're stupid. No wonder you're just a flunky." At Abrial's urging, she kicked Vox in his pride. "How the hell do you think I got here? I dreamwalked. I've been watching you idiots fool around for a while now."

The goblin stood there, still glaring, but he didn't move toward her. Nyssa realized that all this wasn't playing out in the real world, only in the goblin's head. And he likely wasn't used to this sort of vision. He probably half-thought her a hallucination, something he could hear but not see clearly, because he'd still be looking at the real world with his physical eyes, which wouldn't see her because she wasn't really standing there. It was important that she get him out in the open—physically *and* psychically—before his bodyguard got back and figured out that there was a real threat to the boss.

The goblin's eyes tracked past Nyssa and settled on the shack. They widened. A chill passed down Nyssa's already super-charged nerves. This time she threw her rock a lot harder, and aimed for his face. The goblin finally moved, recoiling from the attack. Then, perhaps angered by shame at flinching, he leapt toward her, his first bound landing him halfway up the slope where she stood. Vox's lips rolled back, exposing double rows of sharp teeth. He reminded her of a pouncing spider.

"Half-breed bitch! I'll make you eat that rock."

Vox's bodyguard must have been napping, because in spite of the goblin's angry words, which shook the air around them, his psychic shields were slow to follow. Instead of enveloping him, they streamed like kite tails in a mild breeze, gray shadows trailing after him in a careless fashion. And that was all Abrial needed. In that instant, or something even shorter, he was on Vox, lashing out with his claws and severing the mental connection between the shields and Vox's mind. The shadows floated away on an invisible breeze, and the goblin leader slumped as though he had fainted.

Abrial dragged him closer to the hill and then looked up at Nyssa. She knew it was him, but his face and voice were transformed into something terrifying—something that had enormous teeth. Nyssa dropped her eyes quickly, not wanting to see this nightmare Abrial.

"Go into the shack and bolt the door," he said, his voice altered, and not for the better. "Play yourself back to the physical plane and guard the door until I return. Don't touch my body. It would be dangerous to distract me right now."

Nyssa nodded and retreated quickly. This had been her idea, ambushing Vox here in the astral plane, but she hadn't realized what it would entail. She hadn't known what parts of Abrial she might see.

Abrial's body stirred a short time later. It was only seconds more before Nyssa heard a gunshot from outside. The wind gave a dreary sigh and then momentarily stilled.

"That was Vox? He's dead?" Nyssa asked Abrial's profile as his eyes fluttered open. It had been a relief to see that the dream manifestation of Abrial's body hadn't occurred in the physical world, but she had still been unnerved by the sight of his seemingly lifeless body standing upright near the door. It was like watching a dead man, frozen in place.

"Yes." His voice was again normal in pitch, but it

still sounded harsh. He reached for the door, pulling it out of its warped frame and dropping it on the floor. "The dark is fleeting. I know what I must do. Let's go, before the others return and report Vox's death to Carbon."

He stepped out into the night without looking back. Nyssa wondered if he was disturbed that she had seen him in his dream state. Probably very few people had seen him like that and lived. Maybe no one had. The thought gave her pause.

Chapter Nine

"Goblins, goblins everywhere . . . we really have the king and queen of all pest control problems." Abrial's voice was soft as he studied the goblins milling about. There were a dozen of them, all clearly shocked and uncertain about what they should do now that Vox had shot himself. Unfortunately, they didn't show any signs of climbing in their cars—or into nearby goblin bolt-holes—and leaving. "They have at least two trolls as well, and some human psychics that were supposed to be his bodyguards."

"Too bad we can't just look up an exterminator in the Yellow Pages." Nyssa was trying not to think about the twenty-three people—humans—in the town who hadn't come out at the sound of the gunshot, and who were probably all dead. Their traumatized ghosts would soon feel her presence and begin seeking her out. She also knew that Abrial was still thinking about the benefits of trying to kill the other goblins right now. But she had nixed the idea, reminding him of what might happen to her if he managed to get himself killed, or if anyone alerted King Carbon to their exact location.

"In the Yellow Pages, no," Abrial said slowly. "But there is someone else. . . ."

"Yes?" Nyssa asked uneasily. "You know someone around here who specializes in goblin cleanup?"

"Sort of. Feel like dreamwalking over to my side of the tracks? We're mentally tuned to each other now. It shouldn't be so hard this time." He added: "It won't be nearly so ugly either."

She hesitated. "You can't manage this alone?"

"No, I need your particular skills. The creature I am looking for resides in an unusual part of The Yesterdays. And he is reclusive. We will need music to lure him out."

"What about those psychics?"

"I don't think they are looking this way. Vox's death and his psychics' collapse have them in disarray. If we go immediately, we should be okay."

"Uh, then sure—since you need me and we have very little choice if we want to get out of here. Who are we looking for exactly?"

"The Pied Piper of Hell: my uncle Farrar. Or rather, his ghost—if that is the word for his noncorporeal form, which may be hanging out in The Yesterdays."

"We're looking for your dead uncle?"

"Well, *dead* is as good a word as any. He doesn't have a body anymore."

"That doesn't sound reassuring. Is he a ghost or isn't he?"

"Well, it's difficult to be reassuring without lying." Abrial shrugged. "Farrar is best known for his gig in

Hamelin back in the thirteenth century. You probably heard about that one. Leading a dozen goblins and a couple of trolls astray should be a piece of cake."

Nyssa stared at Abrial, wondering if he was kidding. When she decided that he wasn't, she said with an assumption of lightness: "Your uncle is the Pied Piper of Hamelin? And also of Austria, Poland, Denmark, Ireland, England—"

"Yes, he got around a lot in the Dark Ages. Huge rat problems back then, you know."

"So I've heard." Nyssa shook her head. "You know, Abrial, I'm not sure that I'm ready to meet your family yet. Dead or alive. Isn't there something else we could do?"

"Look, be glad it isn't Dad. Or Mom. Now *that* would be something to worry about. This will be a piece of cake, and is far and away the safest way to handle the trolls since you are worried about me getting killed and leaving you on your own."

Nyssa stared some more. "I really hate to ask this but, since you brought it up, who is your mother?"

"Tienette, sometimes called Theophania. Also known as Tymandra, Tolla, Tora, and, by Dad, as *'that soul-sucking bitch.'* She was a succubus." The answer was prompt and too casual. At least for Nyssa. It was nice that Abrial felt comfortable enough to share this all with her, but she sensed some deep emotions running through him. She understood tangled family relations, and even sympathized, but she was exhausted and needed to focus her attention and energy on getting rid of the goblins. And on finding transport so she could escape from the gathering ghosts whose presence was making the atmosphere thick and heavy. Abrial's fascinating and probably disturbing genealogy had to wait.

"A succubus. Great. So your dad seduced monks, your mom sucked souls, and your uncle kidnapped children. We are definitely never getting married," Nyssa muttered to herself as she crawled for the cover of the rock outcropping. The wind was still moaning theatrically and was full of stinging dust. She went on sotto voce: "The guest list would be impossible, anyway! Half of them wouldn't even be able to be in the pictures because they're dead. And then there's *my* daddy dearest. Oh, Goddess! Think of the children. We'd have monsters instead of babies."

Abrial gave her a startled look, then crawled after her. After a moment he said: "You're getting upset again. Better let me have the PDA. We'll need it."

Nyssa fished the machine out of her pocket and handed it back to Abrial, wondering where in his skintight leathers he was going to put it. "Just tell me one thing: How old are you?" she asked. "I mean, I haven't heard about any succubi—or whatever the plural is—surviving the seventeenth century. And your uncle and father go back farther than that."

Abrial hesitated, then said: "Time is different for me—for all of us from the dreamlands. I lived in others' thoughts for most of my life and didn't really have much use for a corporeal form. And my body was also inside a tomhnafurach. Years, as they pass for humans, did not mean anything to me."

She had a brief moment of mental connection and felt Abrial struggling with his explanation. He was old, and he was young too. But how could he explain all those eons where he had lived in a sort of trance, doing the queen's bidding? He'd been alive but not living.

Eons? she thought. But he was gone again, his mind closed up tight.

"And now?" she persisted.

"Now I walk in the human world." He shrugged, the gesture oddly helpless. "I understand time better now."

"Okay. So how old are you—in round numbers?" she asked again, settling against a fairly flat stone that was out of the wind.

He glanced at her, his expression almost troubled. "Old."

"How old?"

"I don't know," he said bluntly. "I remember Constantine and Julius Caesar. Is this a problem? You're an ageist or something?"

"No, it's okay. Don't get upset. Age isn't a problem. At least, not the biggest one we have." She exhaled slowly, trying to ground herself and finding it difficult to relax with the spirits of the newly dead suddenly massing around her, trying to distract her with their shocked, jabbering voices. It was part of the curse of her mixed and warring blood that she had a hard time finding peace anyplace where men had lived. Or died.

"It's okay?" he asked. Then, with a small show of nearly human exasperation: "Is that an okay as in: You are being understanding about my situation? Or is it okay as in: You don't have any choice at the moment, so it may as well be okay for now?"

Nyssa blinked at the almost anger in his voice and said mildly: "It's okay, as in: I understand. Actually, I don't know how old I am either. I just wondered if you knew. It is odd to meet someone else who doesn't know these things. Heck, I don't even know what month I was born in. I asked Mom, but she just said I could pick whatever month I liked—except December. She didn't think I'd want a party during the Christmas holidays. I liked June. We celebrated my birthday then."

The wind picked up, almost as if it were listening and growing disturbed or excited by their conversation. Abrial looked out at the small whirl of dust forming in front of them and then back at Nyssa. It was hard to tell, but she thought his gaze was troubled.

"I'm willing to bet that I know what day you were born, if not what year."

"Yeah?"

"It would have been on a Saturday, on the thirty-first of December."

Saturday, the thirty-first of December. The date had meaning. Power.

"Why do you think that?" she asked, suddenly nervous and wishing she hadn't brought up the subject at all.

The whirlwind spun faster, as though it were nervous too. The surrounding ghosts' voices rose in protest at the disturbance.

"Two reasons. One, almost all humans with magical powers are born on that day. It's a favorite of vampires too." He turned to stare at the dust devil, eyes narrowed against the sand it flung at him. It was growing taller and darker. "Are those ghosts?" he asked.

Nyssa explained. "Among other things. They are having trouble forming because they are the newly dead, and their spirits are confused. Maybe some of them will move on without manifesting fully." Then, unable to leave the subject when she was so close to learning something about herself, she asked: "And the second reason?"

" *'Among other things,'* " he repeated, his eyes narrowing another degree. Then he said, "I think the other reason can wait. We better find my uncle while we still can."

Nyssa turned her eyes on the dust devil, which twirled like an ecstatic dervish on its dried twig legs. It reminded her of a gruesome old fairy tale, one about a witch who had a dancing broom made with the hair and bones of a long-dead woman.

Suddenly, she was certain that Abrial was about to tell her that all goblins were born in December, somewhere close to the winter solstice, when the days were shortest. But saying that out loud would be a bad thing—bad because there was a strong mental connection between them, and because she would then have to face her suspicions and possibly tell him the truth about her parentage; bad because whatever was guiding that dust devil didn't want Abrial to know that Nyssa was probably part goblin. Part hobgoblin. It would be willing to kill him—or at least attempt it—to keep the truth from being known.

"Okay. Let's go fetch your uncle. Any musical preferences?" Her throat was very dry. It was part dehydration and part fear. She kept an eye on the dust devil.

"Something short would be good."

"How about the 'Minute Waltz'?"

"Fine. See if you can play it in half that time."

* * *

The first thing she saw when she looked up from the music was a small pink toad perched on the top of her envisioned piano. The colorful amphibian watched her with serenity as she moved back the piano bench and stood up slowly. It didn't speak to her, but Nyssa wouldn't have been surprised had it done so.

"This way," Abrial said, touching her arm and pointing at the gates that marked the edge of The Yesterdays. They were for once standing open, as though expecting her arrival.

"Good-bye," Nyssa said to the frog, feeling silly and yet somehow certain that it was best to be polite now that she wasn't in Kansas anymore. Or Arizona.

It was noon and the sun of some spring day past was shining through the new leaves of the woods on the other side of the iron gates, making them sparkle brightly. Everything looked lovely and innocent, but Nyssa was wary. She could sense that Abrial was also especially watchful and alert, though she didn't know what he was looking for.

After a few steps, she identified one thing that was wrong: There were no shadows.

"Wait. This isn't the gate I usually use. It looks the same, but . . . Have you ever been here before?" Nyssa asked, feeling strange.

"No. I've never been beyond the gates of either of the realms. I can only enter this time because we are bound together."

"Realms?"

"This is the land of magick past, The Yesterdays where ghosts of things fey abide."

"Oh. Then certainly I've never been here. At least, I don't think so. It's very pretty."

"It's pretty and it's dangerous. It's also well-hidden from humans. Perhaps you could sing something? I am certain Farrar would like it."

"Sure, but sing what?"

"Do you know any cowboy tunes?" Abrial asked as they stepped through the iron threshold. Nyssa had a moment of gentle vertigo, then felt something brush over her skin.

"Um . . . one. But it's dumb."

"It won't matter if it has horses. Farrar has always been fond of equine songs."

"Horses? Okay." Grateful that he hadn't asked for a song about rats, Nyssa began to sing. Abrial took her arm again and they progressed slowly into the strange wood.

Nyssa didn't know what the Pied Piper of Hamelin would look like, but she imagined some variation of the man she had seen in storybooks as a child. He would be a thin man, with tight hose and a cape like the one in Browning's poem—a cloak half of yellow and half of red—and a silly hat, and of course a pipe or flute. Or maybe two of them. In some legends the piper carried flutes of both ivory and ebony: one for working good deeds and one for evil.

However, the creature they soon came across lounging in the wood bore no resemblance to her fairy-tale notions of what a piper should be. For one thing, he was a centaur, naked except for the buckskin-colored hair that covered his legs. He had human hands though, long ones that were swaying in time to the music in the manner of a lackadaisical conductor. They were attached to muscular arms and an even more muscular chest. She couldn't see if the legs terminated in feet or hooves, because the silky gold hair fanned out above the ankles, covering his lower extremities. And very little else.

Unable to help herself, Nyssa's song faltered. "Goddess! Is that really your uncle?"

"Yes. Hello, Uncle Farrar," Abrial said cheerfully, giving Nyssa's arm an encouraging squeeze.

The giant head perched on the long, muscled neck turned their way. The features were nearly human, except for the eyes, which were equine and black and filled up their sockets so no white showed.

Most ghosts were somber, many confused, and a lot were just plain addled to the point of stupidity. Abrial's uncle Farrar was something else entirely. Abrial was right not to call him a ghost.

"Hello, Abrial." The centaur stood up, putting to rest any doubt Nyssa might have had about either his massive size or gender. The sight was—among other things—awe-inspiring, and it was difficult not to stare. "And who is your musical friend?"

"This is Nyssa."

Farrar's footsteps clopped on the woodland floor, which was paved in cracked white stone. Nyssa looked about quickly and finally noticed that the surrounding trees were actually inside some sort of huge temple that had gone to wrack and ruin. It looked almost familiar, but if she had ever seen it, it had been on a dark, moonless night when bonfires burned.

"Nyssa." Farrar rolled the word around his mouth as though tasting it. It was only at that moment that she realized that Abrial and his uncle were speaking in some foreign language that she could only understand because Abrial was translating subliminally. She began to feel a little dizzy, and was unable to take in all the strangeness. "What lovely tunes you play and sing."

"Thank you," she murmured, finding the correct foreign words with Abrial's help. And though she was reluctant, Nyssa took the hand that was extended to her. She was extremely relieved when all Farrar did was bow over it. She tried not to be unnecessarily frightened, but she had noticed that his mouth was packed with giant, bone-crushing teeth and was large enough to swallow her hand to well past her wrist.

"Uncle Farrar, we have a favor to ask of you. It's a job, really."

"Yes?" The liquid eyes shifted from Nyssa to Abrial and her hand was freed. Nyssa tucked it behind her. Ghosts shouldn't be able to touch her, but somehow he had. If that rule could be broken, there was no knowing what else Farrar could do.

"Do you still have your pipe?"

"But of course." Farrar turned and plucked up a velvet cloak—half of red and half of yellow, just as she had expected—and a small bit of silver that had to be his pipe, though it had no holes. "Who do you need to get rid of?"

"About a dozen goblins and a few hungry trolls. Maybe the odd human or two."

"And you need *me* for this? What's happened to you, boy? As I recall you were able to take on as many back in the Battle of Grasse in thirteen-twenty-two—and did, gleefully."

"They have new weapons these days. They also have mental shields, those humans I mentioned. I can't risk their minds being able to call out for help. Any attack would have to be a physical one, and I don't know that I can kill them fast enough to stop some psychic message from getting out to their king. Anyway, I can't risk Nyssa being hurt or captured if for some reason I fail."

"I see. I won't be able to enter the real world. I've been barred from it, as you know," Farrar warned. "My help would have to be more ephemeral."

"You won't need to materialize. Nyssa can get you inside their minds far enough to make the musical manifestation real. You just need to distract them so they don't even think about putting in a call for help before they take the long walk off a conveniently tall cliff."

"She can get me into their heads? Directly? Without being terrified or bespelled herself? How very interesting." The black eyes were on Nyssa again, and this time they had a gleam that made her uncomfortable.

"Don't even think about it," Abrial warned sharply. "You can ask for any fee you like, except that one. She can't get to you, or you to her, without me as an intermediary, so don't even consider it."

"What a pity. Interesting females are so rare. But if you are feeling protective . . ."

"I am."

"Then so be it." Farrar swirled his cloak over his head twice and then dropped it down over his shoulders. Nyssa couldn't say for sure, because the inside of the cape was a mass of shadows, but she was fairly certain that it was lined with hundreds of rat pelts that had their heads still attached. Some seemed to be moving. "Well, shall we begin?"

"Yes. The sooner the better. We have a clutch of ghosts gathering back in the mundane world. Nyssa is also a human ghost-talker."

"So nice to be bilingual," Farrar murmured.

"I would suggest going after the psychics and trolls first. The goblins will be relatively helpless without them," Abrial added.

"My boy!" The voice was shocked. "Are you actually telling me how to do my job?"

"Sorry," Abrial said promptly. Then he added with a trace of surprise: "Be careful. I don't want you getting hurt either. We have no way of knowing how strong those psychics are. And I have no idea how much psychic damage a troll can do if properly guided."

"It'll never happen, my boy. There has never been an enchanter who could snare me. Now watch and learn. I may yet surprise you."

Nyssa's red piano appeared in the glade—at whose behest, she couldn't say. Certainly not her own. Sensing her unease, Abrial turned to her and raised a brow.

"Ready?"

She nodded, and once seated she began to play them back toward the real world.

"I see them now. I'll take it from here." Farrar's voice was distant. After a moment the piper put his holeless flute to his lips and eerie music filled the air.

Nyssa stopped playing, too unnerved by Farrar's song to try to accompany him on the piano. She sensed that she was able to resist because of her human blood, but if he shifted the song by even a few notes, she would also succumb to its deadly charm.

"Close your eyes," Abrial murmured, his expression grim as he closed up the piano. "I recognize this piece. It's very effective, and you really won't want to see what's happening."

Nyssa did as he suggested, and not a moment too soon. All around them the goblins began screaming, adding their voices to those of the wailing ghosts of Deadly. She didn't speak the lutin language but didn't have to in order to know what was happening. Somehow Farrar had been able to take control of the trolls, and they were busy picking up goblins three and four at a time and throwing them down into one of the nearby ravines filled with knifelike stones. The human psychics had been the first over the cliff. Being less hardy than the goblins, they had mercifully died on impact.

"Oh, Goddess." Nyssa put useless hands over her ears and tried to hold the noise at bay.

"You don't have to stay," Abrial said. "Go back and wait for me in the cabin. Farrar will understand why you didn't stick around to say good-bye."

Nyssa nodded. She didn't rush back to her body though, because she was fairly certain that she would hear the goblins screaming in the real world as well. There was also the danger of opening her eyes to a planet filled with new lutin ghosts—hostile ones. That wasn't something she wanted to face alone. Instead, she cowered in the gray place between the worlds and prayed that Abrial's uncle would hurry.

Chapter Ten

"Word on the grapevine is that King Carbon just lost his right-hand man in a no-name hellhole called Deadly," Thomas reported to Jack. "No one is mentioning Abrial by name, but I'm betting he's behind it. Humana Vox wasn't the type for suicide."

"Keep me posted," Jack said. "And let me know the moment you hear from Abrial. And see what our people in Mexico and New Orleans have to say. I'm sensing activity all over the south."

"It's a good thing we can pirate time on the goblin communication network," Thomas said. "Otherwise our phone bill would be the size of the entire Third World's GNP."

Abrial brought Nyssa a gallon jug of water and a six-pack of Coke and left the beverages to their fate. She was happy to guzzle his gifts while he investigated their transportation options.

It didn't take long. Deadly was, after all, a small town. It was also apparently bereft of four-wheel-drive vehicles that could get them off-road. And since off-road was the only safe way for them to travel, they would be riding what the locals colorfully called shank's mare: They'd be walking.

The countryside they walked through was raw, almost unfinished, and nothing lived there. Only wind and rain had tried to tame it, and those only halfheartedly. The rocks around them were not mere stone but giants' knives, sharp points that promised danger and even death to the unwary who climbed them. They were like the stones that had broken the goblins' bodies. Nyssa and Abrial moved quickly but carefully.

The endless, breathless surrounding ravines were stuffed with tumbleweeds and shattered boulders, and they made Nyssa think of the possibility of being both crushed and suffocated. And of getting lost. Very, very lost. Nyssa hadn't argued when Abrial decided to lead the way. Her usual dependable sense of direction had abandoned her. She didn't know where they were going anyway.

Upward they traveled, racing the sun for the crest of the mountain. Surrounding them now were shadows: patches of retreating darkness that waited expectantly and breathed and whispered as the dry winds occasionally passed: watchful sentinels for someone or something else that didn't like the day. The pressure inside Nyssa's head was also growing, watching, planning.

"Not too much longer," Abrial encouraged.

"You said that before."

Abrial didn't reply, and she felt guilty for sounding so waspish.

It didn't seem possible, but the land grew steadily more steep, austere, and impenetrable after they reached the mountain top. Nyssa slowed her steps and they reached a seeming dead end—which it was, unless you knew the magic word that would open the cliff face before them and let travelers pass through without scaling the last impossible face. And she didn't. Unless the password happened to be *Open Sesame*. Maybe she should try that. It might work, and magic was often more about will than specific words.

"Let me open this. You can fool around with the exit if you want," Abrial said, apparently hearing her thoughts clearly. "Just a bit farther on there will be—"

Water!

Nyssa's gasp interrupted Abrial. She stopped immediately, one foot still raised, and stared hard at the unexpected pool of quiet blackness that appeared on her left and began to spread over the stony ground, separating her from Abrial.

Abrial didn't gasp as she had, but she knew he was shocked. She also knew that the pool couldn't have actually manifested out of nowhere, especially not on the steep slope of an arroyo, for all that it seemed to have done just that. It sat there, still as death and defying gravity with invisible embankments.

"I didn't think there were any springs out here," she whispered, barely hearing her own voice above the ringing in her ears.

The pool was not a spring. It was a dark place where people drowned and monsters abided, but she still found it oddly inviting. In fact, she wasn't certain that she could look away even if her life depended on it—which it might, a part of her realized with sudden alarm.

"There aren't." Abrial inhaled, turning his head slowly as he scanned the land around them. "Nyssa, step back. Slowly. Don't let the water touch you."

"Maybe the rain . . . ?" she offered logically, the words almost coming from someone else. "It looks cool."

"Stop it. Don't you smell the difference? This isn't natural. Someone appears to be *helping* us again. And the list of candidates is very short and very nasty."

"But it can't be goblins. Not after we killed them." Her tone was more wistful than certain as she stared at the life-giving pool and then at the shadows creeping about them. Dawn, that bringer of heat, was close now, and night had begun to slink away. She sniffed the air like Abrial, hunting for danger, and smelled only seductive dampness, the sort of scent usually only experienced deep in underground caves. The impulse to bathe in the water was overwhelming. She knew it would help relieve the terrible pressure inside her skull.

She stepped closer and looked deep into the pool. Things were moving in there.

Something cracked open in her mind, and suddenly she had a glimpse of memory, just the snippet of a vision, but one of those despaired-of moments of recall that she thought had been forever wiped from her mind. The miraculous storeroom of memory, which others took for granted and that was usually locked to her, abruptly opened its door and beckoned.

And the water showed this to her. It was summer. She had stolen away from her mother when she was barely more than a toddler and gone out to the black pool that sometimes appeared in the pasture on nights when there was no moon. A deep voice that came from nowhere and everywhere had told her to go into the water, to drink deeply and long. Her mother had found her before she went in, and carried her away as she cried violently to be let into the black water. Her mother had told her that she had to forget, to shut her ears and mind and heart to the voice that called her, and back at the house had forced a potion on her. Nyssa slept for a long while then, and when she again awoke, it seemed she was older.

Even then, hardly more than a baby, Nyssa had been outraged at what her mother had done. She realized that her natural life cycle had been forced into an unnatural rhythm with an impossibly long sleep. *And it still was being contorted, wasn't it?* Part of it was the war between what-might-have-been and the-things-that-are. Part of the mental distress was the battle of the alien thing inside her wanting to get out, to escape her control. It wanted to be free—she could understand that.

Her true nature and her memories had been secreted both from the human world where her mother hid them after their escape from the goblins and also from herself in large measure. Her mother had forced her to deny certain aspects of her nature, out of fear and out of love. But she had to have known that eventually nature would seek to reassert itself in her daughter. Even as a child, those bonnets and demure dresses couldn't hide the power in Nyssa's eyes or in her body. Surely the woman had a plan for when that day arrived.

117

And all the delusions, rationalizations, and lies from her mother couldn't hide from her the emptiness inside, the loneliness, the incompleteness of her soul. Nyssa was different. She was alone. More alone than anyone in the world. She knew it then and she knew it now. She needed to go home—to wherever, whatever, whoever home was.

She was being called back. It was time to know the truth. All she had to do was step into the pool, and it would take her where she needed to go.

Unshed tears, grown unbearably bitter for being delayed for decades, filled her eyes, momentarily blinding her. Before the rediscovered memory was even half played out, Nyssa had stepped into the water and sunk almost to her neck. She would have fallen under completely, because she had no buoyancy and the pond was supernaturally deep, but Abrial bounded across the water and grabbed her hair. He hauled her out again. As she struggled against him, he dragged her three steps back from the edge and then dropped her on a flat rock, being careful not to touch any of the water streaming off her. It wasn't difficult to avoid because the rivulets hit the rocks and then disappeared without a trace.

"Nyssa!" For the first time Abrial sounded horrified. "That's an enchanted pool—goblin waters. You can't go in there. Who knows what could happen if you actually swallowed any of that stuff?"

"What happens is that I'd feel better," she answered in a voice that didn't sound much like her own, being both slow and deep and somehow unfamiliar with the English language. But it spoke the truth. She did feel a little better for her limited contact. Her skin wasn't as dry as it had been. Somehow, it had refreshed her in ways that merely drinking the water at Deadly had not. The door in her mind was also cracked open a few inches wider. All she needed was a little more water and then she'd know everything. Impulsively, she tried licking her skin, but the water wouldn't wet her tongue any more than it did the rocks.

"Maybe, but look at yourself. Nyssa, please think! Is this normal? Look at your body. Look at your clothes." She did as Abrial asked. In less than a minute, she was completely dry. As the last of the phantom water evaporated, so did the voice that had been calling her home.

Home? What home? The pressure in her head deflated. Suddenly Nyssa was dizzy and afraid.

"Abrial?" she whispered, starting to shiver. "It had me."

"It?" He stared in consternation, for the first time not able to make a mental connection, and obviously not understanding her words.

"Please." But please *what*? She didn't know.

"Shh! You're safe now. I'm right here." Abrial sat down beside her, leaning against a boulder. He looked suddenly tired as he reached for her hand.

"Abrial," she whispered again, loneliness breaking over her, filling up that horrible hole of forgetfulness inside her with something even more terrible. Pain wracked her, body and soul.

She turned to Abrial in desperation. He, the creature of night and bad dreams, a killer and a demon, in that moment also looked like comfort and salvation. He was a monster, but then—she admitted—so was she. Who better to ask for help?

For the second time that night, she gave in to impulse. Hating herself for the weakness, Nyssa moved toward him, reaching out with pleading eyes as well as arms, asking for comfort in the only place that offered. Her need for Abrial was irrational, even insane. But reason and sanity had less and less meaning for her all the time.

"Shh! You're safe now. I'm right here," Abrial told her, wondering if it was completely true.

"But where is here?" Nyssa asked as she crawled into his lap. He looked and was momentarily puzzled by her actions; but realizing what she wanted— needed—he slowly wrapped his arms around her, offering physical comfort as he had seen humans do.

"Try not to worry," he said, feeling wholly inadequate. He stroked a hand down her back. He enjoyed the sensation, and he was fairly certain that he should be feeling some guilt about that. Lust had no place in an offer of comfort. He tried again. "It's all right. I got you out of the water in time. You didn't drink any of it. Don't be so afraid."

But she was afraid. He could feel it inside her: a giant black thing that smothered all other emotions, blotting out his ability to connect with her mentally through the normal channels he used.

"Can I be damned without being dead? Can I be in hell and not know it? Abrial, I feel like I have scorch marks on my soul," she whispered, shaking hard and cuddling closer. "I feel lost—dead."

"I'm sure that you do," he answered, giving in to an impulse and burying his face in her hair. It was thick and smelled somehow exotic. "This has to have been very frightening and very revolting. I'm sorry you saw any of what happened with the goblins. It was never my intention that you be so involved."

"Involved? I couldn't be more involved—or more blind." She laughed humorlessly. "Abrial, please help me. I admit it; I'm lost. I need help to find out where I am. Why I am. Who I am." She looked up, snagging his gaze. "Look inside me. I know you can see me. Tell me what you see inside. I won't try to hide anything now. Tell me who I am before I give in to that voice."

He attempted to do as she asked. He stared into her mind, looking more deeply than he ever had, but all he saw was a whirlpool of nightmare images. And there was a part of her that had a dark veil laid over it, thick, like a shroud. Only that part pulsed with life and intent—and it radiated hostility and fear, the kind of hostility and fear that would be willing to destroy everything when backed into a corner. He retreated slowly, not provoking it.

"I am helping," he said at last. *As much as he could.* "And I will help more when I can. There is some good news in all this, you know."

Nyssa gazed up at him, her eyes unblinking and her expression so bleak he could barely stand to look at it. Then something shifted in her psyche. He could feel her gathering herself, fighting back despair and exhaustion and fear—fighting the black thing that overshadowed her mind. Hope stirred in her and her expression grew less stark.

She would believe him now, whatever he said, because she needed to. The fact shook him. No one had ever been willing to trust him in this way. This sort of faith was reserved for saints.

"I could use some good news," she said softly. "What is it?"

Abrial wished that he knew better what to say, what would offer comfort without deluding her and placing her in even greater danger because she thought she was safe. But all he had to offer was the cold comfort of truth. He hoped it was enough.

"Souls can burn, Nyssa. They can writhe in torment, be made small, or spread thin—but they can't die. You will survive this trial. If you want to. The outcome is up to you. It may not seem like it, but you have a choice."

She nodded once, a reluctant gesture.

"Will I want to?" she asked, her voice barely audible. "I thought I could face anything. But I've been lost for so long. Even now, I don't really know who I am. What I am. I can't *remember*."

Her anguish touched him. She had a direct line into his psyche now, a power cord that conducted heavy emotion—not something he wanted to experience, but he didn't turn away from her pain.

"I don't know what the future holds, what role in the affairs of goblins you may yet have to play. But if you will let me stay in your mind, I will give you the strength you need to find out who and what you are. All you have to do is stay the course and trust me. The answers will be revealed. And soon. I can feel it. For good or for ill, you will know the truth." He could promise no more than that, even though he wanted to. Her grief and confusion made him want to promise all sorts of rash and impossible things.

"I am *something*, aren't I?" she asked. "Not human. You felt it, didn't you? The dark thing inside."

"Yes. You're not all human. But that isn't necessarily a bad thing. Mixed blood can give you strength. We'll have to wait and see what it means. And worrying about it now doesn't help." He wondered if he should mention what he had begun to suspect. It didn't seem the wisest of places or the most propitious of moments to bring up her perhaps being of goblin blood. Did she know that herself?

"Abrial." She sighed and began to straighten. The familiar complaining tone had re-entered her voice, and he was very glad to hear it. Some of the despair that had touched him fell away as she remastered her wayward feelings and stuffed the desperate ones back inside. The black thing in her mind began to shrink, pulling in on itself. "You really suck at this comfort-and-support thing. Can't you lie a little for a good cause?"

"No, not about this." He let his arms drop, and she slid from his lap. He was both relieved and sorry to see her go. He sensed she felt the same way.

"You could try."

"To what end? I know I'm no good at offering comfort. It wasn't what I was made to do. But we're both learning to improvise, so there's hope for this too, I guess." He rose to his feet and then, after a pause, offered her a hand. "We have to go. We need to be through this pass before sunrise or we'll be trapped here all day. The gate only works at night."

"Where are we going?"

123

"On the other side is a sort of encampment where gypsies live."

"Gypsies?" She took his outstretched fingers and allowed him to pull her to her feet. She embraced the change of subject as well as his hand and asked hopefully: "Like golden earrings and Spanish guitars and exotic beauties dancing under the moon?"

"No, like broken-down motor homes with tuck-and-roll upholstery and bobble fringe on the dashboard. And homemade moonshine and the odd meth lab. And sometimes some cocaine and marijuana being run up from Mexico."

"Oh, swell. And we want to go there because . . ."

He found himself beginning to smile. She sometimes brought out the most ridiculous feelings in him, and he had decided that as alien as the experience was, he mostly liked it.

"Because it is the nearest place where we can find another vehicle." Still holding her hand, Abrial walked around where the pool had been. While they had been talking the water had faded away, again revealing the path, but he was taking no chances. Goblins could be canny creatures. They might have some trap that would sense if they stepped on the magicked ground. He didn't want to tumble into a goblin hole. More importantly, he didn't want them getting Nyssa. They would take whatever that dark thing inside was and turn it against her.

"I want transportation as much as anyone, but a motor home with bobble fringe on the dashboard? That won't be a bit conspicuous? And slow?"

"You need to broaden your sense of style. There is

more to the colorful human experience than Prada shoes."

"Well, I don't have those anymore either," she said grumpily, and Abrial nearly laughed. She glared at him. "That just pisses me off. And my purse is gone too. I don't even have a hairbrush!"

"I'll get you another pair of shoes," he promised. "And a hairbrush."

"Not at Camp Bobble you won't," she muttered. "Damn it! Those were my favorite shoes. They were, as the clerk said, *totally deck. Blazing.* Damned goblins!"

"That's it—feel the anger," he urged her. "A woman's rage is a powerful thing."

Nyssa snorted, sounding like herself again. This relieved Abrial tremendously. They would both have to be strong to face what he suspected was waiting for them between here and Cadalach, and he didn't know how to give her what she needed without taking total control of her mind—something that would feel like rape and leave her scarred forever. Her body he could protect from outside threats, and even her dreams. But her spirit and emotions were from realms beyond his ken.

He stopped in front of a blank cliff face and, after glancing at her, spoke in the old language.

This time, she didn't flinch when the mountain split in two and folded back on itself. She was getting used to things, adapting at a rapid pace. He just hoped it was rapid enough, and that she was adaptive enough to stay in control of her emotions and sanity. He didn't want to go any deeper into her mind—for both her sake and his own. To do so was self-demolition. And he didn't know what would happen if he pulled back the shroud of her memories before she was ready to have the hidden black thing revealed.

Chapter Eleven

"So, how do things look to you?" Nyssa asked. Their trek through the mountain had been fast and painless, with none of the vague sensation of vertigo she had experienced earlier.

"Things are pretty good, considering we're on the wrong side of the encampment from the cars, and the place is full of illegal Third-Worlders who wear guns as their basic accessory, and some of whom are obviously schizophrenic and violent—and the rest are drug runners."

"But at least I don't see any goblins or FBI types." Nyssa's voice was properly hushed, but she looked more relaxed than she had before.

"How can you tell?"

"Please! With those ugly suits and shoes the Feds wear?"

"You have a point. So I don't suppose we need to stay here jerking off until we go blind. The sun is already rising over the mountains."

"Jerking off? You spend a lot of time interfering with yourself, do you?" she asked.

"'Interfering with myself'!" he almost laughed. "That's an old phrase. You must have been raised a Catholic."

Nyssa thought about this and answered seriously: "I don't think so."

"You don't think so?" Abrial asked. A bottle shattered around the corner, and two drunks began snarling at one another. "This is more of what we were talking about earlier, about not remembering even your birthday?" he asked tentatively.

"Yes," Nyssa confessed. "I don't remember very much about my childhood at all. Bits and pieces have started to come back though."

"You really don't remember? That wasn't just some metaphor—a way of saying that you had lost your way emotionally?" Abrial looked a bit grim.

"No. I meant it literally. I have no clear memories of my early childhood. I do not know anything about myself before age five. And even then my memories are spotty. They're vivid, like still-life paintings, but lack continuity and context. It's almost as if I was shown random pictures or told arbitrarily selected stories about what happened back then but didn't experience things firsthand. Sometimes I wonder if the memories are real."

"Is this by choice though? Did something horrible happen to you, something you chose to forget? Or has someone shadowed your brain against your will?"

"I don't know for sure. I think it was done to me. It's part of what I've been looking for in The Yesterdays. I want to know who did this to me . . . and how.

And why. I want to know who I am." She shrugged helplessly. "But I'm not there. Or if I am, I can't find me. It's as though I don't exist—not even in the past."

"That is probably because you aren't dead. There are rules about you meeting up with yourself, you know."

"I thought of that. But I can't find my mother either. Or anyone I think I remember: Mr. Granger, who had a farm next to us and died when his tractor rolled over on him; Miss Quinn, my third-grade teacher who passed away halfway through the school year when I was eight. There was a man I called Uncle Bob, a pilot who supposedly died when I was fourteen. I think I remember these people, but no one I think I was close to is there. I've wandered around the dreamlands like that chick in that kid's story asking everyone I find—'Do you know me? Are you my mother?'"

Another bottle shattered, and someone screamed hoarsely. The drunks were determined to get in one last fight before going to bed.

"It's like I imagined them all."

"Damn it. We better go," Abrial said, rising to his feet and giving her a hand. The flames of a distant fire painted his face with wavering red light. "But I think maybe you better tell me everything you recall about your parents—whether real memories or not. I have a feeling that your father may play a huge part in this. It would be—what?" he asked as her footsteps faltered. "What's wrong? You're as gray as the sheets in a one-star motel."

"Thanks a lot."

"Honey, it can't be that bad. Especially if you don't

remember much about it. Just tell me the bits that you do know."

"I don't feel ready to talk about this. I'm going to start crying or something." Nyssa swallowed and took Abrial's hand, trying not to think about the hobgoblin but failing. "I've made a fool of myself once this evening. I don't want to do it again."

"You were a fool twice. But who's counting?"

"You bastard." She punched him in the arm. "That wasn't nice. You can't throw that last moment of weakness at me right now."

"I can't?"

"No. Anyhow, it can so be that bad. Man, you have no idea."

Don't think about it! Don't think about it! We don't want him to know, her subconscious whimpered. *No one can know. He'll think we're a monster—and then he'll leave us.*

"Fine, so it's bad. I'm just saying, why not talk about this rationally? You are acting like . . . like . . ." Abrial stared at her, his brows drawing together for an instant before his eyes went wide. "Oh, Goddess! I've got it now! It's Qasim, isn't it? He's your father. You aren't just part goblin—you're part hobgoblin. Well, damn, girl. That's bad news."

She waited, but that was all he said. There were no gasps and no recriminations. He didn't faint or run away. Nyssa finally sighed and then looked about quickly, half expecting to see that sinister shadow lurking nearby. She was nervous, but mainly she just felt relief to have the matter out in the open.

"I'm afraid so. I don't have hard proof, but the circumstantial evidence points that way, and everyone else seems convinced."

"And that's why the goblins are after you? They want to take you to dear old dad?"

"No—Goddess, no! What are you thinking? It can't be that." She flinched as yet another bottle shattered, this one closer to them.

"What, then?" Abrial began towing her toward the makeshift parking lot at the back of the encampment. "Let's have it all. Even if it's just speculation. I can't protect you if I don't know what's going on." As she hesitated, he added: "We're supposed to be a team. I thought you trusted me."

"I do. Really." Nyssa gathered herself for a moment. The story was one she had learned in bits and pieces while doing her research. It didn't have any place in her conscious memory, but it was still difficult to talk about.

"My mother was raped. She was a wise woman—a Sabine and a healer—who was brought to the Seelie Court to help with faerie births. You've heard of these human midwives?" She waited for Abrial to look back and nod. "Anyhow, she was marked as sacred and no one could touch her. The Seelie and Unseelie Courts agreed to this. At least that's what the stories say. Mother never talked about any of it. Or if she did, I don't remember." She wiped the trickles of sweat from her brow. The sun was still just below the hills, but the heat was already building.

"I see. But Qasim was always a little crazy and a lot wild, and he decided he had to have her anyway. And she got pregnant. I vaguely recall this event now,"

Abrial said. "Queen Mabigon was enraged. He had been her lover, you know. The Seelie Court was in uproar too. King Finvarra demanded Qasim's blood. There was even talk of war."

"Yes. Mother—if it was my mother and not some other healer—had the right to demand my father's death for what he had done. The goblins, who supposedly controlled the hobgoblins, were allies of the Unseelie Queen. They in turn were bound to uphold the sentence of death if the queen insisted on it. And Mabigon did—reluctantly. She simply couldn't risk a war with King Finvarra."

"Like I said, I dimly recall this. Nyssa," he said gently, "you realize that this happened nearly two hundred years ago, right?"

"Yes. That is partly why I haven't totally accepted the story as true. I mean, how can I be two hundred years old? I don't look two hundred. I don't have two hundred years of memory. Hell, I don't have twenty. I barely have ten."

"I don't know why you haven't aged—maybe it's genetics that has prolonged your life. Though, even a pure-blood hobgoblin would normally look older than you do." He shrugged. "Never mind that for now. So, what happened after? Your mother didn't ask for his head on a platter?"

"His heart. That's what was offered, not the head. And she didn't. My mother was a healer. She—or any healer—couldn't ask that he be killed. It would have rebounded on her and destroyed her ability to save lives. I think that is why he chose her as a victim. He knew he'd be safe from retribution. And he knew she'd keep the child. It was the only way he would be

132

allowed to reproduce, since the goblin kings had forbidden the hobgoblins to breed." Her voice was breathless as she trotted to keep up with Abrial. "Anyway, since the goblins were growing frightened of Qasim anyway, they let the Unseelie queen imprison him until the child was old enough to pass judgment on him. As the other victim of his crime, Mabigon said it was right that the child choose in her mother's place. And it was probable that the offspring would not be a healer, not with hobgoblin blood. King Finvarra eventually agreed to this."

"How convenient. And the light dawns," he said, slowing down as they came to a row of cars and he began checking doors to see if any were open. Most looked too derelict to be of any use. "But things went awry. The hobgoblins didn't take this judgment lying down. And when the other hobgoblins rebelled at this sentence against their leader, they were all imprisoned or killed."

"Yes."

"But they didn't have their hearts removed like Qasim did. They were slain by silver swords."

"Yes. The removal of Qasim's heart was a delaying tactic, meant to rob him of power until sentence could be carried out. It somehow put him in a sort of suspended animation—not alive and not dead. Then they shut him up inside a tree in a sacred lutin grove." She added, to herself, "Which those monks somehow found."

"With some outside help, I'm betting," Abrial said.

"Most likely. I couldn't discover whose though."

"So, do you think the goblins, or Queen Mabigon, shrouded your mind so you wouldn't ever recall what

133

happened? That wouldn't be ethical, but that wouldn't have stopped my dear dead queen. She wasn't at all pleased at having her lover taken away." The door to a '57 Chevy opened with a heavy clunk when Abrial tugged. He shoved her into the car and then piled in after her. Nyssa was grateful that the shift was in the column or she would have been impaled. "Here we go. This is just what we need. Next best thing to a Sherman tank."

Abrial's calm, as always, allowed Nyssa to also be almost tranquil as she discussed this horror. The relief of finally sharing her fears was tremendous.

"I don't know who did it. Mom might have arranged it, since she would have believed that patricide would scar my soul. She certainly hid me away from the truth. If it is the truth. And she never encouraged my *gifts.*" Nyssa exhaled. "But I have no real evidence. And I don't dare just walk into some doctor's office and demand they test my DNA. The medical databases aren't secure. If I am what I think I am, the goblins would know about it immediately." She watched as Abrial broke open the Chevy's steering column and began hot-wiring the car. "What I suspect now is that the goblins will do anything they can to keep me away from this newly resurrected weapon."

"Keep you away?" Abrial looked at her. "When did you have this insight? After your dip in the pool? Something seemed to happen to you then. It was like your brain disappeared. For a moment, I couldn't find you, and then when you came back you were frightened."

"Yes. I had a memory then of when I was maybe two or three and went out to another dark pool to try and swim. My mother stopped me before I could go to Qasim."

"And you're convinced that the goblins are sure that you'd do what your mother couldn't manage and kill him? And they don't want their tool taken from them?"

"I'm not convinced of anything—that's the trouble. And it's too late to make nice now anyway. What *they* can see is that we probably killed the goblins back in Deadly. No one is going to buy that it was some suicide pact that made all of them jump off that cliff, you know. A dozen dead goblins and a few trolls and psychics is suggestive of our intent, don't you think? I mean, if I were the goblins, I would take this as a sign of hostile inclination on our part toward their species and plans."

"True."

"So they don't have to be convinced of what I'll do," she pointed out. Her voice was steady, but only with an effort. It was difficult to articulate the likelihood of one's own death. "They can't afford to take the risk that I might forgive him. Or might not. Either way, it's potentially bad news. One way, he gets all his powers back and is stronger than they are because he is of pure blood. The other way, he dies and they can never make use of him—supposing they want to."

"And H.U.G.?" Abrial nodded as the engine caught and roared to life. Nyssa looked about nervously. Surely the car's owner would recognize the distinctive roar and come to investigate.

"Well, I'm guessing, but if they aren't trying to use him for their own ends—and even if they are—they probably don't want to take the chance of me forgiving dear old Dad and making him truly immortal either. That was the other side of the sentence Mabigon passed, you see. I forgive him and he gets a free pass—forever." She added, "It's probably why King Carbon sent Vox and the goons to deal with this. He wasn't leaving anything to chance." She added: "Losing Vox is going to really piss him off. We're going to have to be extra careful."

"You're telling me." Abrial dropped the transmission into reverse and began backing out. He shot her a quick glance and asked: "Is that even a possibility? That you would forgive him?"

"It doesn't matter," she said again, not wanting to face the question yet. "They can't risk it. After all, if I forgive him, the last of the shackles Queen Mabigon laid on him will be broken. As it is, he can't approach or enslave anyone from the Unseelie Court, and not the goblins either. Not even other hobgoblins, should any have survived. The others are all protected by the queen's sentence as long as things remain as they are."

"Yes, they would be." Abrial threw the car into first and then quickly changed up through the gears as they left Camp Bobble behind them. "So that's why H.U.G. is going after you with such diligence. You threaten the balance of power. Especially if you know where Qasim's heart is. Everyone will be wanting that too. And I'm not sure what would happen if he was given his heart back. He might not need your forgiveness then. A half loaf might be enough for whatever he has planned."

"Quite possibly." Nyssa made her hands stay still and not reach for the scar on her chest. "H.U.G. faces the same conundrum as the goblins. If they want to use Qasim, they can't afford the risk that I'll kill him. And if they want him dead eventually, they can't take a chance I'll make him immortal." She looked away from Abrial, pretending to study the nonexistent view from the passenger window. She didn't ask about air conditioning; there wasn't any. "What I haven't figured out is why Jack—or the shian—wants me. They are the real jokers in the deck. What's in it for them?"

"Ah—a good question," Abrial admitted. "At least you know that they want you alive. Jack wouldn't have sent me otherwise. At least, not in the flesh."

"You know, you are taking this very calmly. Hobgoblins and H.U.G. and the FBI. I wouldn't believe any of it, and would panic if someone convinced me this story was true."

"Calm is the only way I take anything. Anyhow, I had begun to suspect half of this stuff. Only I was thinking it was the goblins running interference on our behalf, not Qasim himself."

Nyssa stared at him.

"Qasim?" she said stupidly. "You think *he*'s helping me?"

"Isn't it obvious? Most hobgoblins can control the weather and from great distances. Qasim also had a way with ghosts. One of his favorite parlor tricks was raising the dead so Queen Mabigon could torment her enemies' spirits."

"Damn. I didn't know about that. It wasn't in the records."

"This is a new wrinkle. More than ever, we need to get some feedback from Jack. Maybe he knows more about what's going on by now. We've got to get to a phone or radio ASAP."

"We still don't know anything for sure," Nyssa pointed out. "It's all guesses and supposition, a real house of cards."

"Yeah, but they're good guesses and suppositions. And whatever the answer, the situation for us hasn't changed. We are left with the same problem we had before."

"Yeah, we're on our own, in the middle of the desert, miles from help, and everyone wants me dead."

"Not everyone. Not Qasim. Not Jack. Probably not ninety-nine percent of the people we meet, including those in law-enforcement and even H.U.G. But we can't trust any of the players—whatever they offer us in the way of deals or shelter. It would be easier for everyone—except maybe Qasim—to have you dead right now. And we can't count on him wanting you alive for long, even if you forgive him."

Nyssa finally tuned to look at Abrial. "Like I said before, you really suck at this comfort-and-support stuff. Couldn't you at least hold my hand while you deliver the bad news that I'm a real insurance risk?"

"I'm busy driving. And I know that I suck at this. But maybe I'll get better." He added under his breath: "I suppose I'll have to now. I'm well and truly hooked."

"There you go again! I hate it when you're cryptic," Nyssa complained. "You aren't hooked, you know— not the way I am. And even if you can't hold my hand, this would be a good time for you to start practicing saying reassuring things in clear, declarative sentences. I'm scared here and starting to panic. Throw me a bone."

"Clear sentences? That's a tall order given the obscurity of the problem, but I'll try." He raised one finger. "I am pretty sure Jack doesn't mean you any harm. But like I said, it wasn't he who decided to bring you to Cadalach. To a degree, we all take our orders from a higher power."

"He really didn't want me—he isn't after power or something?" She looked back at Abrial. They were running without headlights, so she couldn't discern his features as easily as she would like. "Then who did? Who is the higher power?"

"No one. It's like I said. It was the shian itself that wanted you brought in. These tomhnafurachs have minds of their own—wills of their own. Agendas too, I suspect. It's just that we can't understand them." He added to himself: "Maybe Cyra will know. The mound talks to her."

"The *shian* wants me? Not Jack? Really and truly?"

"Yes."

"But why? How? I still don't understand why it would care about the goblins or the fey or anything so small. It's like—I don't know—like Mother Nature caring about a flea."

"I don't know why." His head turned her way. He said clearly and concisely: "But I can promise you that I won't let anything bad happen to you, flea or not."

Nyssa thought about this as she stared out the dusty windshield. She finally said: "You swear? Not even if Jack decides I need to die?"

"Take it to the bank," he answered, turning his attention back to the road. "Now get some sleep if you can. I can't be reassuring you all day. This is some-

139

thing I need to work up to—maybe even read a how-to book or something."

Nyssa sighed. "I'd love to sleep, but is that wise? Two sets of eyes are probably better than one. And you know how I sometimes dream."

"You'll be okay. I'm with you now, remember?" The velvet thing in her mind gave a soft caress. Was it affection, reassurance, warning? She couldn't say. She had almost forgotten that it was there; Abrial hadn't been using it.

"Okay," she agreed, giving in and letting her body slump down in the seat, trying to make herself comfortable against the car's heavy door. "But wake me in an hour and I'll spell you. You're tired too."

"Here," he said, reaching for her and pulling her down across the bench seat, settling her head into his lap. His long fingers brushed her hair back from her face. The gesture seemed thoughtful, perhaps even affectionate, but Nyssa knew it could mean anything. Abrial still baffled her.

"Try not to get in a head-on, will you?" she mumbled through a yawn. "I don't think my looks would improve for having a wheel embedded in my face."

"I'll do my best," he said, returning his hand to the steering wheel. "We wouldn't want to make it too easy for the bad guys anyway. Now get some rest. And *don't worry*. This old car's electrical systems can't take you in full-fret mode."

"Shut up, already. You're ruining the moment."

"Are we having a moment?" She was sure there was a smile in his voice.

"We could, if you'd let it happen. Sheesh, you have to ask? We're almost sleeping together. I've bared my very soul to you. And we've committed a dozen felonies together."

"So we have. Maybe we'll have another moment later, when it's more convenient."

Nyssa relaxed, and so did he. She knew that he could feel it: a lessening of the pain of the secret she had carried that had overshadowed her heart. Who would have thought it, but teasing and brutal truth from this cold person was actually helping. Perhaps he *was* getting better at comforting her. And maybe she was getting better at accepting what reassurance he could offer.

"Do you ever live for the moment?" she asked.

"Yes, for all of them, every precious one of them." His voice was definite.

"I'd like to know more about you, Abrial. If you'd like to tell me. I've never met anyone like you. You're . . . different. Your family is different too." Her words were beginning to slur. Abrial gave her a tiny nudge in the direction of sleep, and she didn't protest.

"Yes, I'm different. And my family's very different. Very, very different. In fact, too damned different. So let's concentrate on you for now. There are great powers in you, as yet inert. I can feel them. At the right time, they will come alive. It will probably be exciting to find out what they are." His voice was dry.

"More excitement. Oh, goody." She tried but couldn't manage to sound as dry. Probably it was the yawn that was threatening to escape her. "But I want some breakfast first. A big breakfast, with pancakes and steak and eggs. You don't feed me enough. Adventurers need food as well as water."

"I'll try to do better at that too."

"Good." She yawned again. "I hope I don't dream of Farrar."

"That would be best. He'd never be able to resist the invitation, and I have enough to worry about as it is."

Chapter Twelve

Abrial? Cyra asked, listening as the faerie mound amplified the night demon's thoughts. Even with the shian's help, his voice was only a faint vibration in the back of her mind.

Yes, at last. I've been trying to get to Jack, but the psychic barricades are up. We are almost to town now. I'll be able to use the PDA once we're there.

He'll be relieved to hear from you. Qasim and the goblins are both on the move—the goblins in massive numbers—and Cadalach is under some kind of psychic siege.

How are you getting through?

I can only talk to you because I am at Ianna Fe's elfin stronghold. It's the shian where Thomas and I met, and the goblin psychics haven't discovered its location yet. Thomas has some files to send to you, but they'll have to go electronically.

Give me a couple hours. And take care. Many of those elfin mounds were booby-trapped in a last de-

fensive maneuver to preserve them from the humans and goblins.

I know, we discovered that on our first visit. The Goddess be with you both.

There was a moment of surprise and then he answered: *And also with you.*

The old Chevrolet ate up the miles without complaining as they headed for Last Chance, another small mining town miles off the highway. They were passing through an area called Forgery Flat for some long-forgotten reason that probably had something to do with ironwork but might equally have had to do with some other criminal behavior. They were alone on the dirt road, but people had been there before them and in great numbers. Their discarded beer bottles littered the side of the road with shards of glittering glass that hurt the eyes.

There wasn't much in the way of vegetation to break up the stony monotony, just some warped Joshua trees that were permanently bowed from trying to duck away from the savage sun. It was still morning, but the air was so thick with heat that the Chevy had to push through it, and Nyssa was certain she would be able to see the turbulence behind them if she looked back.

The land had long since passed from magnificent to frightening. Moonlight gave the landscape a severe, transcendental beauty that wasn't possible in the light of day. The only magnificent thing to look at right then was Abrial, and she didn't dare take her eyes off the road long enough to appreciate him.

As if hearing her thoughts, Abrial's eyes opened. It

was a little unnerving to watch him sleep because his body did not seem to relax. He looked much as he did when he dreamwalked, alert but with his eyes closed.

"We're going to need gas soon," Nyssa said in a rusty voice.

"We'll leave the car outside of town," Abrial answered. "It has probably been reported as stolen by now. We'll find another."

Nyssa suppressed a sigh. She didn't like stealing cars, but she had had quite enough of walking in the last day. And night.

"Were you able to find Jack?"

"No, there are psychic trip lines everywhere. But I raised Cyra since she is in another location—some elfin hideout the goblins aren't watching. We'll have to collect some newspapers in Last Chance and see what they have to say about news of the world. It sounds like Qasim is on the move and doesn't care who knows it. Everyone at Cadalach is nervous."

"Swell." The thing about being focused on one thing—even on something horrible—was that it shrunk your world down to something that felt almost manageable in size. Qasim she could deal with—intellectually. "Okay, we ditch the car and read the newspapers. And then?"

"And then we pray the PDA is working. I'd like as much intel as possible from Thomas about what and where the goblins and Federal boys are amassing. I don't know how long we can go on avoiding highways, missiles, and bullets by blind luck alone."

"That all sounds good to me."

"I bet a shower does too." He turned and smiled at her.

"Be still my heart! Don't tease me, Abrial. You know how I love my water."

"No teasing. I think a brief stay in a motel would be wise. We shouldn't have you out in the sun any more than necessary. You're incredibly strong, but the daylight is taking its toll on you."

"I'm okay," she reassured him. "I can go on if it's best. Daytime is the best for avoiding goblins, isn't it?"

"I know you can go on. It just isn't necessary right now. We'll take a few hours to rest and get clean— and to find out where the bad guys are lurking. We'll also find you some new clothes. Those are looking rather the worse for wear."

"Bet Forgery Flat has never even heard of Prada."

"We actually aren't stopping until Last Chance. But I bet you're right. So we won't be conspicuous and ask for it."

The only motel in Last Chance was not a four-star model. In fact, it would have been stretching things to give the six-room motor court two stars. But it had indoor plumbing and a bathroom floor that, while badly bowed from water damage, did not actually collapse under them. The beds might have been more like hammocks than mattresses, but the sheets were clean, and the room only vaguely smelled of smoke. It had a working phone, and it managed semi-warm water from the bathroom's rusty pipes. And best of all, the manager didn't ask for ID, home addresses, or anything besides twenty bucks. Nyssa and Abrial couldn't ask for anything more.

"How's your Spanish?" Abrial said as Nyssa emerged from the shower looking pink and scrubbed.

146

It was an easily achieved look, because the water was thick with abrasive minerals.

"Pretty good after my stay in Mexico. What have you got there?" Nyssa wrapped the threadbare towel around her hair and came over to the small desk.

"Since we are short on international newspapers here, Thomas just sent me a piece that appeared fifteen days ago in *El Universal*." He knelt beside her and offered the PDA, but she shook her head.

"The batteries," she explained. "I don't trust myself when I'm so tired."

"Right. Well, it seems Qasim has been doing ritual killings as he works his way north."

Nyssa scanned the lines quickly. With an effort, she managed to keep her voice calm. "Yes, this sounds like a hobgoblin ritual murder, the bodies all laid out in compass points with their heads missing. H.U.G. had some files on this from the hobgoblin slayings in New Orleans. I wish we could get more details. If only I could dreamwalk. I could just stroll into H.U.G.'s office and get what I want. I know just where the files are."

"No. We got away with our metaphysical stunt last time because the goblins didn't expect you to sneak through The Yesterdays, or for us to employ Uncle Farrar as a tool. But you can bet they've posted psychic watchers now—and H.U.G.'s spies in L.A. have probably passed the word on as well. Those files will be booby-trapped."

"I guess. It would just be handy. I feel rather useless. Like I've been lamed or blinded."

"It would be very handy but very unwise. And you are far from useless. I would never have made it into

147

The Yesterdays without you." Abrial pushed a button, and another piece sprang up on his PDA's tiny screen.

"Bernalillo—that's in New Mexico, isn't it?" Nyssa asked, after reading the second gruesome account of a mass murder. She swallowed hard.

"Yes. That happened eight days ago." Abrial pushed the button again. "And this happened in Pahrump last night."

"That is Nevada, isn't it?"

"Yes, near Sin City. There are a couple of other stories as well." Abrial switched screens again.

"The day just gets better and better—and it's hardly even begun." Muttering, Nyssa read the various reports of strangling and shootings as Abrial slowly scrolled through them. "At least no one seems to have found the bodies in Deadly."

"No one in the press, anyway. I suspect that place may turn into a mystery spot where everyone thinks the inhabitants just got up one morning and left."

"Like a ghost ship."

"Yeah. So, looking at this, we know where the goblins have been. Just play connect-the-strangled-corpses fanning out from the City of Angels," Abrial said. "And clearly Qasim isn't being coy about his activities either."

"And what about all the bodies with bullet holes in them? Those look fairly mundane."

"Those would be the FBI or H.U.G. Don't know what Thomas saw that made him flag the stories, but he wouldn't have sent them unless there was a connection."

"And, as you said, the decapitations are probably all Qasim."

"Greedy bastard. Humans, the other white meat. I've been thinking about this. These killings seem excessive, but he may need a steady diet of victims to keep going. Not having his heart has to be slowing him down."

"But so many? And so often?"

"He's building his strength, preparing himself for a magical confrontation."

Distraught, Nyssa looked up from the PDA. "Abrial, is he heading for Cadalach on his own? Or am I leading him to your friends?" she asked abruptly.

"I don't know," he answered frankly. "And neither does Thomas. It might be that he's going to Las Vegas rather than Cadalach. The hive there is reorganizing and in need of a leader. It may be someone's plan that the remains of the Sin City hive join forces with another hive. Or all the other hives. Carbon has watched a lot of TV. He's seen the 'reach out and touch someone' ads too."

"Yeah, and *'Double your pleasure, double your fun,'*" Nyssa said, feeling suddenly both ill and certain that Abrial was right. Humans had been fortunate that the goblin hives had refused to cooperate with one another so far, but their luck couldn't hold forever.

"Most likely Carbon or whoever will want Qasim to join together all the western hives—the ones who don't have firmly established leaders like in Santa Fe and Phoenix. But we have to assume that he is probably also heading toward you—killing two birds with one stone, so to speak." Abrial looked at her, pity in his dark eyes. "Sorry, Nyssa, but you're going to have to make up your mind soon, you know. Whether or not you want to forgive him . . . or even meet him."

149

Nyssa stared at him, knowing her face was filled with the strain of the ongoing dread of confrontation and not bothering to hide it. "How did you know?" she asked in a whisper. "I haven't allowed myself to think about it."

"I haven't been eavesdropping on your inner thoughts," he promised. "It's just that I think it's natural that you'd want to meet your father—whoever he is, whatever he is."

"You think? I'm not so sure. Consider what he is— what he's done. He's a rapist and a mass murderer. Any sane person would want him exterminated." Her voice was bitter and angry. The bitterness was for Qasim, the anger for herself.

"I *am* thinking about it. And I am certain that when he opens his arms and cries *'My beloved daughter, how I have missed thee!'* a part of you will want to believe him. It's unfortunate, but it's natural. No one blames you for being conflicted. I, least of all."

"But it will all be lies, won't it?" she asked, willing herself not to cry. She had rejected the right to feel sorry for herself when she embarked on this quest; she wasn't going to give in to self-pity now. Abrial had already been forced to buck her up once, and she wouldn't ask it of him again.

Abrial didn't answer, and she went on: "Because I'm *not* loved. Daddy dearest isn't coming back because he misses me. He just wants his heart back and he thinks I know where it is."

"Yes, and I'm afraid he'll probably lie to you to get what he wants. Probably because he can't just take back the heart without your consent. That was part of the sentence laid on him—no full reprieve without your forgiveness," Abrial responded, as always refusing to blunt the truth just to comfort her. "But you're wrong about one important thing."

"What?" she asked, blinking hard. Then, touching a hand to her chest, feeling the scar through her shirt, she clarified: "What am I wrong about?"

Abrial got to his feet, shutting off the PDA. He didn't look at her as he said, "You are loved. Just not by him."

You are loved. Just not by him. She had made no comment about that, and he hadn't pressed it. Probably she thought he meant she was loved by her mother, or the Goddess, or something.

Abrial had had a belated epiphany and, perhaps because of it being so long in coming, it was a doozy, a Technicolor burning bush with a full orchestral score. He wasn't *interested* in Nyssa. Wasn't *intrigued.* Wasn't *fascinated.* He was in love. *In love!* Mabigon had warned him it would happen someday, and she had taken malicious pleasure in the thought of her coldhearted Executioner finally being smitten.

Of course, it wasn't his being in love that was the problem. It was that it was practically ordained by Karma that whomever he loved wouldn't be able to love him back. Those who dwelled in darkness were always drawn to the light, but the light nearly always shunned them. That was what had given the spiteful dark queen so much pleasure when she considered the matter.

The only question now was whether Nyssa would reject him herself, or if death would claim her before they knew any happiness at all.

Not death! He wouldn't allow it. Rejection would be terrible enough, but Nyssa's death? No. *No.* He'd brought death to so many—surely he could find a way to keep it at bay. Just this once.

"Did you unplug the TV and lamp?" Nyssa asked sleepily as she curled up in the swaying bed. Dawn was close. "I forgot to."

"I didn't." Abrial smiled a bit wistfully. Hurt, frightened, exhausted—she looked so young, so fresh and unjaded. And he wanted her as he had never wanted anything in his life.

"Good." Then, perhaps picking up on his stray thoughts about the dark queen: "Can you tell me about Mabigon? About what it was like when she was alive? Are you sorry that she is dead?"

"That isn't a particularly pleasant bedtime story. What about the one with the three bears?"

"I've heard that one. Besides, I'd like to know about her, since it's important to you."

"*Was* important. Long ago."

"*Was*, then. Please, Abrial. Talk to me for a while."

"As you like. I suppose it is as good a place to begin my story as any." This time, his smile was bitter, but she didn't see it. "You're thinking that we were lovers, aren't you? That this is why I had such a strong connection to her. But for all our mental closeness, the queen didn't choose me to grace her bed. I think perhaps my job made her a little nervous."

"Yeah? Why? She's the one who gave you the job. And you're way less scary than a hobgoblin—and she slept with one of those."

"I'm glad you think me harmless," he answered. "But others did't share your confidence. Mabigon liked danger and pain, but not when it was directed at her." He thought for a moment and then added: "Well, not fatal pain. She didn't mind a spot of bondage and torture when the mood was right."

"And you were really that dangerous?"

He hesitated, then said: "Yes." And he still was. Bad things sometimes happened when a night demon was in your head.

"Even though she was your queen? That's weird." Nyssa sighed. "I don't understand any of this bizarre stuff about the Unseelie Court and know that I probably should. But I'm thinking that I'm pretty much glad I missed all that growing up. My mother was right to hide me from them. And the Seelie Court too, though as far as I know they were never particularly interested in me."

"But, lucky you, you can go back and see it all, if you want. You have a permanent ticket to The Yesterdays."

"Yeah, lucky me." Her voice was flat.

"It's a gift, Nyssa, albeit a dark one. I know people who would give anything—*any*thing—for this power."

"And I'd just as soon pass on it, thanks. My own past—what I can recall of it—is quite bad enough. I don't need to see anybody else's. And anyway, I already get to talk to ghosts. They're reminder enough of things and days gone by." She shifted, trying to get comfortable, and pulled the old bedspread up to her chin. He found it touching that she pouted when she slept. "What about your family? Your dad? Do you miss him?"

"Miss him? Sometimes. I'm not entirely sorry that things have changed, though. Dad and I weren't exactly what you'd call close. And I have a lot more autonomy now with Queen Mabigon dead. In fact, I stand a better chance of surviving with her gone. I was a useful tool for her, but she also feared me. And Mabigon had a habit of making those she feared disappear." He saw Nyssa's hand move beneath the blanket, and knew that she was again touching her chest. That worried him. He had seen her do that before, as though her heart pained her. "Mostly, I just try to forget about that time. It's dead—dead and gone. It has no power over me."

"And I wish that I could remember," Nyssa said, her voice slurring. "I just have this giant blank spot where my childhood should be. And I can sense that it holds terrible power over me."

"I wish you could remember too. But maybe you needed to forget in order to survive."

"I don't want to just survive anymore." She sighed softly. "I want to live."

"You will," he promised. "I'll do anything I must to see you're safe, I swear it. But go to sleep now. You're exhausted."

"I'm also frightened. What if I have a nightmare? The bad thing is very close now, trying to get out."

"Don't be frightened. I'm right here, guarding your dreams. If a bad one comes, you won't face it alone."

"I wouldn't mind if you guarded me a bit more closely," she said diffidently, eyes slitting open for an instant and then closing hastily. "If you wanted to. The bed isn't that bad. And I've had all my shots."

Surprised and pleased, Abrial walked over to the bed and lay down behind her, tucking her into the curve of his body. She felt perfect, like she had been there all his life.

"Thank you," Nyssa said softly, wiggling a bit closer. "I know I'm being a coward, but this is nicer. I'm so much more comfortable now."

"Yes, much nicer," he agreed, touching a hand to her hair. "Now, go to sleep."

"Okay. What is it with you guys? You never want to talk about anything important."

"Maybe we differ in our definition of 'import,'" he said, but she was already asleep.

Abrial sighed and looked at the ceiling. Nyssa was wrong. The bed was dreadful: full of broken springs, it smelled of smoke and many, many bodies. Comfortable was the last word he'd use to describe it.

But it didn't matter. As she snuggled against him, Abrial thought that he'd never enjoyed a mattress more.

Chapter Thirteen

"I look like I lost a bet with a clown," Nyssa complained, staring with disgust at the assorted stains on her shirt—red earth, green sap, and something in a disgusting shade of snail yellow all streaked her top. Fighting both the FBI and the goblins was ruining her very limited wardrobe.

"And a damned messy bastard he was too," Abrial agreed solemnly and got a punch in the arm for his trouble. Nyssa might have snuggled with him last night because she needed comfort in the dark watches of the night, but she was her independent self again once the sun was up.

"You already owe me new shoes. I hope your budget will run to new clothing as well, because my purse and all my money were vaporized."

"Of course," Abrial answered. "I'm on a limitless expense account. The handy thing about having a hacker friend with back doors into the goblins' empire is that our funds are more or less unlimited."

"Good, because I expect breakfast too. After I get a new shirt."

"Of course, or whatever passes for breakfast around here. It looks like the sort of place that does bacon and eggs and bad coffee all day long."

They had found fresh clothing for her at the Last Chance Post Office, which doubled as a general store. Unfortunately, the only T-shirt that more or less fit her was one that said ASK ME ABOUT GIRL SCOUTS. With her hair pulled back in a ponytail, she looked about fourteen years old. But since she was looking crabby, Abrial refrained from mentioning this.

"Do you think goblins designed this shirt? It doesn't fit right. The armholes are at the wrong height." Once outside, she reached up and tore out her right sleeve. It took some effort but, pleased with the result, she reached around and tore at the other. She then tore the hem and tied the shirt up under her midriff.

"Is that better?" she asked.

Abrial eyed the womanly chest she had stuffed in the now much tighter shirt. Though interested in her curves, his keen eyes also detected the end of a long scar that split the midline between her breasts, almost as if she had suffered open-heart surgery. "Could be. They move in mysterious ways," he answered absently, but staring with concentration.

"Like God?" she asked with a raised brow. "Surely not."

"Sort of like God. Only not nearly so benevolent or just." Unable to help himself, Abrial asked suddenly: "What caused that scar? Can you remember?"

"No. But I've had it since I was a child. I think . . ."

She swallowed and turned her back to the light. "I can't remember, but I think goblins did it to me."

"They really aren't very nice, are they? They might have thought about your limited options for swimwear." Abrial smiled in an effort to be reassuring. His touch was gentle as he ran a finger down her too tight shirt. The ridge of scar tissue was firm, much harder than the rest of her skin. It hadn't been created by a surgeon, or anyone who took pride in their work. He wanted to ask her why they had done such a thing but knew it would be a useless question. It was probably part of the dark amnesia that lived inside her.

"Finding an evening dress is a bit of a challenge too," Nyssa said, ducking her head and then rubbing a hand over the scar, as if either to wipe out the feeling of his fingers or else to rub the scar itself away. "Is it very noticeable with my top tied up?"

"No, my eyes are exceptionally keen. No one else could see anything." Though he had the urge to once again try to smooth the pain away, he dropped his hand and turned the conversation to a more comfortable subject. "Shall we get you some breakfast?"

Nyssa's hand dropped as well.

"Yes, please." She smiled up at him, eyes still a little troubled. "I'm actually hungry today. Bad coffee, eggs, and bacon sound perfect."

It was fortunate that this was all Nyssa wanted, because eggs dressed in various manners was all that the menu offered until eleven o'clock.

This limited selection didn't seem to thrill the pair of hunters who had the table across from them, but that might have been due to the hangovers they had.

Abrial didn't mention it to Nyssa, but their bleary eyes were the result of nightmares as well as beer. The two men had gotten noisy only a few minutes after Nyssa had gone to sleep, hurling insults at their dogs and at each other, and when that wasn't enough, they had taken to throwing boots and empty cans as well.

Annoyed, Abrial had waited for them to drift off again and then slipped into their dreams and gave them something unpleasant to think about. Another person might have found the vision of wild boars hunting naked humans with rifles amusing, but he knew for a fact that neither of these two men had enjoyed the experience.

"Are you being a pussy and sayin' we shouldn't go huntin' 'cause you had a dream?" the older hunter demanded, slamming his coffee cup down on the battered table. He reached for the tin of cherry pie he had demanded from the waitress.

"I'm saying my damned shin hurts! Look at this!" The second hunter hauled up his pantleg and pointed at his badly scraped leg. "I stepped right through that damned drain pan in the shower. That sonofabitch was rusted clean through. I should sue someone. I'm probably gonna get tetanus."

Abrial sincerely hoped so, especially when Nyssa started watching the men with obvious consternation. He wondered if he shouldn't see about hastening some disease or accident for these two.

"You ain't gonna get tetanus. You're just bein' a frickin' pussy because of that dream."

"I am not. But it is goddamn weird that you had the same dream."

"Pussy!" In jest, the man gave a plaintive mewl.

Enraged, the younger hunter jumped to his feet. Grabbing for his belt, he brought out a ridiculously sized hunting knife, that he brandished carelessly.

"Shut your yappin' mouth or I'll cut out your heart and shove it down your throat!" he shouted, and he stabbed the blade into his companion's pie. The blade sank through the tin and right into the table, splashing red filling everywhere.

Nyssa gasped, her eyes going wide and dark even as her face paled.

"Nyssa—honey, what's wrong?" Abrial asked, his attention turning instantly from the hunters. "You aren't frightened of *them*, are you? Don't worry. They'll never get close to you. I'll drop them in an instant if they take a single step this way."

Nyssa's lips parted, but she didn't speak. When a full minute had passed and she still hadn't moved, Abrial got up and reached out a hand. She was freezing cold, both in body and spirit. He could almost see her aura bleeding into the atmosphere, and it had turned a dark gray. He asked again, this time with both his voice and mind: *"What's wrong?"*

What had happened?

The hunter's knife had flashed down and a lightning bolt of memory illuminated the dark secret in Nyssa's brain, the thing her mother had most wanted her to forget. The thing that had been trying ever since to escape, and that was finally succeeding.

Nyssa sat very still, her hands clasping the edge of the table, wondering if that outward manifestation of control would calm her inner turmoil before she started screaming. She had sensed all along that her

161

life had a blueprint, a preexisting plan, but she couldn't see it because of the fog in her brain. The fog was always there, confusing her, diverting her thoughts down vacant and dead-end pathways when she got too close to the truth, too close to her memories. But in an instant, with the wave of a knife, all that mist had been stripped away and she was left with a jumble of nightmare images.

Again and again, she saw the hunter's blade plunging downward. Only it wasn't made of metal and it wasn't stabbing into a cherry pie; it was jabbing into her chest. And she heard a voice saying: *"We've ripped his heart out and now must put it somewhere safe—someplace he can always find it."*

"What's wrong?" Abrial asked, coming around to her side of the table and kneeling, blocking her view of the hunters. He put a dark hand over hers and squeezed gently.

Abrial. The sight of him helped Nyssa reel in her bloody memory and ground herself back in the present. Some of the dreadful cold around her heart—her *human* heart—receded as she drew warmth from him.

"I remembered," she whispered, licking her lips. *Remembered*—what an inadequate word. This was like an earthquake in the brain, shaking loose memories that permanently damaged the careful constructs her mother had created for her. She hadn't had a childhood. After the goblins had stolen her for the dark queen and performed their ritual on her, she had gone into a coma, a sort of hibernation. Bysshe had stolen her back from the Dark Court, but it was too late. The damage was done.

Every once in a while, her mother would rouse her

and they would leave the Seelie Court and she would live in the human world for a while. But always the ghosts and the horror had caught up with her, and her mother would again put her to sleep and return her to the Seelie Court.

That had worked until the time of The Drought, when all the feys at King Finvarra's court died.

"Yes?" Abrial said gently. "Can you tell me what you see?"

"I remembered *it. This.*" She turned her head and looked him full in his strange eyes. She didn't attempt to hide her thoughts—couldn't have. The shock of the memory of having her chest cut open with an obsidian dagger and her condemned father's torn-out heart sewn up inside of her was too overpowering, too awful to attempt to bury again. The memory just had to lie there and bleed.

"*She* did it." Nyssa's voice was a whisper.

"Mabigon?" he asked, but he knew the answer—saw it. *Felt* it. Her pain filled him with new rage. And she knew that he had never hated his dead queen more. She didn't like Abrial's anger, but she drank it in anyway, grateful for the warmth and the strength it gave her. Anything was better than cold terror.

"Yes. Mabigon did it." She swallowed and then asked in a stronger voice: "How did she ever think I would give it back? Was she insane?"

"She probably was. But I don't believe she thought you would give it back. If anything, she was trying to make it difficult for you to return his heart. No one wanted Qasim walking around completely free after he was pissed off and feeling vengeful."

"Well, I can't give it back now, can I? Not even if I

wanted to. Without her magic, the ritual, I'd die."
Nyssa put a hand to her chest.

"Possibly." Abrial nodded. His expression was as
grim as she'd ever seen it.

"But Qasim is going to want his heart back anyway,
isn't he?" she whispered. "They said that he would always be able to find me."

"Yes. He will want it back."

She exhaled slowly. "It's so strange, I always
thought I'd be relieved when this mystery was
solved." She shook her head. It took an effort, but because Abrial was there, she managed to reel in some
more of the panic and horror that had stunned her.
More of the terrible cold dissipated from her body and
soul and the memory began to still, turning into something like a painting. Perhaps it had bled itself out.

Nyssa turned and looked at Abrial, trying to see
into his mind. "What are you thinking?" she asked.

Abrial also exhaled, and he chose his words carefully.

"William Faulkner once said that the past wasn't
dead. It wasn't even *past*. I think he was right." Abrial stood up. He didn't say anything more, but Nyssa
was certain that Faulkner wasn't the only thing he
was thinking about. She had the impression that
he was still thinking about Mabigon and other unpleasant things. "Come on. I want you to go back to
the room while I do something."

"Faulkner? What are you really thinking, Abrial?
Do you hate me now? Are you disgusted? Is that why
you turned away from me—because you sensed I was
unclean?"

"Stop. Right now. Listen carefully. I could never hate you. What I am thinking right now is that, more than ever, we have to get you to Cadalach. Maybe there is some way they can get that thing out of you before Qasim gets here. There has to be. Thomas will know something about this. Zayn too. He's a first-rate healer."

"So you don't despise me?" she asked, wanting to reach for him but not quite daring. "Because I'm contaminated—a carrier of evil?"

"No. I never blame the victim. And you won't be a carrier for long." His voice was definite, and though the answer was blunt and unadorned with declarations, it was also reassuring because Abrial didn't lie.

"I'm glad. That makes me feel better. I have to think that someday I'll be clean again."

"You aren't unclean. And don't thank me yet. Getting that sucker out may be unpleasant. And I am very afraid that the heart draws Qasim like a magnet. And you'll never be free of him as long as he is alive and you have that thing in you."

She nodded jerkily. "Where are you going?"

"To find a car. And to try once more to raise Jack. Zayn, our healer, may need some time to prepare a counter-ritual. He's pulled off miracles before. His wife was torn apart by gargoyles, but she lived. Maybe he can meet us somewhere on the road."

"What can he do for me out here? Heart surgery in the back of a Taurus? That would be one for the *Guinness Book of World Records*," Nyssa joked, trying for humor but failing. "It sounds a little unhygienic."

"It wouldn't be my first choice of options," Abrial

agreed. "But believe me, it's still better than letting Qasim find you and take his heart back himself."

Nyssa bowed her head. His answer was terrifying, but she knew it was true.

NAME: _____

ADDRESS: _____

_____

_____

TELEPHONE: _____

E-MAIL: _____

_____ I want to pay by credit card.

__ Visa   __ MasterCard   __ Discover

Account Number: _____

Expiration date: _____

SIGNATURE: _____

*Send this form, along with $2.00 shipping
and handling for your FREE books, to:*

Love Spell Romance Book Club
20 Academy Street
Norwalk, CT 06850-4032

*Or fax (must include credit card
information!) to: 610.995.9274.
You can also sign up on the Web
at www.dorchesterpub.com.*

Offer open to residents of the U.S. and
Canada only. Canadian residents, please
call 1.800.481.9191 for pricing information.

If under 18, a parent or guardian must sign. Terms, prices and conditions
subject to change. Subscription subject to acceptance. Dorchester
Publishing reserves the right to reject any order or cancel any subscription.

Chapter Fourteen

Thomas looked from Cyra to Jack.

"This isn't the best news in the world," he said.

"But it's a damned tempting proposition," Jack countered. "Opportunity is definitely knocking."

"It sounds like a job for super-kloka," Thomas said, looking at his wife.

"Io and I could easily lure the Feds away. Making them believe that we are Abrial and Nyssa won't be a problem." Her voice was calm, unafraid.

"We're agreed then?" Jack asked.

Both Cyra and Thomas nodded.

"I want that bitch," Thomas said. He was speaking of Lilith. "She should have drowned along with her supply of dirty bombs when we took out her Sin City hive."

"Her survival is bad news for all of us," Jack agreed. "Okay. Send Abrial the plan and we'll see what he says."

* * *

"What took you so long?" Nyssa demanded crossly. "You've had time to walk to Las Vegas and back."

Abrial looked around the room. The alarm clock was dead and there was no light on the phone. Her nerves had been busy sucking up power.

"Missed me?" he asked.

"Not exactly. Where have you been?"

"I wanted a decent car. And one that wouldn't be reported stolen right away. You need to learn patience. Some things just take a little time."

"Yeah, yeah—and *good things come to those who wait*. Easy for you to say. You haven't had a rattlesnake terrorizing you." *Or been worried about having your father's hobgoblin heart removed from your chest with a ritual dagger.*

"A rattlesnake has been terrorizing you?" Abrial sounded amused. It was good that this further bad news didn't send him into a panic, but sometimes she both loved and hated his careless attitude.

"After a fashion." She tried for some dignity.

"And what fashion would that be? A metaphorical one?"

"No, I mean this quite literally. It's in the bathroom, coiled around the toilet. It came out of the shower drain. I tried to shoo it out, but it won't go. And I haven't been able to . . . to . . . shower or *any*thing." She added under her breath, "I wish I'd never touched that vile coffee."

"Ah. Well, that is serious. I'll go take care of it. I think you should be really nice to me though. Usually I charge extra for working with animals."

"Can you die of rattlesnake venom?" she asked with feigned concern.

"No. It just hurts a bit."

"Then I hope he bites you."

"She won't," Abrial said, looking in the bathroom door.

"She?" Nyssa peered around his shoulder, also looking at the annoying reptile. Its face somehow looked smug as it gazed back at them. "This is a friend of yours perhaps? Maybe an old girlfriend?"

"Not exactly, but I had an aunt who was a lamia."

"Naturally."

"Well, I do come from a very large family. It's a pity I had to kill her when she made an attempt on Mabigon's life," Abrial said casually as he reached for the snake, being gentle as he shifted its coils.

"You killed your own aunt?"

"It was my job, to protect the queen—whether she deserved it or not," Abrial said shortly, and then he murmured something in a strange language. The snake went limp, and he began unwinding her. The body was nearly five feet long and had an impressive set of rattles.

"You never sweet-talk me that way," Nyssa complained, leaving the matter of his aunt for another day—a day when she might be better able to face unsettling answers from this man she was coming to care about deeply.

"Would you like me to?" he asked, turning his head to look at her. "Should I charm you into pliancy?"

For some reason, his expression made her heart contract. Belatedly, she recalled that his powers could do precisely that: charm her into pliancy. She also recalled that she had enjoyed—intensely—those few, brief moments on the back of his motorcycle.

"Just get the snake out before I pop," she said hurriedly, looking away before she embarrassed herself. She also didn't answer the question since she didn't want to lie but didn't want to say *yes* either. She hadn't forgotten how their lovemaking had been aborted outside the faerie cave. She was pretty sure that things had changed between them since but wasn't sure enough to talk about it at the moment. To cover up her thought, she added: "Honest to Goddess! I can stand the goblins and the G-men and being a car thief—even the bad food. But the lack of proper sanitation facilities is making me crazy!"

"I'll make a note of that," Abrial said, looking away.

"Please do. And then you can tell me what Jack said." Her annoyance was cooling.

"Do you want to pet her?" Abrial asked, backing with the snake out of the bathroom. "I know she looks scary, but not all ugly things are dangerous or evil."

Nyssa began to automatically refuse, but then she paused. She wasn't sure what Abrial was really saying, but it seemed important to him that she not reject the rattler.

"Are you sure she won't bite?"

"Very sure," Abrial said.

The snake did look very relaxed. It was doing everything but snoring.

"Okay," Nyssa said, reaching out a tentative hand, and she stroked down the snake's surprisingly firm body. She kept well away from its triangular head.

"See, not so bad. Most beasts are reasonable. You just need to know what to say to them."

"Really? There's something I could say to make snakes go to sleep?" Nyssa asked, instantly intrigued.

"Yes." Abrial seemed to have one of those moments where he wrestled with himself. Then he repeated the strange phrase he had used in the bathroom. If possible, the snake went even more limp. "Wait. Let me get her outside before we put her in a coma. Repeating it three times would probably kill her."

"Take her around back, away from the parking lot," Nyssa suggested. "We don't want her to get run over."

"Okay. I'll be right back."

Abrial didn't come right back, but he was gone no more than five minutes. And that was fine with Nyssa. It gave her time to use the long-denied facilities.

"Ready to learn some serpent?" he asked, shutting the door behind him when he reappeared.

"Yes. But first I'd like to hear what Jack said. I just realized that you were looking cheerful, and I could stand some good news."

"As you surmised, I was finally able to get hold of Jack. He wasn't thrilled to hear about you carrying Qasim's heart, but he had just about reached the conclusion that this was what the hobgoblin is after, and that you must have it. He thinks that Zayn and Thomas may be able to help you. Eventually." Abrial stopped smiling.

"Eventually?" Nyssa sat on the side of the bed, ignoring the tortured springs' shrieking.

"Well, Jack has a plan. It's a good one—very tempting. But also potentially dangerous." Abrial sat down in the chair across from her. "I told him I couldn't speak for you on this. It is something you'll have to decide for yourself. And he agreed."

"I see. So, what's the plan? I take it that it doesn't involve sending Zayn to do impromptu surgery on me."

"No. Jack thinks they can divert the G-men and H.U.G. operatives away from this area by sending out a decoy on a faerie road to the north of the state. That would give the goblins and Qasim a chance to get close to us without human interference. It would, in fact, make them very bold."

"And this is a good thing?" she asked.

"It is, if there's a trap waiting for them."

"And the trap works."

"Yes, if it works."

"Will it work?" she asked.

"We wouldn't go near it if it didn't look ninety-nine point nine percent sure." He didn't say whether the trap was supposed to be sure of catching goblins, or sure of being safe for them.

"Who would we be trapping?" Nyssa asked. "Qasim?"

"Yes. But also King Carbon." He paused. "And Queen Lilith."

"Lilith?" She repeated blankly. "But she's dead."

"So we all thought. She should have died when her Sin City hive flooded. But it looks now like General Fornix's men were able to secret her away after the explosions. It seems she is the one who went to King Carbon and got him interested in you—as her apology to the hive master for trying to turn California into her personal radioactive playground without consulting him first. She is also the one who wants to control Qasim. As well as—surprise, surprise—the military."

"Could Lilith control him?" Nyssa asked. "Could the military?"

"Not a chance." Abrial was emphatic. "But it wouldn't be any better if she could. Lilith is one of the less sane goblin leaders. And would you really want the military using hobgoblins? Recall that they have no natural enemies left—and very few unnatural ones since the Great Drought killed off our kind."

"It's a fluke that Qasim's alive, isn't it?"

"Yeah. It's pretty damned ironic that the hobgoblins survived because of how they were imprisoned."

"Okay." Nyssa exhaled slowly. "So this plan would get all of them—Qasim, Carbon, and Lilith?"

"Yes."

"Before they got us?"

"Yes."

"So . . ."

"Yes," he said a third time.

"Is Jack waiting for an answer?"

"He is. If you agree, he is dispatching another fey that has experience killing hobgoblins. His name is Roman, and he has a magicked sword that supposedly worked really well on one of Qasim's cousins."

"So, Jack and this Roman guy know what they're doing?"

"Jack says so. And I believe him."

Nyssa looked into Abrial's eyes, but she couldn't read anything there.

"And if I don't want to do this?"

"Then I take you to Cadalach as planned and we try to get the heart out and destroy it there." He added slowly: "Or anyplace else that you feel might be safe. If we can't get the heart out, then Roman and I will

173

find a way to kill the hobgoblin. Either way, we *will* make it safe for you."

Nyssa smiled a little, knowing what the offer cost him. Abrial obviously felt high regard for this Jack Frost and didn't want to disappoint him. He also really wanted to take out King Carbon and Queen Lilith. Which was understandable. Lilith had been ready to set off dirty bombs and irradiate every human in California.

"I'm guessing that my role in this is mainly being bait."

"Mainly." Abrial added: "Understand, no one is asking you to kill Qasim yourself. You wouldn't have to kill anyone—physically or psychically. We wouldn't ask it of you, not now, when I know how much it would hurt you."

"Yes. Killing anyone, let alone my . . . father makes me feel a bit sick. I guess I have a bit of my mother in me after all. Who'd have guessed?" Nyssa touched her chest. She had felt a cold weight inside ever since remembering how Qasim's heart had gotten there.

"And thank the Goddess for it," Abrial answered. She appreciated his words but suspected he might be wrong about what she would have to do. She didn't know the exact terms of the sentence passed on her father, but it had involved taking his life in payment for his crimes. That was why her mother couldn't do it. And why the burden had passed to Nyssa. Maybe she could employ an agent in this affair, but maybe not. Magic could be awfully specific.

Either way, it didn't matter. Qasim had to be stopped. Carbon and Lilith too, if they were bent on teaming up with him and possibly resurrecting all the hobgoblins. Abrial was right: Hobgoblins had no one to prey on them, nothing to keep them in check with the Unseelie queen gone. They weren't afraid of the hive masters and were psychically invulnerable to humans. An army of them would be impossible to stop without the use of massive magic, and nothing she had seen or heard in any of her investigations led her to believe that any such powerful enough shamans still lived. Abrial was the deadliest thing Nyssa had ever imagined, and even he couldn't stop a troop of hobgoblins. It had to end now, with a preemptive strike that would stop those hobgoblins from being resurrected.

"Okay," Nyssa said. "Tell Jack that I'll do it. But he'd better be ready to cough up some really good shoes at the end of this business."

Chapter Fifteen

"You should try to sleep," Abrial said when he got back from wherever it was he went to contact Jack.

"I don't think I can." Nyssa sat on the edge of the bed, but she was not relaxed. Her heart was beating in odd flurries and she felt warm.

"Are you afraid you'll dream?" he asked.

"Dream?" She laughed without humor. "I haven't just dreamed in more than two years. My eyes shut, but I'm not resting. I'm searching, thinking, trying . . ."

"For?"

"For everything. For answers, for my mother, for memories—and for some understanding of the sequence to put those few memories in. I've reached the point where my sleeping world is more real than the one I am in when my eyes are open. And it isn't just that I spent so much time there. The things I see in my sleep are more real—more true. There is no deception there, because people don't know there is a witness to their thoughts and activities. They are themselves, if you know what I mean. They don't think to lie. It's all very nice, but completely backward. I have no reality that humans can understand."

"I know." Abrial nodded. He had obviously found this truth as well. The thought of their common bond helped her go on.

"I knew you would understand," she said. "It must be that way a lot for you when you . . . work."

"It was. I spend less time in the dreamlands now. Things are less clear out here, but they're a damned sight healthier."

"I hope that I can stop soon. I just want . . ." She trailed off.

"Yes? What do you want?" His gaze was intense. "Tell me."

Nyssa swallowed. She wanted to go on, to tell him, but she was fearful that her composure would crack, that her control would blow apart, pinwheeling crazily as all the ugly emotions and doubts inside tore her mind to little incoherent bits.

"No," she said softly. "I won't let that happen. I've been strong so far. I can be strong now."

"What won't happen?" Abrial asked. "What are you thinking about?"

Unwanted images of recent events rose in her brain, racing by in a blur. Most were ugly, but not all. Not Abrial. Yes, he had known darkness—he *was* darkness—but he was also at his core an honest person. Or so she believed.

Because she had no choice but to believe it? It would be easy to delude herself, to see good in him, to see strength when there was none.

Nyssa shoved the shadowy doubts and emotions away: self-pity, fear, doubt, suspicion. They had no place here. The only way to survive her next trial was to remain calm and focused. The goblins might defeat her and Abrial, but she wouldn't defeat herself.

"Talk to me, Nyssa." He came and sat beside her. His presence was comforting. And there was something else as well. He made her heart beat faster, her breath come more quickly, her skin heat. Her very nerves had begun to tingle.

"What an odd expression you're wearing. Have I grown a second head?" Abrial asked her.

"We could die tomorrow, you know. We really could," she told him. "Or I could. I don't know if you can die. I don't know anything about you really. And yet I trust you."

There was no fear in her voice, but there was urgency. Abrial frowned.

"You won't die. And it's good that you trust me."

"You don't know that I'll live. I don't know that either. I can look at the past in perfect detail, but I can't see the future. Neither can you."

Abrial didn't argue. What she said was the truth, and he wouldn't lie.

"What do you want from me?" he asked. "What do you need? Ask and I'll give it, if I can."

Nyssa swallowed. She wanted to look away but didn't. He had asked what she wanted, what she needed. There wasn't time for her to be anything but direct. "I want two things—but I need one of them if I am to go on."

"Yes?"

"First, I want your promise that you won't let Qasim get me. No matter what." She gave him a look fraught with meaning.

"You're asking me to kill you," he said, his body still, his face blank, "if the only other choice is surrendering you to Qasim?"

"Yes, if there is no other way." She waited, barely breathing. It was hard, asking someone to kill you when you so very much wanted to live. When you were just learning there were things to live for. "You can't let him have this heart. Whatever you did—however you chose to . . . well, it would be kinder than what he would do."

"All right," he said finally. "I swear that I shall keep this heart from him at any and all cost."

"Thank you. I'm sorry that I had to ask it of you."

"That's okay. But please tell me that your second request is something easier. Maybe cherry pie with ice cream. Or a steak dinner. Or spending next Easter in Rome." He reached out and took her hand. His fingers closed over the pulse in her wrist.

Surprised by his near levity, Nyssa laughed once. She didn't understand how horror could be so mundane. It also baffled her that she could be contemplating death and still feel desire.

"Nyssa?"

"I shouldn't. It's crazy."

"So, it's crazy. Spill."

"Look, what I want might be somewhat sweet, but I suspect not entirely. And there is nothing cherry about it. Neither of us is that innocent." She could feel herself coloring.

"Go on," Abrial said, beginning to relax. "You are

180

looking very flushed, and I am intrigued. What larceny are you contemplating?"

"Not larceny." Nyssa looked down at her hands for a moment. How odd that this should be even more difficult than asking for death. Taking a breath, she rushed on: "I know that you don't want a physical entanglement between us because of the bonds you think we'll form." Seeing his mouth open, she added, "But I would like to know you anyway—in my dreams, if nothing else."

"What?"

"You are the person I am closest to in this world—in any world—and I want to see who and what you truly are. I'm sorry to be so blunt, but we don't have much time."

He was still again. At another moment, she might have felt smug at managing to startle him. Now, she was too nervous.

"You want to meet in a dream because you think that you will know the real me if we meet on the metaphysical plane," he finally said.

It wasn't a question, but she still answered. "Yes, in the right dream."

"Am I being dense? Or do you mean . . ."

"Yes! I want to meet as lovers. Maybe I can have you there without all the consequences you fear. In any event, I want to see you once when you aren't . . . battling."

"There are always consequences," he said slowly. "Always. I don't think you know what you're asking—of either of us."

"Probably not. But I do want to know you. And I also know that if I end up strangled by goblins tomorrow, I will really regret that I missed this chance." She looked at him, willing him to understand. "Maybe I'm not as important to you as you are to me. Maybe I don't appeal to you. But it isn't like you'd actually have to touch me, if that's what bothers you."

Abrial snorted.

"Come on, Abrial, say yes." She looked full into his eyes, willing him to agree. "You're supposed to be a ruthless son of a bitch. You're risking your life for me. Whatever happened to the warrior's recreation? Take me. I want you to."

When Abrial remained motionless and speechless in the face of her offer—her plea—a suddenly ill Nyssa got up and moved away from him.

"I see. This was rather stupid of me. I don't know why I thought things had changed between us." Embarrassment choked her and she couldn't go on. If it was possible, she would leave. But there was nowhere to go.

Except the bathroom.

Nyssa moved slowly. She closed the door quietly, not bothering to turn on a light. There wasn't anything in the shabby space to take her mind off what had just happened. Or not happened.

So he still doesn't want you. You're a job, nothing more. Get over it.

"Shut up," she whispered to the voice in her head. "You never say anything I want to hear."

Throttling both tears of humiliation and curses directed at pigheaded overly scrupulous night demons, Nyssa decided to try to drown her humiliation at a second rejection in the ancient shower.

* * *

Abrial sat on the side of the bed, still in shock, when the shower turned on with a familiar asthmatic wheeze.

Nyssa's proposition had come at him out of the blue. Not since that moment on the bike outside the faerie cave had she evidenced any desire to be intimate with him. He had assumed that earlier moment of intimacy was an aberration caused by his manipulation of her. Her request stunned him.

And she had not asked for any old thing. She had asked for the union he wanted and dreaded the most—to let her know the real person inside. Not just sex, not just talk, but *knowing*.

Intuitively, she had understood that she would see more of his true nature in a dream state. He could control his body on the physical plane and often on the metaphysical one as well. But he couldn't always control his mind, his thoughts.

She had seen some of his true form on the night they met in her concert hall, and also when he went after Humana Vox, and he had frightened her then— both his form and his actions.

Would she be frightened now? She was more used to him, had seen the truth of what he could do and not turned from him, in spite of her gentler nature. Was it possible that he could actually go to her and give her what she wanted: not just his body, but the whole truth about who he was?

The temptation to attempt a union was strong. His contact with Nyssa had opened up old channels of emotion in his brain, reawakening his dry heart with floods of protective feeling. He'd been alone for so long—always in dark places, doing dark deeds, shut off from the warmth of civilization and the love of family by what he had to do for the queen. He hadn't realized until that very moment how badly he wanted there to be someone who knew him completely and wasn't repulsed or afraid.

But she didn't love him: he was almost certain of that. And without that, he couldn't go to her as she asked. Any bond they formed would be forever. And he knew how women reacted to the Executioner. Only the deepest of attachments would keep her from turning from him when she knew the truth.

Nyssa worried that she was part-monster. Abrial knew he was monstrous.

And even if he wanted to take the risk, the danger was simply too great. The goblins and H.U.G. would be watching for her now, waiting for her to step into dreams.

"Damn it." And he would need her trust tomorrow. If fear of his true nature made her hesitate at the wrong moment . . . They couldn't chance it. Especially not when they were so close to capturing Qasim and setting her free. That had to be their first priority.

But he couldn't just walk away from Nyssa's words either. There had to be some middle ground.

The thought was barely formed when fierce and sudden desire slammed into his body. For a moment he wondered if it was his own longing finally breaking free, or if some enchantment was being thrown over him from the outside. He had never felt anything like it. It was death and life and hope and terror. As the wild need built, he decided that it didn't matter where it came from. The call had to be answered. Or he had to flee—run from it and never look back.

And he couldn't walk away. Not if Nyssa would die without him, not when he wanted this—needed this—union as much as she did. Possibly even more.

He got up quickly and walked toward the bathroom door, shedding clothing as he went and wondering what he was going to say to the only woman he had ever loved—a woman who didn't and couldn't love him back. It wasn't a situation covered by greeting cards.

Abrial opened the bathroom door and then turned off the one functioning bedroom light. Nyssa had known he was coming and had watched through the curtain, breath held as his silhouette, outlined by the faint moonlight from the other room, walked toward the shower. The curtain was pulled aside.

"Abrial?" She didn't think to cover herself and would wonder about this lack of modesty later.

Plastic rustled, rings clacking on the rod above and letting in a small eddy of cooler air. And then Abrial himself appeared. For a moment he blocked the water, but then he turned her so that she was near the stream.

"You said you wondered what I'm like . . . in dreams. You wanted to know what it would be like if I came to you in your sleep." His voice was soft and deep.

"Yes." Her own voice was closer to a whisper. Heat, but not from embarrassment, was again climbing through her body.

"I can't show you that now. It isn't safe. H.U.G. and the goblins will be watching for us. And I'm . . . not sure we're ready. That you're ready. This is as close as

I can come to giving you a sex dream, without giving you a sex dream."

Sex. Not love.

"I see." She tried to think, but her thoughts were suddenly mired by the blind want of her body. The need running through her was unlike anything she had ever known and she felt dazed. "But what about the bond you said would form between us? Can we—can you risk it?"

"I think we can finesse that to a degree. Things needn't go that far—not if we don't want them to. Will you trust me to know when we should stop?"

Her heart skipped a beat.

"Abrial, I wasn't just looking for sex." She hadn't been, but now she wasn't so sure. "If you don't—"

"I know." He paused, as though trying to decide what to say, then added: "But sex is what I can offer now. You can't *know* me yet. Not completely. Not the way you want. Will you trust me anyway?"

"Yes," she said again. "Of course."

He exhaled, and Nyssa wondered if he was actually nervous about being with her.

"Close your eyes. You don't need them here. A dream isn't about sight or sound, or about other waking senses." Abrial laid hands on either side of her head, covering her ears.

Nyssa did as he asked. The sound of the shower almost completely disappeared, and all she could hear was the thudding of her heart and the rush of her breath as it pulled life into her lungs. She was closed into a cocoon where all she could feel was the warm rain, and all she could hear was her own body, telling her of its mix of fear and excitement.

And then Abrial was there too. His mouth covered hers, gently, softly, but it was enough to slow and then stop her breathing for a long moment. He tasted like the night just after sunset in the summer deep in a forest.

Then, just as quickly as that last light of day, he was gone again.

She couldn't use her eyes to know his dimensions, to define his shape. But still she needed to know him. Automatically she raised her hands, wanting to understand him with some other sense.

No. Don't tempt me. The words were in her head but didn't arrive there through her ears. And her hands laced for a moment with fingers much longer, much harder than her own, and were pushed back down to her sides where all they could feel was the random patter of water.

Unable to help herself, Nyssa's eyes sprang open, but the tiny bit of light in the room didn't help. The shower was still running, but it was just white noise. She was still in a small space—or perhaps a large one; she couldn't truly be sure—where everything was warm and wet and male.

Would you care to make use of my mouth? That, we can have, the voice in her head said. And before she could form an answer with either mind or lips, something was there, biting down not quite gently on the side of her throat, easing up while it scraped down to her collarbone. The touch grew lighter still as it slipped down her chest until it had all but disappeared as it grazed her breast.

Then all trace of him was gone again, and she was in a void which only the dictates of logic assured her was still a shower and that her feet were still on the floor.

"This is real, is it?"

Yes, and it can be like this forever, an endless half-dream, an endless taunt, an endless longing. Is this what you wanted?

"Abrial," she whispered, reaching for him, less nervous now and more aroused. "Maybe I don't want any dream after all. Surely it can't be that dangerous for us to . . . to touch just a little more."

"To touch? Oh, I think that might be very dangerous." But he let her lay a hand on him this time, in spite of his words, allowed her fingers and sense of touch to translate who and where he was for her confused mind. She sensed that it took an effort, but he kept his body still as she explored.

Reassured by his restraint, she stepped forward a few inches and leaned into the solidity of his chest, enjoying the feel of his flesh but also relieved to again be anchored by at least one sense. Arousal without it was terrifying.

"Would I fear you in dreams?" she asked. "Is that really why you hesitate?"

"Perhaps. I don't know anymore."

"I find that hard to believe—that I could fear you. Nothing about you is repulsive. I can't imagine being frightened of any part of you."

His mouth was at her throat again. He murmured something that vibrated against her skin, and then penetrated it, making her nerves thrill and surprising a small gasp from her.

Then he was touching her, understanding intuitively what she wanted, or perhaps moved by the impulses of her mind. She had known that the bond between them was growing even without any sexual contact. Every hour they spent together brought them closer. With anyone else, she might have thought that they were falling in love, sharing that almost psychic understanding that some lovers had. But it couldn't be that. Not with Abrial. Not with her.

It wasn't that she didn't believe that love was possible, but for her it was like some imaginary horizon that slipped ever farther from her whenever she pursued it. And yet, what else could this be? Magic?

"Don't think about it," he murmured. "We'll hunt for explanations later. You've brought this feeling out of me. Let's just enjoy it."

But had she brought this feeling out? It had appeared so quickly—so violently. She had started by speaking of death and ended by asking for love. That couldn't be normal.

Nyssa started to object, to warn him that she could feel something new happening between them— something otherworldly and immensely powerful— but her thundering heart snuffed out her voice. Her legs betrayed her next, and she started to sink down onto the floor.

"No," he said, and his hands were around her waist, lifting her. Her eyes sought his out, his gaze suddenly a deeper darkness in the black that was around them. She tried to see into his soul, to know his mind, his past—above all, his future. But there was nothing there to see. Nothing but desire: deep, dark, vast as anything she had ever known. It was something cataclysmic. Dangerous. The knowledge that she had called it forth humbled her.

It really was almost like love.

Unable to think clearly anymore, she gave herself over to it.

Abrial carried Nyssa into the bedroom, watching as the veil of steam pulled away from them and left their skin naked. She was beautiful, scar and all.

Nyssa smiled dreamily and curled herself around him as he knelt on the bed. "So hard," she murmured, turning her face into his thigh and biting not quite gently.

He quickly lay down beside her, framing her face with his hand. He looked at her for a long moment. The lush mouth, slightly bruised from their last kiss, smiled at him. Her beautiful eyes watched him, her expression at once carnal and yet dreamy. She reached out and caressed his chest, and he felt a rush of fire that ran roughly from collarbone to knees.

"Kiss me again." Her voice was husky.

"Absolutely," he agreed, lowering his mouth to hers. Again, sensation raced through him like an arc of electricity stirring feeling so fierce and primal that he didn't have words for them. It felt right, but it also felt magical.

I know. And I don't care anymore.

He didn't care either. He broke the kiss, shuddering with the mix of pain and pleasure that touching her brought. He fought for control, to have some say in the pace of this joining, but she flexed her hips against him—once, twice, and then a third time—and he knew he was lost.

"I lied," he told her. "I thought I could control this. That we could stop it."

"I don't want you to control it," she answered. Her eyes were blazing and she wore a flush from breasts to hairline. "I don't want anything to control it. Can't you feel that this is right? Why have we been fighting it?"

"I don't know. Stubbornness? Stupidity?" Abrial groaned and buried his face in her neck. She sighed, allowing him access for a moment, and then turned her own head, again using her teeth as she bit his shoulder. Blazing streams of passion burst out from the bite, making even his fingertips tingle. Abrial knew she felt his response and was pleased to have drawn it.

"I don't know why I bit you," she said, running a tongue over her lips. "But I enjoyed it."

"I enjoyed it too." He tried not to think about why she might have enjoyed biting him. This wasn't a moment when he wanted to consider her mixed blood and how goblins had sex.

Feeling both very hungry and very hard, he lowered his mouth to her breasts. He felt her hesitate for a moment as he brushed over the scar that bisected her chest, but her eyes closed and she breathed a soft sound of encouragement as he began a slow stroking of her breasts. He drew her into his mouth, using teeth and tongue, being less gentle that he usually would be. Her nipples hardened immediately and she gave a soft gasp.

"Abrial!"

Yes, he felt it too. This was lovely, but they needed more. The desire—a mix of pain and pleasure twisting inside him—was pouring through them, sweeping them along, demanding he continue. Somewhere a floodgate of sensation had been opened, and they were both in danger of drowning as the tide overtook them.

"I'd like to hold you down and devour you." His voice was rough.

"Please do." He looked into her eyes, trying to determine whether she meant it. Mind and body gave the same answer: She wanted him.

The invitation was dangerous. It made him want to unmask, to reveal who and what he was—and the consequences be damned.

"So show me," she whispered. "I won't be afraid."

"How you tempt me."

He watched her closely as he settled his hand over the soft curls between her legs and then eased a long finger inside her. No hesitation, no fear. She rocked against him, inviting him into the heat of her body. Her own hands began sliding down his back, kneading as they went. The tiny pricks of her nails biting into his skin were her sensual goads.

His uncontrolled and uncontrollable response to her was at once reluctant and yet exactly what he needed—had always needed—to be whole and sane. He moved down her body, enjoying the slight concavity of her abdomen and then the tenderness of her inner thighs as he settled between them. He kissed her gently, subtly parting her legs as he neared the heart of her. She didn't resist; she was willing to let him touch her any way he desired.

He gave her leg a last small kiss and then a sharp bite. It didn't break the skin, but the quick pain had her rearing up, her eyes blazing and her hands flexing into the muscles of his shoulders.

No, she wasn't feeling gentle. The thing that rode them was far from tender and tame. It could probably face who and what he was. Probably.

He allowed himself a moment more to savor her, to let his fingers and mouth play a game of advance and retreat, tantalizing both of them. But it wasn't enough. He slid up her body.

The sound she made when he pressed against her core was broken, her thoughts equally incoherent. The only clear words were *now* and *more*.

He paused for an instant, poised above her as something shifted in his brain. Then, around them a dark cloak fell, and Abrial realized that his wings had manifested themselves. Nyssa had called them out of him against his will. He looked down quickly, shocked speechless and afraid of what he'd see, but his claws were sheathed. He hadn't transformed into the beast.

"Abrial, I'm not afraid," she told him again. Her eyes were wide, blazing with desire. Her words weren't entirely true. He realized that, while she wasn't afraid of his appearance, she did fear that he might stop again.

"Not this time," he told her. Then he sank into her, the sensation somewhere between the sublime and the savage.

Nyssa wrapped herself around him, leaving herself undefended as he pounded into her until he had to accept that he could go no deeper.

He wanted the moment to last forever, but of course it couldn't. He felt the flash fire of climax explode through her body, and his own immediately followed. And one small part of his brain thought: *This may have been the biggest mistake of your life.*

The rest of him answered: *The best mistake.*

Chapter Sixteen

Thomas leaned through the jeep's passenger door and kissed his wife. He was grateful that she had Io with her. Io was able to bend magic and rework it into spells; if Cyra ran into trouble, Io would be the best person to help her out.

"You take care. Give the Feds an hour to chase you and then cut off on the nearest faerie road back here."

"Have you found the dragon yet?" Cyra asked.

"I think I know where he is," Jack answered, appearing at the driver's side of the jeep. He was wiping his hands on an oily rag.

"We'll start modifying him as soon as we get back," Io promised.

"I hope we won't need him," Thomas said. "But better safe than that other thing."

Jack slapped the side of the vehicle. "This sucker can go like a bat out of hell if you need it to, but take it easy if you can. It won't do any good if anyone figures out you aren't who we want them to believe you are."

"I'll be careful," Io promised.

"The Goddess be with you both," Thomas said.

Cyra touched the medallion that had been a gift from her husband the first time they faced the goblins. "And also with you."

Abrial and Nyssa made love and then dined on a simple meal of smoked gouda, a *pan rustique,* and an oaky wine, which they sipped at cautiously, since alcohol tended to provoke strong reactions in feys and goblins alike. Their meal done, they made love again.

Yet, even after that, Abrial found that he still had appetites: that he wanted to eat, to devour, to drink Nyssa in and down, to make her part of him forever, so that all those cold places she warmed would stay alive even after this night had passed. And then he realized that he had taken her in. For better or worse, the attractions between them had mixed with some dark magic and bound them. And sexual satiation could never be achieved and would never be enough.

Nyssa sensed this permanent bond too. And she somehow feared it, and feared for their future. This blend of trepidation and spiritual magnetism made her feel a bit like a fish that had swallowed a golden lure. The hook of her attraction to Abrial had gone deep and would not come out without pain and possible internal injury—assuming it came out at all.

"You don't look much like a fish," Abrial consoled her, sensing her thoughts, almost hearing them word for word, though he was making no particular effort to listen in. "Only a bit around the eyes, and I've always liked sockeye salmon."

"To eat maybe," she grumbled, trying to smooth her hair, which had become as abandoned as her desire.

"But of course." His smile was not at all nice, and yet it was so very sweet as he tumbled her back onto the bed. Nyssa decided that perhaps she didn't need to start the extraction immediately, that maybe it wouldn't be so bad to face the day with desire in her heart.

Though their time together seemed infinite, it was not. The hour for leaving the hotel and facing down the lutins finally arrived.

"Please return your seats to the upright position," Nyssa muttered, looking at the light moving through the crack in the curtains. Fortunately, she didn't feel nervous. Yet. She seemed to have found some lingering benefit to the chemical lobotomy caused by the hormonal storm of their lovemaking. She also knew what Abrial was feeling. This was both comforting and odd.

"I was prepared for this attraction to be many things," she told him. "I just didn't expect we'd be connected at the frontal lobes."

"That may prove a benefit today," Abrial responded. His voice was guarded, and he sent a psychic wall slowly sliding up between them.

She rubbed her hands down her arms, attempting to smooth the gooseflesh that was rising there. "So you can control it—our mental connection?"

"When I concentrate, yes."

"Well, don't. Not yet." Nyssa turned and wrapped her arms around him. "I wasn't complaining about having you here."

They stepped out of the hotel room, and the first thing Nyssa noticed was the strip of lawn colored a startling shade of avocado green. Then she looked at the sky. It seemed off-color too—brighter and harder, as if everything was made of crystallized turquoise.

She turned slowly. The entire world looked different, bolder of color and yet more ominous. It took her a moment to realize that she was seeing it with Abrial's senses as well as her own.

Wary yet fascinated, she turned toward the west, where the old cemetery marked the end of Last Chance with a small enclave of weathered stones. Most people would feel that the six feet of earth that separated the living from the dead would be enough to keep them at bay, but Nyssa knew better. The bodies might be six feet under, but any spirits who hadn't moved on would be much closer, and the restless ghosts would be waiting for someone to venture near, someone who could give them strength. Abrial apparently didn't see them, but she did.

"No, I can't see them, but I can sense them. They just add to the general unpleasant atmosphere. Really, this place has all the charm of a hemorrhoid," Abrial joked, closing the door behind them. "I can't say that I'm sorry to leave it behind."

"I suppose it might be heaven for a herpetologist," Nyssa said doubtfully. She sniffed at the air. It seemed to her that the slightly sulfurous odor was rising, and beneath that there was something else, something rancid.

Beside her, Abrial stilled, and his mental shields came back up, wrapping around her in a protective wall. His gaze fixed just above the horizon. Nyssa turned and followed his line of vision.

"Is that skywriting?" she asked, staring at the thin

stream of stuttering clouds that was moving swiftly across the sky.

"Yes." Not having seen it for a few days, Nyssa realized how profoundly disturbing Abrial's usual enigmatic expression was. It probably meant that she needed to get a game face on too. One never knew what sort of psychic eavesdroppers might be nearby.

"What does it say? I can't make it out."

"It's in Lutin." Abrial paused. "You aren't going to believe this."

"Or probably even like it, but go on."

"Loosely translated, it says: 'Nyssa, go home or face your doom.'"

"It does not!"

"It does."

"I guess this means they didn't forget about us after all. I was kind of hoping they'd just get tired and go away."

"I don't know what it means, but I do know that I don't like it. Why write that in Lutin? It makes no sense if they are really trying to warn you."

"Neither do I—understand it, I mean—and just where the hell do they think *home* is, anyway? They chased me out of my old life. Where can I go?"

"Anywhere except Cadalach would probably suit them fine." Abrial touched her arm and forced a smile. "This way, m'lady. Your coach awaits."

"What model of coach is it this time?"

"A safari-style jeep. The open top and sides will be annoying in the daylight, but I figured we might need the four-wheel drive."

The jeep was old but fairly well maintained. Best of all, no one seemed to notice them taking it.

If they had truly been bent on escape, they would have gone off-road at this point and disappeared in the desert, but since the idea was to allow the goblins to get close, they stuck to paved surfaces and didn't drive particularly quickly.

Somewhere to the north, their doubles were racing through the desert, luring H.U.G. and the FBI away. Abrial had said that the decoys were actually the spouses of two of his friends, one of whom was a kloka—a conjurer who was a master illusionist. Nyssa said a brief prayer for their well-being.

Nyssa didn't particularly like country music, but she supposed they were lucky to be getting any reception at all, and the short songs did break up the tedium of staring at the blank desert and waiting to be attacked. It was just that the sadly dogged voices on the radio called to things inside of her—stupid things she'd just as soon forget. But all alone, now that Abrial had withdrawn from her mind, these memories resurrected themselves, pointing and laughing at her. She had made a fool of herself once—or twice—over a man, of course. And, little as she wanted to consider the idea, she had to wonder if she was doing it again. Big time.

After all, Abrial wasn't a real candy-and-flowers sort of guy. Dear Abby would not approve of him. And though their relationship differed from anything humans had ever encountered, it was in many ways the same old situation outlined in nine-tenths of the love-gone-wrong songs they'd been listening to. Girl meets wild boy, girl loves wild boy, girl blurts out she loves wild boy, and wild boy says thanks, but I've got to be free, and rides away.

That was it in a nutshell. The depressed crooners irked Nyssa because she suspected that though her feelings for Abrial were not entirely unreturned, they weren't sufficiently requited. How on earth could they be? What she was feeling was crazy—overwhelming— two things that Abrial never was. And though she wanted to, mentioning them now just didn't seem wise. There were, after all, life-threatening problems pressing in on them.

She sighed. She was grateful that he couldn't hear her thoughts, but she was feeling very alone now that Abrial had his mental wall back up.

If only she wasn't trapped with the same old feelings, the same old fears, the same damn ugly desert that had been with her for days.

A new song began. It was the worst one yet. Nyssa stared at the radio with loathing.

"You're awfully quiet," Abrial said. "What are you thinking about? You aren't worried, are you?"

Nyssa shrugged, unwilling to admit to her maudlin train of thought. Truly, if there was ever *not* a moment for a relationship discussion, this was it.

"Just the same old, same old. I'm stuck between a hammer and an anvil. Only one of them means me harm, but it doesn't matter when the two collide. I also don't know if we're coming or going," she told him, knowing she sounded slightly dazed but unable to help it. "But in any event, we aren't wasting a lot of time along the way—which is good. Less time to brood and worry." Then she added quickly, "Did he just really say that his heart got caught in the kitchen door?"

"No." Abrial turned back to the road.

"Oh." She caught the next line, something about being swept up off the floor. "Are you sure about that? Door would rhyme with floor."

"Yes. He didn't *say* it, he sang, '*My heart got caught in your kitchen door.*'" Abrial crooned the line, complete with thick accent and nasal twang.

"You really do that rather well for a . . ."

"Basso profundo?"

"Well, yes. Have you ever considered a career in music? It wouldn't have to be country or the Beach Boys. You could do more mainline rock and roll."

Abrial's lips twitched. "No, I've never considered it."

"Maybe you should. You'd probably be a hit as a rock star. You have the look."

"I'll keep it in mind."

Nyssa sighed again and began doodling in the dust on the dashboard. Who would ever have thought that the combination of worry and terror and potential heartbreak could lead to boredom? She was almost looking forward to the final showdown. Almost.

Abrial sensed Nyssa's restlessness and didn't know quite what to make of it. He'd seen similar symptoms in soldiers before battle, but he doubted that pre-battle adrenaline was what was making her so fidgety. He considered opening up a crack in his mental wall to see what was going on in her head but decided against it. He needed to stay focused. There was only one logical place for the goblins to waylay them—but since when had goblins been logical?

He saw her writing her name in the dust on the

car's glove compartment, and then rubbing it out again. He realized that her name was also written on his heart, only it wouldn't be so easily removed if she decided that she wouldn't stay with him.

Abrial heard himself and almost snorted—*written on his heart? How poetic.* And what was worse, he meant it. He usually believed in calling a spade something slightly worse. It was just more colorful and it kept one from hoping too much or longing for impossible things. But this time, he wasn't willing to look things in the eye and calculate the odds. He needed Nyssa, more than he had ever imagined needing anyone. He wasn't open to entertaining any notions about her leaving him through free will or death.

She was understandably afraid, because of their situation, and holding back from him because she didn't believe that they would be able to rid her of Qasim's heart.

But everything was going to go just like clockwork. They'd kill off the bad guys and Zayn would remove Qasim's heart in a complication-free surgery. Once liberated from that awful burden, she'd promptly announce her love and eternal devotion to him. They'd get married, have a honeymoon in Hawaii, then a baby—though that little detail might already have been taken care of. Feys didn't conceive without magical assistance, but the magic had been with them last night.

Should he mention this to her? No, probably not. She needed to focus too.

Maybe later he'd take her suggestion and look into a career in music. They'd travel and do all the normal things that couples did, and everything would be just fine.

It would.

It had to be.

Chapter Seventeen

Just as anticipated, the attack came in the late afternoon, when the expected storm rolled in with an unseasonably harsh downpour that clattered against the windscreen and their heads like the keys of an old manual typewriter. The rain should have smelled fresh, but it didn't. The air grew sulfurous, and the damp also made the skin sting. Abrial stopped briefly to lace up a makeshift tarp. He only barely had it in place when more of the eerie lightning that had chased them through the desert that first day began dancing in the sky. The color was depressing, but it made the nerves sing with alarm.

"Here we go."

"That sounds like an epitaph," Nyssa muttered, and her eyelid started flickering in time with the lightning. She looked over at Abrial. In the reflected glare of the headlights that bounced off the road, the streams of harsh water running down the windows seemed also to be tears running down Abrial's face. She knew that she must look the same and thought it fitting that someone or something wept for them.

Though the storm before the attack was anticipated, what was not expected was that the goblins would fire some sort of anti-tank missile into the jeep miles ahead of the target area. They had all assumed that the lutins working with Qasim still wanted Nyssa alive, and that therefore they would be somewhat cautious of how and where they attacked her.

Fortunately, Abrial was not distracted by the rain and his senses were working overtime. Catching a stray hostile thought, he knew what was coming almost from the moment of initiation. Grabbing Nyssa, he launched himself into the air, shredding his clothing as his body transformed into battle form. The clawed wings and taloned hands she hadn't seen since their first dream encounter were back again. Nyssa thought at first she was seeing a psychic portrait of Abrial because their minds had reconnected but soon realized the transformation was at least partly physical. Abrial didn't just look deadly; he *was* deadly.

Behind them, the jeep exploded with a loud whoosh and started burning merrily in spite of the rain.

"Stay here." Abrial shoved Nyssa behind a stand of rocks and then seemed to disappear, a blurred shadow heading at impossible speed toward the troll-goblin cross who had ambushed them with the rocket launcher. The creature was huge and could have brought home Olympic gold any day of the week if trolls were allowed to enter weight lifting. Fortunately, like most trolls or troll half-breeds, he was slow and not particularly bright, and simply stood there, staring joyfully at the big explosion he'd caused.

Abrial materialized again, but only an instant before he struck. Before their mental connection, Nyssa would not have seen him or the troll-cross at all, let alone the strike that killed the awestruck creature, so fast was Abrial. But as it was, she could see all that she wanted—and much that she didn't. Unable to look away when Abrial was in danger, she watched, eyes wide, as Abrial's claws sprang out another two inches, and as his jaws contorted into something that belonged on a large cat. She saw that he aimed for the troll's femoral artery. One swipe and the creature's leg disappeared in a spray of blood. The troll fell over, dead, and everything was finished so fast that there was no time to feel alarm.

In what seemed less than an instant, Abrial was back at her side, again reappearing like something conjured out of thin air. He didn't have much gore on his pants or chest, but what there was clung like tar and smelled dreadful even when damped down by the rain.

Come on. There are more of them posted all along the road. We need to get inland.

Feeling stunned, she asked: *But why did they try to kill us? I thought they needed the heart.*

That troll wasn't from the Sin City hive. He wasn't one of Carbon's either. I think he is one of Lobineau's pseudo-Christians. Abrial hauled Nyssa to her feet and started into the rocky cleft that climbed steeply behind them. His mouth shifted back a few degrees and he added aloud: "We need to reach the plateau and get across the stream while we still can. We can't afford to get cut off by the flash floods."

"Okay." She thought about asking why the head goblin in New Orleans might want her dead, but it didn't matter which reason Abrial picked off the list running through his mind. The desire and plan were there. The troll's rocket launcher had said it all.

Though there was no indication that the troll-cross had been anything other than a lone scout on that part of the road, and she and Abrial were promptly covered in red mud that had to be an effective camouflage, Nyssa still felt as conspicuous as a chief clown in the center ring of the circus as she clung and scuffed her way up the mountain. She also began to tire, and had to question whether she and Abrial should have made love that fourth time; those lost hours of sleep and muscle repair were beginning to be missed.

"You know," she panted, "I am rethinking the wisdom of taking this job as lure. The pay is lousy and the working conditions suck."

"But you have me," Abrial pointed out, planting an unromantic hand on her rear end and boosting her onto a high boulder.

"I suppose that's true." And at least they wouldn't dehydrate. The cold rain was keeping them plenty wet. And it was getting darker all the time. That was good for the skin, but pretty soon the only way to locate the numerous chasms would be to fall into them. And while that would probably save the goblins a lot of trouble, and might be better than what Qasim had in mind for her, Nyssa didn't really want to end her life that afternoon, smashed into bloody fragments in the middle of nowhere.

"You do know where we are going, right?" she gasped hopefully.

"Yes. We are headed to the nearest faerie road. It's where the others are—or will be shortly. We'll rendezvous there."

"And how near is the *nearest?*"

"Just keep climbing and head west."

Nyssa looked at the cliff in front of her. It looked treacherous. She stuffed her hands into the thick trickle of muddy water that was rapidly turning into a waterfall, and did as Abrial suggested. She also stopped talking, since there wasn't any way to open her mouth without getting it filled with red sludge.

She wasn't clear on where west was, since there were no astral bodies to navigate by and she had somehow managed to forget to pack a compass, but Nyssa soon figured out that as long as she kept the cold stinging rain beating directly on the back of her neck and running down her spine, she could pretty well stay pointed in the right direction.

She had only one mishap, thanks to Abrial's watchful eye; but while he was turned away, studying their back trail, she slipped on a patch of loose shale that made up the lip of a narrow ledge, and ended up tumbling down the hill until caught in the rescuing arms of a dead manzanita bush perched on the edge of a cliff.

Abrial was there an instant later, helping extract her and running hands over as he searched for broken bones. He took one look over the cliff and then pulled her two steps away, turning her so she couldn't see the drop.

It took her a minute to get her lungs functioning again. Having the air knocked out of her by the dead shrub was no fun, even it had kept her from screaming and giving away their position to anyone who was following them.

"Thanks," she wheezed, beginning to shiver from a mixture of cold and adrenaline ebb. She felt like a bowling ball at the end of a hard-played tournament but made herself say: "Really, I'm okay. I think I hit every bush and boulder on the way down, but it's just splinters and bruises. I'll live."

"I'm sorry. You aren't used to the mountains, and they are perfidious in this rain."

"Perfidious? You mean, the mountain did that on purpose?"

"Maybe. We're in their territory now." Abrial smoothed back her mud-clotted hair. He plucked out some dead twigs. "I'll take the lead now."

"It's okay," she assured him. "I'll be more cautious. And I'd rather have you there to catch me if I slip again." She also preferred to have him watching the trail behind them in case someone took up pursuit.

"Are you sure?" His eyes searched hers, but he didn't look inside her brain. The fact that he was holding back on mental contact probably meant that she had frightened him even more than she had herself, and he didn't want her to know how close she had come to ending up as red stuff on a rock.

"Yes." It took an effort, but Nyssa forced a smile and turned back to look up at the hill that needed retaking. "Anyway, I'll be damned if this stupid mountain is going to beat me now. We're almost to the top."

That was a slight exaggeration, and the last third of the trail was narrow, a chute between tumbled boulders that had been snagged by the mountain gorge on their way down to the valley floor. The mix of thick scrub and loose debris that held the suspended rocks in place did not inspire confidence. One foot placed wrong and the whole lot could come unstuck. And the water rushed down relentlessly, gaining strength with every minute the unnatural precipitation kept on. Nor had Nyssa forgotten Abrial's words about the land possibly working against them. Nyssa kept her eyes closed as much as possible, climbing by feel.

The last boulder was an irregular plug at the top of the gorge. It held back much of the water from the flash flood that wanted to cascade down on them, but it also canted outward at a fairly severe angle, and Nyssa would never have made it over the giant step if Abrial had not been there to help her with another well-placed shove in the nether regions.

He joined her a moment later, barely winded and heartlessly hauling her to her feet when she showed no sign of rising on her own.

"We have to cross the stream now," he told her.

"Okay. I'm coming . . . I'm coming."

The *stream* Abrial had been concerned about was more like a river in spate, thick with red soil and swollen to twice its seasonal height. The water pushed against him and Nyssa relentlessly, and strong as Nyssa was, she knew that without Abrial, she would have been swept away. As it was, they had to shove their feet along the bottom through the rounded rocks, taking small shuffling steps so that they never shifted their center of balance by more than a few degrees.

The water was abnormally cold and numbing, but not entirely sufficient as an anesthetic, since they still felt every shattered tree limb that swept past them and knocked into their already bruised bodies.

Eventually they reached the other side, and Abrial allowed Nyssa a short rest. While she slumped on a flat rock, he remained standing, turning about slowly and watching the horizon with wary eyes.

"The rain is easing," he said at last. "But the clouds are still thick."

Nyssa nodded.

"I know you're tired, but we have to go on. I can carry you, if you like. The ground is flatter here. It should be safe."

Nyssa looked at Abrial and then at the wild country around them, the same landscape he was studying so carefully. It looked like the world's most likely spot for a sniper. Or several of them.

"I'm fine," she said, forcing herself to her feet. "Let's go find your friends. I'm ready to see something other than trolls and goblins."

Abrial nodded and then pointed in a direction that she assumed was west.

"I'll go first. Stay close and keep your eyes open. We should be safe here, but . . ." He didn't have to say anything more. They should have been safe on the road too, until they reached the obvious ambush

212

point. All bets were off now that there were new players in the game.

Once again she thought of Father Lobineau and the New Orleans hive, and wondered what the hell was going on.

Chapter Eighteen

Cyra looked into the dragon's flat gold eyes. They hadn't seen each other in more than a year. By choice. Theirs was an uneasy relationship.

"You wanted something?" the dragon asked. "Perhaps help with a little green problem?"

"Yes," Cyra answered. "And I'm willing to make you stronger if you'll help us deal with King Carbon and Lilith."

"Lilith? Ah, I see. She *is* unfinished business. What's the job specifically?"

"Eating goblins," she said deliberately. "Lots and lots of them."

The dragon smiled. It was unnerving, as was the joy in his voice when he asked: "When do we begin?"

"Now." Cyra took off her jacket and began walking toward the serpent. "How would you feel about being able to breathe acid as well as fire?"

"Stop," Abrial said, as if his abrupt halt wouldn't have been signal enough.

Nyssa was about to ask why, and then she saw the two creatures loping toward them through the rain. Their eyes gleamed an eerie black and red, lit from inside by some unwholesome fire.

"Stop," Abrial said again, and this time he put the full force of his will behind the word and cast his command toward the two goblins. He added: "Or I will have to eat your livers."

The threat, or something, worked. The pair, male and female, halted. Nyssa recognized King Carbon; the female she was less certain of. Clearly she had the size of a hive master, but she was badly scarred and didn't resemble any of the photos of goblin leaders Nyssa had ever seen.

Abrial and the goblins stared at one another through the veil of unnatural darkness.

"Just give us the girl, Executioner. We have no quarrel with you," the female said. Even her voice sounded mangled, a bit like a smoker's voice, but one who had been smoking napalm.

"Sorry." Abrial didn't sound it. "No can do. I'm afraid that we really can't have Qasim getting a hold of that heart."

"He won't get it," Carbon said urgently. "Give it to us and we'll see it's safe. Qasim can be controlled. But we have to have the heart first."

"I feel doubtful about this," Abrial said. "And more than a little pissed about being shot at, even if it was Lobineau's creature who did it."

The two lutins exchanged a glance. Apparently the news about Lobineau being involved was something they hadn't known about.

"We didn't try to kill you, Executioner," Carbon

said. "You are Unseelie—an old ally—but you must give us the girl. Now. Before Qasim or anyone else gets here. If you don't . . ."

Nyssa felt that she should say something, since it was her fate being discussed, but she drew a large blank in her script when faced with the two hostile lutins who wanted her dead. Or for something worse. It was also a little unnerving that Abrial didn't contradict them about that old ally stuff. She had known that he was a servant of the dark queen but hadn't ever thought of him as being a goblin collaborator. It was a shock to think that he had been a goblin ally at the time of her kidnapping and mutilation.

Before Abrial could answer the unspoken threat, he and Nyssa were joined by two other feys, a tall male with black hair and the gold eyes of a dragon, and a long lanky man roped with obvious muscles that somehow made Nyssa think of a horse. There was nowhere they could have come from except the rocks behind them, which meant they had been using a faerie road.

The goblins looked unhappy with the company.

"Friends of yours, I presume," Nyssa managed to say. It was difficult to look away from the lutin hive masters, neither of whom looked friendly or pleased, but she gave both men a quick smile. "So glad you could join us on our romp through the desert."

"You're late," Abrial said. "The moon is almost up. Thomas, Roman, this is Nyssa Laszlo. Nyssa, Thomas Marrowbone and Roman Hautecoeur."

"Sorry, Roman and I were delayed fighting what looked like the entire goblin nation. I had to go round up some extra help to deal with the flying fecal matter

217

fresh off the New Orleans fan. I can't believe that ungrateful bastard Lobineau has gotten involved."

"And Jack?"

"Our illustrious leader's still a little busy closing off the road from L.A. so no others can get in the pipeline." Thomas's voice was calm and relaxed, but his eyes were keen as they studied the two goblin leaders in front of him. He didn't look at or speak to Nyssa—a fact that didn't offend her. She wanted everyone to keep their eyes on the goblins.

"I could be wrong, but I don't think it's visions of sugarplums that are dancing in their heads," Roman commented.

"It never was. . . . You know, she's even uglier than I remembered," Thomas said. Then: "I wonder why they came alone."

"Why do goblins do anything?" Roman asked. Then: "She really is hideous."

"They won't want her at Vogue now that you've scarred her, that's for sure. I take it that you found your pet dragon?" Abrial asked. Then, before Thomas could answer, he ordered, "Nyssa, get behind us."

He waited until she had moved, then continued. "I think they're here alone because they don't want anyone to know that they are after Qasim's heart. It would piss the hobgoblin off if he knew about this bit of attempted backstabbing, and he has spies everywhere."

The words were barely out of his mouth when the two goblins decided to strike. They dropped down on all six limbs and ran at them. Their speed was shocking, but not as horrible as the teeth suddenly jutting from their giant mouths and their appalling gait, which resembled scrambling beetles. Somehow they had unhinged their jaws, making their mouths even wider, and gave the impression that they were planning on biting off someone's head.

Thomas and Abrial also leapt forward, and Roman was only a beat behind, drawing out a long sword covered in runes. But before the enemies could join in battle, something gigantic and even faster came crashing between them. It landed just slightly in front of the two goblins and about thirty feet from Abrial and Thomas.

Nyssa knew instinctively what—who—she was looking at. The creature was horrible to behold, a conglomeration of nightmares: barklike skin that curled back from an open wound in its chest, giant tusks that resembled a boar's—except they were longer and sharper and made of green bone. And there was a terrible stench that was horribly familiar. But worst of all was the mouth. It was as though someone had stuck a shark's mouth in a Neanderthal's head.

Both parties stopped the attack, involuntarily arrested by the sheer power that came rolling off this thing. Neither Thomas nor Abrial had ever encountered such raw psychic miasma. Roman had experienced something like it before, but not from a hobgoblin. The creature that he had been forced to use every last bit of courage and will to face had been a master vampire.

Nyssa was immune to most of the psychic shockwave that rolled off the hobgoblin, but she quailed at the thought of this creature turning his will upon her. Fortunately, though he studied her for a moment, he made no attempt to take over her mind. His resolve seemed directed at the goblins.

"You weren't thinking of starting the party without me?" Qasim asked, swinging around suddenly to face Lilith and Carbon. He used rough English, suggesting he wanted all of his audience to understand his words. His voice grated on the ears like claws on a chalkboard, but it was brutally clear. "It couldn't be that you were going to take my heart from this child and keep it for yourselves. That would make me very angry."

Before the shocked goblins could answer, Qasim's arms whipped out and slammed the two hive masters together. He picked the stunned lutins up by their hair and shook them the way a terrier would a rat whose neck needed breaking. Unfortunately, goblin necks were rather thicker than rodent ones, and all the shaking did was hurt them.

Satisfied that he had the goblins' attention, Qasim turned back to face his daughter and Abrial. He never once looked at the sword Roman was carrying—perhaps it had no power over him because he had no heart to pierce with it.

"Carbon's army has split into three parts and is coming fast. They are using the faerie roads. Your Jack has closed off one, but the other two are still open. You can't escape that way. And neither can I." His eyes again focused on his daughter. Terrified at his words, his presence, and even his gaze, Nyssa still looked back. His next words were even more shocking. "Your mother isn't dead."

"What?" she whispered.

"Carbon had her. I'm afraid that I spent valuable time liberating her before I came here. She is safely stashed away now, enjoying the sun and the sand."

220

"Why did you save her?" Nyssa heard herself ask, and felt Abrial glance her way.

Qasim laughed, and she suddenly knew it was a stupid question. Intuition told her that the only reason he would have bothered with Bysshe was so that he would have something to give in exchange for the heart he wanted back. Her mother's life for Nyssa's own: That would be the trade he offered. Nyssa was very glad that she hadn't been faced with that choice, because she didn't know what she would do.

"I wish that I could visit more since it's our first reunion, but I really have to be going. The goblins have actually discovered a rather nasty drug that doesn't agree with me at all—some form of menispemaceae, I believe. It's made me a little slow. The dragon didn't seem to like it either, but I think he managed to escape along with Mr. Frost." Qasim turned around and stepped toward the cliff that overlooked the river, taking the goblins with him. "Come along, my faithless friends. Don't you know what today is?"

The two goblins struggled and hissed pleas in Lutin, but in vain. Their claws, though formidable, couldn't penetrate the hobgoblin's scabrous hide. Nyssa sensed that they were sending out mental pleas for help, but the hobgoblin's psychic mire was deadening their psiwaves.

"That's right," the horrible voice went on, the tone almost jovial. "It's the solstice. It's the day I've returned, and the day I've learned of all the treachery in the world. And that means that today is your day to die!"

Qasim strolled deliberately for the long drop, but turned back once more at the edge of the cliff.

Nyssa saw the fey tense—Abrial, Thomas, Roman—prepared to attack if Qasim dropped his burdens or changed direction. But all the hobgoblin did was to look deep into Abrial's eyes and issue a parting instruction.

"You keep my treasure safe, Executioner. Don't you let any goblins or humans get her. You owe me that for getting rid of this little problem."

Not waiting for a reply, Qasim leaped off the cliff, carrying his two shrieking lutin captives with him. There was an audible splat about three seconds later.

"Well, damn," Thomas said, and all of them hurried for the ravine's rim.

It took only a moment to spot Carbon and Lilith's bodies. They were impaled on a stand of rocks at the river's edge, with several stone spears piercing them through. It was a few more seconds peering into the gloom before they spotted Qasim being carried downriver by the raging flow. The giant body appeared limp, but there was no sign of blood in the water.

"Is he dead?" Roman asked.

"I wouldn't count on it," Abrial answered. "The cloud cover isn't breaking up. Nyssa? Can you tell if he's really gone?"

The three men turned to look at Nyssa. She knew she needed to respond, but for the moment all she could do was shake her head.

"Nyssa? Are you okay? Did he hurt you?" Abrial began an internal check, rushing through her brain, looking for injury either physical or psychic. Her nerves were raw from their exposure to Qasim, and the contact hurt.

222

"I don't know if he's dead," she said honestly, forcing her mouth and brain to function. Immediately, Abrial retreated. "I don't feel anything. I'm numb."

"If he isn't dead now, he's badly wounded. How long can he hide from the goblins, humans, and fey?" Thomas asked them.

"Too long. And he'll heal fast if he finds someone to sacrifice," Abrial answered. He turned back to face Nyssa. He was still clawed and fanged, but his appearance no longer frightened her at all. Nyssa doubted that anything would have the power to truly scare her again.

"Where's my mother?" she asked. "She has to be nearby. He said he rescued her."

"I don't know. Somewhere that the goblins can't get her would be my bet."

"If he wasn't lying about that," Thomas interjected.

"He was telling the truth. The trade was to be my life for my mother's." She was certain of this.

"I'm sorry, Nyssa," Abrial touched her arm as he spoke. "But she needn't be physically close. You know how the faerie roads work. She could be anywhere."

Thomas said, "In any event, a search will have to wait. The dragon and Jack were doing all they could to delay the hordes, and Qasim bought us a little time by killing Carbon and Lilith, but the goblins will soon reorganize, and they'll be out for revenge. And there is that bastard Lobineau. Who knows how many trolls or goblins he may have sent this way? There's an elfin shelter about ten miles from here. Cyra and I went there once. It's a stronghold of Ianna Fe's. If we can reach it, we'll be safe."

Safe from goblins, he meant. But Nyssa knew that she would never be truly safe until Qasim was dead, or the heart was taken out of her and destroyed.

"Let's go," Abrial said. "Sorry, but you'll have to run some more. The cloud cover and increasing darkness should help. It's the only reason to be glad that Qasim isn't dead."

"He isn't doing it for us," she snapped. "He's making it dark for himself. He doesn't want the moon to find him."

"I know, but it will still help."

Nyssa nodded, saving her breath for the ten mile sprint. The four of them turned their backs on the river and began to run. Then Nyssa thought of something.

"What is *menis*—whatever—Qasim mentioned that the goblins had?"

"Menispemaceae. Curare, real nasty stuff," Abrial answered. "It would probably work on us too, so we better keep our distance."

"Trust me, it works," Thomas told them. "I've had that pleasure."

Abrial looked thoughtful. "Still, it's an idea. We'll need something to slow that monster down if he comes after us later."

Thinking of the ease with which Qasim had disabled the two giant goblins, Nyssa could only agree.

"So, you were planning on greeting the horde that is probably waiting for us at the bottom of the hill wearing nothing but your usual, unnerving smile?" Thomas asked Abrial. "Or were you thinking of using some actual weapons this time, Executioner?"

"What do you think?" Abrial asked. This once, Nyssa didn't chide him for his sarcastic tone.

"I don't know about Abrial, but I want a gun. A big gun," she said.

"I want one too," Roman agreed, putting up his sword. "This thing is useless. I might as well have been waving a fish at him."

"Jack thought you might feel that way." Thomas shrugged off his pack as they jogged, and quickly produced four strange handguns, which he distributed. Even before she touched it, Nyssa could feel the dark magic hovering around the weapon. A magic handgun?

Abrial whistled softly. "Jack does have a way with these things, doesn't he?"

"It's practice. Fixing these weapons exhausted him and he had to have Io's help. The ammo isn't endless," Thomas warned, handing them spare clips. "Shoot straight. And not at each other. I don't think any of us would survive the experience."

Suddenly, right behind them came the sound of splitting rock, and then the loud noise of hundreds of dry rattles. Nyssa and Abrial looked back and started swearing. Thomas and Roman didn't bother; they just picked up the pace.

"I don't believe it," Nyssa said, watching the trail begin to boil behind them as hundreds of snakes erupted from the faerie road.

"Believe it. They've found some human or goblin serpent master, and rounded up every damn snake in the desert and sent them after us." Roman sounded revolted.

"We'll be okay if they don't get ahead of us," Thomas assured them. "There's a river about half a mile on. It's pretty shallow this time of year, but the current is strong. It should deter most of these things."

"It will be more than okay, river or not. They miscalculated." Abrial suddenly began chanting, repeating the phrase he had used on the rattlesnake back at the hotel.

"It's working!" Nyssa said. "They're stopping!"

"Yeah, but that's not all that's chasing us." Abrial was grim as he stared into her eyes.

"What do you mean?" In answer, large tarantulas began plopping down on them, throwing themselves off the cliff face that ran along the right wall twelve feet above them. A rain of scorpions followed.

"Sorry, I don't have any power over arachnids," he apologized. "No spider gods in the family."

"Those sneaky bastards—this is cheating! First the damned mountain and now this!? They can't just use humans against us!" Nyssa said, her voice hard with anger as she swatted the giant spiders away. The bites hurt but weren't incapacitating. Yet. Who knew what would happen if they were bitten hundreds of times? Maybe her hobgoblin blood would protect her. But maybe not.

"They are, though. Humans collaborate with the goblins all the time."

"Well, we'll just see about this."

"What are you doing?" Abrial asked as he felt a jolt of mental energy coming from Nyssa. Instantly he began feeding her some of his own power, which she broadcast into the dark.

"See that cavern over there?"

"That black hole?"

"It's a mineshaft. I'm going to use the ghosts there to fight the goblins."

"Did you say ghosts?" Roman asked.

"Dead miners. They died in a cave-in. The spiders won't bother them a bit, and I bet any human allies of the goblins around here won't like seeing them. Humans are scared stiff by spirits." Nyssa closed her eyes and began concentrating, using what she had learned from Abrial to direct her power outward. Abrial didn't argue; he simply took her arm in case she stumbled as they ran.

Nyssa looked at the ghosts with her mind's eye. The hovering spirits seemed pleased with the rush of energy, and they began to produce wonderful ectoplasmic manifestations and loud moaning. They were quite hideous looking, and also quite willing to leave their mineshaft to head for the lutins when she asked them.

"That's impressive," Roman said. "I've never seen a ghost before."

"They're still kind of insubstantial. They won't be real effective against the goblins once the lutins get over their surprise," Abrial pointed out.

Nyssa opened her eyes. She sounded breathless as she gasped, "No, but they'll buy us some time with whoever is up there with those spiders, and any other human spies they're using—and maybe we can lose them in the panic and confusion. Just tell the ghosts where to go."

Thomas pointed, eyes narrowed. "That way, about five hundred yards and closing fast. I recognize two of the goblins, Thetis and Andivak. He's the one with

227

the voice like a sonic boom. This isn't a good sign. They're troll handlers that specialize in tracking."

"Swell. It only needed that," Roman said.

"There's an outcrop of rock about a quarter of a mile ahead, a sort of stone stair. We can watch the show from there for a bit before we cross the stream."

"Though it might be entertaining, stopping wouldn't be wise," Abrial answered. Nyssa was too busy guiding the hungry ghosts to participate in the conversation, but she agreed. She didn't want to stop until she had something substantial between her and the goblins and all the goblins' allies.

"I thought we'd also get in a spot of target practice while we're there. There won't be a better spot to bag some baddies."

"That's worth stopping for," Abrial decided. "Especially if we can kill the troll masters before the bulk of their troops gets here. Unsupervised trolls could do as much damage to the goblins as to us."

"Let's hear a resounding *Amen* for that," Roman answered.

Chapter Nineteen

Abrial did his best to hide his thoughts from her as they prepared for battle, but it was difficult when their impulses were so perfectly aligned. The task at hand was to inflict the most damage with the few weapons they had. That meant thinking coldly about things like trajectories and bullet ranges. Once this would have appalled Nyssa, but not anymore; Abrial's greater experience was an aid to her.

The four of them—she, Abrial, Thomas and Roman—were laid like railroad ties on the top step of a natural stair that offered minimal cover. The wood of her gun's handle was polished smooth, but it was heavy and fit awkwardly into Nyssa's hand. She understood what she needed to do, though, and as soon as the others began firing she squinted down the silver sights of the gun, choosing her target and firing carefully.

The results were terrible and fascinating. Every bullet was fatal—sometimes twice over, since they often passed through their first victim and found another target—but there were simply too many goblins for the gunfire to have much overall effect.

The short but constant barrage left Nyssa feeling shattered, and her ears continued ringing even after the last shell was spent.

"Time to be moving on," Abrial said, handing his empty weapon back to Thomas. Nyssa followed suit, relieved to be parted from the wood and metal bringer of death.

"Damn! I wish they didn't have those drugged darts." Abrial's gaze was intent.

"Feeling feisty, are we?" Roman asked with a grin. "But I'm with you, my brother. These greenies are beginning to piss me off. Glad the old hobgoblin warned us about the curare, because I'd be tempted to go kick a little lutin ass otherwise."

"Laudable impulse, but it's time to move and then some." Thomas, who was not given to Roman's bursts of high-spiritedness, pointed south and they could see in the veiled moonlight yet another column of goblins was advancing. Mixed in their ranks were the larger trolls, who carried something that looked like rifles.

"Not rifles," Abrial answered Nyssa's thought. "More dart guns. Carbon's hive still plans on taking you alive, I guess."

"Should I be grateful?" Nyssa asked, rubbing her forehead.

"Probably not."

Thomas muttered something that Nyssa was certain would qualify as profane. She added a similar phrase in English.

* * *

"Abrial, I feel something." Nyssa obviously tried not to sound breathless, but she was winded and way past what an aerobics instructor would consider her ideal heartrate. Calling the ghosts, and the almost constant running, had drained her. Abrial could feel her exhaustion and it worried him.

"What's tickling you?" he asked.

"Ghosts—lots of them. Organized. And I would say evil. They're coming in this general direction, and fast. Maybe they felt what I did earlier and it attracted them. Or maybe they can just feel *me*. Storms always make things worse, remember." Nyssa looked guilty.

"That's great—can you use them? I can feed you extra energy," Abrial said. But not endless amounts of it. He hated to admit it, but he was tiring too. The only one who seemed to still have endless reserves of energy was Roman. His river horse ancestry allowed him to run long distances without tiring.

"I don't know. Maybe."

"You might want to try if you can think of a way," Thomas said, his voice and eyes both flat. "The goblins are using several old Unseelie roads as shortcuts, and they are gaining on us."

Nyssa's brain turned over, grappling with that further bad news. It was feeling sluggish and as exhausted as the rest of her, but it managed to grasp a lifeline of thought.

"It's the solstice," Nyssa panted. "That's what Qasim said. The solstice is the goblins' night to die."

"Right. So?" Abrial, still partially wrapped up in her thoughts, answered himself. "The Wild Hunt? Here? Did he bring them?"

"That horde used the faerie road to get to America?" Thomas asked. They began to slow their pace. "But how? They died out ages ago. No one has seen them in the last two hundred years—and never here."

"I think Qasim must have found a way, for their ghosts at any rate," Abrial answered. "He always was clever with spirits—the bad ones anyway."

"Qasim did this? Damn. So this is what you might call a classic good-news/bad-news situation." Roman looked at Abrial and then Thomas.

"Yeah. You might also call it a damned-if-you-do and damned-if-you-don't situation." Nyssa barely managed to get the sentence out with one breath. "I can try to call them this way. It would bring them down on the goblins for sure. But listen—if they come, we have to stop immediately and look away. Get down flat on the ground. If we don't—"

"We know the drill. We can face them if we have to," Thomas answered. His voice was uneasy though, and with good reason. Fey sometimes rode with the Wild Hunt, but not on the solstice. That was reserved for the souls of the damned who went out collecting sacrifices for their grisly midnight feast. It was the one night when their spirits were again made flesh.

"Shall I do it?" Nyssa asked, one last time.

"Go for it." Abrial was positive.

"I have to stop running," Nyssa said. "I'm sorry, but—"

"It's okay," Abrial answered as they all halted. Both Thomas and Abrial were breathing hard. Even Roman had finally broken a sweat.

Abrial looked back once. In the moonlight, they could see the goblins coming. There had to be nearly a hundred of them in each column. Some were battered and scorched after their battle with Thomas's dragon, but they were still coming, marching like zombies under a dead general's command. It begged the question of who was controlling them.

"Call the Hunt. Now."

Nyssa closed her eyes. Instead of conjuring her piano, she pictured a giant hunting horn, on which she gave a mighty blast. The horn shook her to the soles of her tired feet. She blew on it three times and then waited.

"Is it working?" Thomas asked after a minute, not able to follow Nyssa's thoughts as Abrial did.

"Yes!" Nyssa gasped, and that was all the warning they had before the air filled with a long eerie howling and a pale blue spirit light. "Here they come."

Nyssa, Thomas, Roman, and Abrial knew what they were dealing with and promptly dropped flat, making obeisance to the hellhounds that ran before the horde. They watched intently until the riders drew near but were careful after that to keep their eyes turned away from the headless specter that led the Hunt, and the corpselike woman on the black stag whose body was pierced with glowing nails. Almost no one could encounter Hel's eyes and live. Those who did, regretted it.

The feel of spectral cloven hooves and the paws of the baying hellhounds treading over their bodies was painful and disconcerting, but the fey lay still, not looking up until the horde had passed.

"Goddess!" Thomas gasped, as the last of the phantom steeds thundered by, blue fire splashing up from its hooves as they struck the stony ground.

"No, that was the Devil," Abrial answered, rolling

to his feet and pulling Nyssa up beside him. He kept his arms around her, offering what comfort he could. All four watched expectantly as the hunters bore down on the goblins.

If the goblins had been versed in the ways of the furious horde, they would have known to throw themselves flat until the Hunt passed by. But Carbon's creatures were very much of the modern age, and instead they either froze in horrified fascination or else raised useless clubs and dart guns against the host bearing down on them.

The dead riders were unperturbed by the show of strength from the lutins and rode right into them. Those goblins that fought were torn apart by the hellhounds that bled red fire from their eyes, or were gored by the stags' antlers and then pierced with iron spears. Those lutins and trolls with simpler minds were snatched up by the headless rider and his host of the damned, and were quickly swept away.

Goblins or not, Nyssa shuddered at their fate; they would be the main course at the horde's hideous feast that midnight.

The last they saw of the Hunt was as it disappeared over the rise. There came a flash of red lightning, and then a small fireball came hurtling their way. Thomas and Roman jumped nimbly aside. Abrial followed suit, pulling a less graceful Nyssa with him. A small sack of charred leather landed where they had been standing. The smell of burning flesh was strong and nauseating.

"What is it?" Nyssa asked, trying not to gag.

"Your reward. Twenty pieces of gold stuffed inside

234

a goblin heart," Abrial answered. "But don't touch it. The Devil's gifts are always dangerous."

Nyssa nodded, shuddering. She didn't want a reward.

"Okay, one group taken out and only three more to go."

"Three more?" Nyssa asked, dismayed.

"Yeah." Thomas looked grim. "Carbon was dead serious about getting his hands on Qasim's heart. But cheer up; there's an ancient faerie road ahead. It was used sometimes by the Unseelie Court so the goblins can take it, but the place is a maze, riddled with tunnels made by an underground river. We should be able to lose them and still come out close to Ianna Fe's stronghold."

Nyssa hoped he was right, because her strength was flagging and she knew that Abrial wouldn't leave her to the goblins—not alive. And certainly not with Qasim's heart still inside her.

Thomas was correct about the entrance to the Unseelie road being nearby. It was set at the dead end of a tight gorge in a vertical outcrop of red rock. The base was also honeycombed with disorganized but obviously recently mined entrances whose dimensions were greater than human size. Someone—or many someones—had searched diligently for the ancient entrance.

It was dark inside, but both Roman and Thomas had torches. Roman offered her one, but Nyssa declined. She was exhausted and would suck the batteries dry in an instant if she touched it.

They ran down the main tunnel, flashlights moving erratically on the uneven floor. But sometimes they were aided by the moonlight that shone through the crack in the cavern's fractured roof, and they made surprisingly good time.

They eventually entered a chamber that resembled a cathedral in its dimensions, but the space felt more like an abandoned tomb than a place where living people worshipped. There were five openings into smaller tunnels leading from the chamber. The space beyond was a shade of impenetrable blackness that suggested the dark of magic and not the mere absence of light.

"This is where the faerie road begins—and where we part company," Thomas said. "Roman and I will try to lead the other armies off. I think that path to the far right will take you to Ianna Fe's stronghold. Cyra and Lyris are there waiting for you."

"Thank you," Abrial said formally, refusing Roman's torch with a shake of his head. There was no point in giving the goblins a beacon to follow.

"Be careful," Nyssa added, wanting to say *and don't get killed, because it will be all my fault*. But she didn't.

"See you soon." Amazingly, Roman grinned at her. "Don't worry. Believe it or not, I've been in tighter spots and made it out alive. You guys will be fine."

"I hope you're right."

"I am," he assured her. "I always am. Anyway, Jack'll be coming with backup. I bet he and Cyra between them have made that dragon into something awesome. I, for one, can't wait to see him."

Thomas rolled his eyes.

Roman laughed and gave Abrial a casual salute, then dropped a kiss on Nyssa's cheek. Thomas embraced Abrial and then Nyssa, and then he and Roman were gone, each racing down a different tunnel, creating the maximum amount of believable noise.

"Your friends are weird, but I like them," she told Abrial.

"They're not my friends. But they grow on you," he admitted.

Chapter Twenty

"Where are they?" Lyris asked. "Shouldn't they be here by now?"

"Yes, they should," Cyra answered. But it's easy to get lost in the tunnels. I'm not ready to panic yet."

"I am," Lyris muttered. "But I don't suppose it will do any good."

Nyssa's lungs worked harder with every step, even though they were no longer running. She wondered at first if fear and the eerie dark of the faerie roads had finally gotten the better of her, but soon she realized that there was actually a shortage of oxygen in the tunnel. The air was being replaced with something else that didn't agree with her lungs, something that prickled like the stings of a million tiny ants. Presently, the long corridor began to glow green, and they smelled the dusty odor of an ancient goblin hive.

In spite of their noses' warning that they were in the realm of lutins, their sudden encounter with a band of roving goblins was startling. For both parties.

Reason momentarily abandoned Nyssa when they turned the corner and faced the dozen green creatures only twenty feet away, but Abrial's instincts were much better. He was able to twist about like a cat and push Nyssa down another corridor before the goblins were able to recover and properly aim their blowguns. Only a few darts sailed their way before they took another branch—and then another—leaving the chattering goblins and their green light behind.

"Were you hit?" Abrial asked, his voice hushed and urgent as he guided them through the dark.

"No—you?"

Abrial didn't answer for a moment. "Just a couple of times. Don't worry. They barely scratched me."

"Abrial!" She tried to turn to face him, but he pushed her on without slowing.

"Hey, if the darts were lethal I'd have dropped down paralyzed seconds after they hit me. I don't think they'll affect me much, except maybe to slow me down a bit. Thomas got shot by one once and he managed to run through the desert for an entire night and half a day. I'll be fine."

Nyssa's heart began to hammer, and she started to feel dizzy. She put a hand out to touch the wall she knew was beside her, wanting something solid in a world that suddenly had become too terrifying.

"There'll be more of them roaming around. And the air is foul. We have to get out of these tunnels," she whispered. "Fast."

"I know. We had to detour a bit, but there should be a way not too far ahead. The tunnels start widening like this when you get near an exit." Abrial didn't say where the exit would lead, and Nyssa almost didn't care. Anything was better than running into bands of goblins inside this stony trap.

They turned another corner and Abrial stopped abruptly.

"What is it?" Nyssa barely breathed the words. Suddenly, she was feeling very claustrophobic, and a sensation of massive but invisible weight was beginning to press down on her.

In answer, Abrial opened up a channel in her mind and let her see the cave-in with his eyes.

"Oh, Goddess."

The last turn in the tunnel ended in a colossal pile of fractured rocks. The rock slide looked natural, probably the result of the same earthquake that had broken open the cracks in the tunnel's ceiling, but the powdered stone was not in its natural state. Mixed in with the stone shards and boulders were bits of glowing green phosphorus, suggesting that the exit might have once opened into a goblin hive.

If that wasn't enough to give them pause, the slope of the pile angled off at nearly forty-five degrees and they couldn't see a summit, though it looked as though it ended before it touched the roof of the rock cavern.

Behind them, they heard the distant sound of goblin hunters. The noise was getting louder.

"Do we go back?" Nyssa asked. "There may still be time to find another way."

"No." Abrial held out a hand. "I feel fresh air—clean air. This is our way out."

"Okay." She exhaled slowly, fighting off the darkness that pressed in on her mind. She started for the slope.

Mathematicians and wise bookies would have given them long odds of making it up that incline in anything under an hour—and an hour was something they didn't have. But Nyssa and Abrial immediately started to claw their way upward, thrusting and pulling with the last of their strength, and making forward progress in spite of backsliding. Their fight was both against gravity and the loose shale that gave out under them in tiny rock falls, but the sound of their goblin pursuers armed with their curare-tipped darts proved inspirational enough to overcome nature's sharpest obstacles.

They didn't so much climb down the far side of the slope as slide and tumble, but they reached the tunnel floor with nothing broken. Once they were down, Abrial pulled back as much as he could from Nyssa's mind, trying to conserve his strength. The goblins' poison was slow to work, but it was beginning to take hold of him, and keeping his mind clear was a struggle.

"Straight ahead," Abrial said, shaking out his wings. "It isn't far now."

"Good." Nyssa couldn't tell if she was actually hearing goblins scrabbling up the landslide behind them, or if it was a panicked hallucination. Either way, the goblins would shortly figure out where they had gone and would eventually follow. If they brought in trolls, it wouldn't take them long to clear a path.

The ground was fairly flat and not especially cluttered with loose stone, so they were able to jog toward the place Abrial said was an exit.

"Here it is!" Abrial muttered something in a foreign tongue and the mountain opened.

They ran out of the dark labyrinth and into a high meadow pasture that was still clinging to its spring green, and that sparkled coldly in the moonlight. There was also a grove of pine trees and an old barn silhouetted on the western rise. The scene was almost pastoral and, after the caves, a little slice of Paradise.

Nyssa had never been inside a faerie mound, but she was pretty sure that shians didn't look like this.

"Any guess as to where we are?" she asked Abrial. "Or when?"

"I think we're in the Sierras. Probably near the California-Nevada border." Abrial rubbed at his neck where the dart had gone in. Nyssa could see that the wound had stopped bleeding, but it wasn't healing as quickly as it should on a fey.

"We overshot the stronghold then," Nyssa said softly. "Damn."

"They may not think to look for us here," Abrial suggested. "The rockfall was pretty daunting. They'll try other paths first."

"Split up and find them!" Andivak's distinctive voice growled, and the long passage's acoustics brought Nyssa and Abrial the clear vibrations of the footsteps of several large bodies. Nyssa looked back into the dark. She couldn't see anything yet, but she sure could hear them.

"They thought to look for us here. Can you shut the door and lock it?"

"No. And they brought trolls. Those're worse than bloodhounds. We have to keep moving."

"But where? Goddess." Nyssa, desperate and exhausted, said to the moon: "Now would be a good moment for you to reveal some divine plan of intervention, because I haven't got one."

"Lovely idea, but not practical," Abrial said. "Leaving their rarity behind, miracles usually take time and come in the form of nasty double-edged swords."

"We may get one anyway. We've got to catch a break soon. How else are the good guys going to win?"

"I'm sure that we'll get our miracle eventually," Abrial agreed gently, kindly—and, for the first time, untruthfully. "But while we're waiting on Divinity, let's keep moving."

Because there was no other choice, they began sprinting silently along the cushion of fallen needles that lined the woodland floor, but it was a slower sprint than before. Abrial was slowing down.

Nyssa wanted to cry. She also wanted to hurt someone for endangering Abrial. Perhaps, she thought feverishly, they could find some sort of weapon in the old barn before the trolls caught up with them. It wasn't a totally forlorn hope, she assured herself. Who knew what kind of things a farmer might keep in an abandoned building? There could be another jeep. Or maybe a cache of dynamite. Why not? Farmers used it to blow up stumps and things.

As a last resort, she could use a pack of the motel's complimentary matches to torch the barn. The desiccated timbers would likely make an impressive beacon to guide whatever passed for law enforcement and the fire department to their side.

The thought of playing firebug almost made her smile, in spite of their grim situation. It was true that she had no previous experience with arson, but she was resourceful—and determined—enough to keep from ending up as the tragic footnote of a really short love affair to make a good job of it.

"I do love your vivid imagination," Abrial said. His voice was beginning to slur. He'd resisted as long as he could, but the goblins' drug was finally affecting him both in muscles and in mind. "And I've never had any ambitions of ending up as a footnote, either." Feeling her worry, he added reassuringly: "Don't worry. Jack will get here with help soon. We just have to hold out for a few minutes longer and then we're off to that happy-ever-after you want."

"Right." Nyssa could lie too.

But Abrial's slurred pep talk added another bit of impetus. The poison was acting on him, but not as swiftly as she had first feared. She had forgotten about Jack Frost. But Jack *would* come. She told herself that she still could get away and get help for Abrial. She had to. No way was she dying without at least one torrid night with him in a water bed.

"A water bed?"

"We all have fantasies."

The wind had shifted with the waning of the moon, and fresh clouds were crowding the horizon. They looked like mildewed cauliflower and held the threat of lightning. What a pity that bad weather wouldn't deter their pursuers.

They ran to the edge of covering woods and paused for a moment. Not liking being forced into the open, Nyssa took another breath for courage and then plunged into the field, dragging Abrial behind her. The land had once been civilized but had reverted to a wild state and was littered with stunted manzanita that grabbed at their clothing as they staggered by the shrubs with increasingly heavy feet.

"Come on," she gasped, urging herself more than Abrial. The slight incline up to the barn was causing her to labor. Nyssa was grateful that she wasn't wearing a skirt and heels; she'd never have made it up the hill in her beloved Pradas.

The decrepit building grew steadily closer until they were near enough to hide in its crooked shadow. They circled it quickly, putting the weathered clapboards between themselves and the cave's opening before allowing themselves to fall to the ground and rest.

Nyssa managed three lungfuls of pungent air before noticing that there was a triad of strange tracks, right under her reddened nose. She reared back on her heels and stared at them.

"Cross your fingers, Abrial. We may just have gotten lucky." It was apparent that, though run-down, the barn hadn't been forgotten. The strange furrows led right up to the giant doors, and there was at least one set of recent footprints disturbing the dusty red earth.

"What is it?" Abrial asked. His eyes were closed and his face was deathly pale. He was losing ground faster now.

"An airplane maybe. And unless I'm mistaken, a large stash of marijuana."

Abrial's eyes opened.

"And you think this is *helpful?*"

"It rather depends. I'm just wondering about booby traps and alarms set by our illicit dope grower. And if we can use them on goblins." Of course that would mean she would have to find a way around any such traps first—hardly her field of expertise. But maybe she could maintain a mental connection to Abrial and he could tell her what to do. He would have done this sort of thing before, wouldn't he?

It took an effort, but Nyssa stopped her noisy wheezing and listened intently, trying to hear whether anyone was inside. She attempted to calculate whether she was up to facing any fresh danger that might be lurking in the barn. She decided that it probably depended on the danger. It was unlikely that the marijuana was guarded by a band of armed Honduran mercenaries. Or that the old shack was a high-tech processing center filled with crazed dope growers with orders to shoot trespassers on sight. However, an electrical wire with a lethal current was not out of the question.

Still, it didn't matter what precautions the owners had taken; she needed into that barn. They had spent several minutes and all of Abrial's energy getting to the shed and were now scraping the bottom of the barrel for alternatives to being a troll's dinner. Trapped on a mountain, separated from Thomas and Roman, miles from help unless Jack managed to find them, they needed a miracle. Or, at the very least, a place to conduct a defense until help arrived. This was it.

"I'm going in. Wait here."

"I can safely promise to do that," Abrial said, letting his eyes close again.

Nyssa hauled herself to her feet and grabbed hold of the rusted latch with both hands. Nothing happened—no shock, no ominous whoops of alarm.

Cautiously, she swung one of the warped doors open and prepared to run again if anyone began shooting.

Nothing. Just a soft fall of dust from the rafters over the door and the rustle of wings.

"Okay then." She leaned in a foot or two and looked around. Her moonlit shadow lingered behind her as she peered into the barn and was swallowed by the musty interior. It took a few seconds for her eyes to adjust to the greater gloom and to process what she was seeing. A UFO wouldn't have been half as startling.

"What's in there?" Abrial asked. He was pulling back from her mentally, trying to conserve strength and not muddle her thinking with his dulling wits, but he didn't dare let go completely in case someone made a psychic attack on her.

"A miracle," she answered. Then added to herself: "If it's still armed."

Squatting in the middle of the barn was a giant wooden stork—a Fieseler Storch—just like her courtesy uncle had flown. The ridiculous-looking high-winged plane had changed German history when it zoomed into the aeronautic scene after the first World War. It had an eight cylinder, invert-V, air-cooled engine, a fifteen-thousand foot ceiling, a stall speed of thirty-two miles per hour, and a two-hundred-forty–mile range. And one machine gun.

"Goddess, thank you! I never doubted you'd come through."

She took a step forward, feeling tentative about trusting her new luck, in spite of her words about having faith. It was her experience that good things came to those who were cautious.

Nyssa could be forgiven for thinking in terms of miraculous deliverance. The Storchs were rare—mythical almost. She hadn't seen one since the Watsonville Air Show back in '92—always assuming that was a real memory and not one her mother had implanted in her. Whichever it was, fantasy or memory, the plane was lodged in her spotty recollection of her pre-teen years. The plane's history had been Uncle Bob's lifelong love and obsession, and he had shared it with her on those rainy afternoons when she wasn't able to play outside. Truly, it seemed like an answer from Divinity that it would be sitting right here in the middle of nowhere. Nyssa didn't know how she'd get the machine gun off its mount, but she'd find a way if no other weapons offered themselves.

First though, she would look for a handgun or rifle. It seemed likely that a drug dealer would have one stashed nearby.

Nyssa took a few more steps inside the barn and forced herself to circle the plane. In spite of the suggestion of divine intervention, it was difficult to shake off the notion that she was in a mescal-induced nightmare, playing the stock part of the heroine from the horror film where it was a given that lone females were supposed to die a horrible death at the hands of a psychopath. Part of it was Abrial's changing perceptions under the influence of the drug, but part of it was genuine intuition that they had at least one more monumental task ahead of them.

"Don't be a coward." Her voice echoed in the timbers and made her flinch. "Think of Linda Hamilton. What would she do if Arnold was chasing her around the barn?"

Fortunately, nobody answered as she continued her futile search for a weapon.

There was an ancient red bicycle leaning on the east wall. It was missing both its chain and its handlebars. Since she and Abrial couldn't ride it or hide in it, she rejected it right away.

She found an old scythe happily rusting on the same wall, but Nyssa didn't put much faith in its frail wooden handle that had split into so many pieces that it looked like the wisps in a broom. And no matter what Linda Hamilton might do, Nyssa couldn't imagine herself using the browned blade as a boomerang. It was too dull to cut wheat, let alone through several fully-armored trolls.

She spun around desperately. The rest of the barn looked like an abandoned warehouse, with piles of old crates, webbed and dusty, stacked every which way along the interior walls. And there was the expected pile of marijuana, neatly bagged and ready for transport, piled on a crude table made of a sheet of plywood and two scarred sawhorses.

Nothing! Nothing!

To underline the fact that time was running out, Nyssa began to hear the sounds of shouting coming from the direction of the cave. They weren't right outside the barn itself—yet. But she had to do something, and quickly. Trolls were slow and lumbering, but they were not the Keystone Kops. And this Andivak was bound to be very angry about Carbon's death.

So, it was the machine gun after all. She'd have to find a wrench or screwdriver. Nyssa turned back to the airplane. She circled it slowly, coming up on its right side. And was bitterly disappointed. The machine gun was gone.

"Damn it! This is no time to be teasing me," she said, addressing the air and the Goddess. "We're in trouble. You can't want the goblins to get Qasim's heart! Help me out here."

Nothing and no one answered.

Maybe there was something inside the plane—a handgun or a rifle. She pulled open the small door and began to search around the pilot's seat. Then she moved to the passenger's compartment.

Still nothing. Not a tool, not a gas can, not even a heavy flight chart she could heave at someone's head.

"Damn. Damn. Damn." Nyssa hit the stork with a weak fist. Then she hit again, a little harder. The taut canvas echoed like a drum. It sounded like it was chuckling.

"Some talisman you are! What the devil am I supposed to do with an empty airplane? You don't even have your machine gun anymore."

The mechanical stork sat there with spread wings, placid and sturdy in its halo of moonlight. It looked like an awkward angel poised for flight.

Nyssa stared at the old bird, gooseflesh rising on her arms. She backed up three steps and repeated selective parts of her last two sentences.

"What am I supposed to do with an airplane?"

An unspoken answer floated down from the rafters overhead, settling on her with a feather-light touch.

Pigeon feathers. Was this Fate's perverse answer to her prayers for rescue? Not a gun, but an airplane?

"I can't," she complained, feeling an increase in her already panicked pulse. "I haven't been in one for years. If I ever really was in one. I could kill us both if I tried."

But she was thinking hard even as she protested. The Storch was the airplane that had been used to rescue Mussolini from the roof of an alpine castle. The female pilot who had conducted the daring mission had struck a parapet on takeoff and lost a wheel, but she still managed to land the plane safely. It was also used in several other rescue missions, because it was stable and easy to fly. Uncle Bob had often said that someday he would teach his dog how to land one.

There was more shouting from outside. She couldn't tell if the voices were any closer, but they had increased in volume and number. And viciousness. The trolls had finally caught up with the goblin hunters and were anxious to start pursuing their dinner.

"Abrial?" Nyssa reached for him with her mind as well as her voice.

"Here." But his tone was desperately faint. "Did you find something?"

"Oh, Goddess—please be with us . . ." She raised her own voice. "Yes. Hang on. I'll be right there."

Nyssa moved forward and dragged the chocks from under the wheels. It took another thirty seconds to race to the front of the barn and shove open the other massive door. The old hinges complained loudly at her rough treatment, but Nyssa was beyond caring about damage to property and if anyone heard her.

She turned and reached for Abrial and hauled him to his feet. He was staggering but could still carry most of his own weight.

"What the hell is that?"

"A Storch. Get in." She half rolled and half shoved him into the passenger seat.

She scrambled up into the cockpit and adjusted the pilot seat. She looked at the vaguely familiar array of instruments and prayed that she could remember her one and only formal flying lesson in Uncle Bob's plane. If only she had time to go to The Yesterdays, she could ask for help there—she could even get the Red Baron to help her!

"Don't try it," Abrial whispered. He was trying to stay alert and help her, though it obviously caused him tremendous pain. "They'll be waiting for you there too, and I can't protect you now."

"Don't worry, I'm not crazy." She laughed once. What a lie. Of course she was crazy. She was about to try to fly a World War One airplane without any training.

"Nyssa, you can do this."

"I hope so."

"I know so." He sounded sure. Sure and exhausted. They had to leave. Now.

"Okay. Battery. No, master switch first." She repeated Bob's instructions. "Fuel valve on . . . mixture—full-rich. Prime it. Slowly . . . one, two."

Nyssa looked at the floor. There were pedals. Clutch and brake?—No, rudders. And the stick was for the elevators or ailerons.

The sound of troll war cries got her attention. This time she wasn't unsure about the sound. The screams were loud in the air and close by.

She didn't bother to analyze the other bewildering dials. One was for airspeed and the other an altimeter. As she planned to be going flat-out and at as low an elevation as possible, neither would be needed for consultation.

"Mags on." She pushed the magneto switch and hit the starter.

Nothing happened.

"Who am I? The new Job?" she demanded of the silent Goddess, toggling the master switch. "You just like jerking my string, don't you? Filling me with false hope?"

Something moved through her mind, and suddenly she remembered Bob taking her to the airshow. Some of the old planes had to have their propellers turned over by hand.

"No!" she insisted. It didn't make sense that anyone would have a plane like that for smuggling. You couldn't always count on having a cohort around to start you up.

Nyssa hit the starter again.

"This has to work. Make it work, please."

The plane belched. Then it coughed. Then it began a bronchial wheezing—but it started. To Nyssa, the engine sounded dangerously asthmatic, but she didn't wait for it to stop sputtering. The bad guys would know exactly where she was now. It was time to make like a birdy and fly south before the storm.

"Now would be a good time to start praying," she told Abrial, but he didn't answer. Maybe he was already lost in Divine appeal. She didn't try to feel what he was feeling, didn't want to know how bad his pain and confusion were.

She released the brake and advanced the throttle forward. The stork waddled out of the barn, pretending that Nyssa was in control. She didn't entirely trust it but decided that it was now all in the Goddess's hands. Either they would get away, or they'd end splattered all over the mountain.

Nyssa knew that she was supposed to take off into the wind, but she hadn't a clue which way that was. And anyway, there was only one clear path that led from the barn. It was a case of using that runway or not running away at all.

It was a very short path. Nyssa knew that in the hands of an experienced pilot, the plane could get airborne in just under one hundred and sixty feet. But her path looked rather shorter and she was certainly anything but experienced with ancient airplanes.

"Beginner's luck," she reminded herself, as she pushed the throttle as far as it would go and began reciting prayers. Uncle Bob had been absolutely correct when he insisted that there were no atheist pilots when it came time to solo.

The Storch waited politely for her *Amen* and then quit lumbering. Suddenly it leaned into the moonlit sky and went leaping forward. It ran, screaming mechanically as it raced along the dirt path, weaving like a chicken trying to avoid the chopping block. Nyssa tried not to worry about its slewing about in a mild slalom while she got the feel of the rudders. She had to learn somewhere, and on the ground seemed safer than in the air.

Something slapped against her windshield. Nyssa looked up from the floor and saw that the end of the dirt road was coming up fast. A previously unnoticed split-rail fence was approaching at a sickening speed. If she'd had a horn, she'd have leaned on it with all her might. Instead, she contented herself with screeching.

"Geez! Oh, Geez!" Almost on top of the fence, Nyssa hauled the stick back into her lap, clutching it like a teddy bear. The plane gave a lurch and then entered into the spirit of things. It leaped for the sky with a choking squawk and nearly pulled a loop-the-loop before she got the groaning engine and ailerons back under minimal control.

Nyssa caught a brief glimpse of the milling trolls as she pelted the tops of the trees only inches above the highest branches. She was lucky that this wasn't old growth forest. If the trees had been any taller, she would have plowed into them.

Then she noticed something else that almost made her jaw drop. Apparently Thomas hadn't been kidding about having a dragon. The mountain had just erupted a new door, and a beast from legend stalked through it, breathing giant gouts of fire as it went.

She had never thought to see the day when facing a dragon head-on would be reassuring. But it was, because it also probably meant that other help was coming.

"Abrial! It's a dragon! Thomas found him again! And he's torching the trolls."

The dragon's head slewed around as she roared by. So did everyone else's, but only the reptile looked happy to see her. An almost human expression of delight crossed his reptilian features as she buzzed the remaining goblins.

Everyone else seemed either angry or alarmed or downright panicked.

Nyssa tried to give the dragon a reassuring smile,

but it was all bravado backed up by the adrenaline of terror, and she imagined that she must look a great deal like the screaming skull tattoo favored by death-metal fans.

Then she passed the field and was sailing downward again, this time toward a sheriff's car, which was racing up the mountain road she was following, and there was no more time to think about dragons. Once more, she pulled up on the stick and prayed.

The airplane climbed, but the stork's engine was again sounding unhappy and her airspeed was falling off. She wasn't a mechanic, but she knew that if she didn't do something, she was going to have a shorter flight than the Wright Brothers' first plane had had. Maybe she could turn back . . .

Nyssa looked over her shoulder and saw that the barn and the field around it were ablaze. There were also piles of bodies on the makeshift landing strip.

"Damn." There was no going back to try to land now. And landing in the other direction would be a very bad thing, given her current location. The road was still free of flames and trolls, but it had narrowed. It was flanked by pines on the left and a row of car-sized boulders on the right. She had a forty-six-foot wingspan and about a twenty-foot-wide road. The math was wrong even without a calculator.

If she couldn't get to an open, boulder-free area before the engine quit, she and Abrial were going to be red pancakes. The thought made her already upset stomach clench in a distressing manner.

Before despair could settle in, the Goddess answered her once again. Ahead, Nyssa could see lights from what looked like a highway.

She bit her lip, feeling increasingly queasy and light-headed. Uncle Bob said that a good pilot could put a Stork down on a fifty-foot runway, but she couldn't class herself as good, or even competent. But before dawn on an early Thursday morning—if it even was Thursday anymore—the road wouldn't be that busy. And surely anyone who was there would get out of her way when they heard her coming.

Forced into the last terrifying ditch as her alternatives dwindled to one, Nyssa exhaled slowly and pushed the left pedal. The Storch reluctantly did as she asked and banked counter-clockwise. She was headed for the highway and her best hope of a safe landing.

She didn't want to think about the odds of putting the plane down unscathed. So far luck had been on her side. There was no reason—except deep cynicism—to think that it would desert her now.

"I love you, Abrial," she whispered, feeling stupid for not mentioning this while he was still awake. She really wanted him to know this, though she knew it was better that he was unconscious. It would be terrible for him to see them die in a ball of fire if things went very wrong.

She started to hum Uncle Bob's favorite flying song, "Coming In On a Wing and a Prayer."

"Damn!" Roman shouted to be heard above the fire and the dragon's roaring. "Was that Nyssa flying that plane?"

"Yes." Thomas's stunned gaze followed the funny-looking aircraft as it barely scraped over the pine trees and banked south. "And Abrial's in the back. I think he's hurt."

"That was some tricky flying! I didn't know she was a pilot."

"Neither did I." Thomas raised his voice. "Jack, we gotta go. Leave the prisoners for the dragon to snack on. I think Nyssa's going to try to put that thing down on the highway."

"What! No way. She's probably heading for the airport. It's only about ten miles south." Jack joined them. He was a mass of shallow bleeding cuts, but his eyes were bright and alert.

Thomas listened to the sputtering engine and shook his head. "Something's wrong with the plane. And I can't believe that Abrial isn't flying it. He must be badly hurt. It could be that damned curare. Call Zayn—we may need him sooner than we thought."

"He's already on his way. He's bringing the helicopter. We have to get them away before the media arrives. There is just no explaining this."

"Looks like we have company already," Roman said. His eyes were glittering. He had been standing downwind of the barn when the marijuana caught fire and had breathed in almost as much smoke as the dragon.

A sheriff's car came barreling up the dirt road and slammed on its brakes when it reached the edge of the smoking grass. An alarmed deputy tumbled out into the charred field. Clearly he was upset at having death fly at him out of the sky.

"Damn! Some crazy-lookin' plane just tried to tear the lights off my car! It's the *damndest* thing I ever saw." Then the deputy looked over and noticed the dragon. It was standing dead center in the bright headlights and gulping down the bottom half of a barbecued troll. Apparently the cop suddenly had a new *damndest* thing to think about. "Holy shit! What the hell is that?"

"I knew this would happen." Thomas reached for the horrified officer as the man fumbled for his revolver. A quick word and a mental push had the policeman toppling to the ground—he wouldn't remember anything when he woke up.

"Let's take his car, shall we?" Roman suggested, opening the door. "I always wanted to use a siren."

"Let me send the dragon away. That creature has no discretion, and now he has the munchies." Thomas's tone was exasperated. "He's high as a kite and he'll still be eating when the news crews arrive."

"No time," Roman said, his smile fading. "That engine sounds worse."

"He's right. Hang on, Abrial my friend," Jack said quietly, trying to reach for Abrial with his mind but failing to find him. "We're coming!"

Mercifully, the highway was free of traffic. Nyssa was ten feet off the ground when she lost the engine. The Storch came down hard on its tiny tail wheel. She bounced once and the landing struts screeched with pain, but they held valiantly.

Feeling drunk and nauseous, Nyssa wanted desperately to assume the crash position but forced herself to try to keep the plane on the road. The manmade stork slowed swiftly, living up to its fifty-foot promise, and Nyssa coasted to a stop at the Hoodsville city limit sign. She was blocking both lanes of westbound traffic.

"Oh, Goddess, we made it. Thank you! Thank you! Abrial?" she called, trying to see into the compartment behind her. The streetlights overhead were bright, but Abrial's face remained in deep shadow.

Nothing, not verbally or mentally. But she could hear his labored breathing, so she knew he was still alive.

Behind her, she heard the first shrieks of a police siren. It was coming fast. It was probably that sheriff she had almost beheaded.

"Shit." It was probably a patriotic lawman—the goblins wouldn't have reason to corrupt a small-town cop—but friend or foe, it didn't matter. What would come, would come. She had nothing left to fight with except her bare hands. She would use them too, if she had to. She was strong enough to kill a single human male.

"Abrial, wake up. We made it," she said softly. Tears finally started to fall. Unable to control her turbulent stomach, Nyssa fumbled for the latch with shaking hands, opened the right side door, and threw up on the white line that marked the shoulder of the road.

Chapter Twenty-one

Her first meeting with Zayn and Jack was a bit of a blur; they were busy forcing some bluish fluid into Abrial, and then, noticing her own gray color, pouring a bit of it into her as well. It seemed that she had had some sort of allergic reaction to the bad air in the cave, and the blue fluid was a form of antihistamine that functioned as a cure-all for goblin ailments.

Abrial had revived enough by then to hold her during their terrifying ride to Cadalach, which was in some sort of combat helicopter that Zayn flew with great—and Nyssa suspected unnecessary—panache.

The blue potion had helped with her breathing, but she still felt queasy, and the weight in her chest—her father's unwanted heart—had grown crushing and seemed to be pressing on her other organs. She wondered if somewhere, some malignant being wasn't sticking pins into a voodoo doll made in her image. Or if the heart was expanding and about to burst like a rotten appendix. She supposed that it could happen if Qasim died before they got the organ out.

Since she was having trouble walking upright when they landed, Abrial carried her into Cadalach and then into a room that looked more like a church than a surgical theater, though the altar was draped with sterile white linens and lit to a state of painful brightness.

It was there that she met Io, Cyra, Lyris, and Chloe. Her gasps of pleasure at the introductions were polite but clearly lies, and they didn't try to engage her in extended conversation. Abrial waited until Zayn approached with a metal tray that had both a scalpel and some sort of stone dagger, and then he entered her mind, shutting down most of her emotions and all sensation to her body.

"Can I put her under?" he asked Zayn.

"Better not. There are ritual answers she has to make."

Abrial nodded, though Nyssa knew he didn't like the answer. She wanted to tell him not to worry, because she wasn't frightened, but that was too big a whopper to even attempt. She was nearly blind with terror.

Her filthy shirt was cut away, exposing her chest and belly. Under other circumstances, Nyssa would have objected to being undressed in front of a room full of strangers, but she sensed neither revulsion nor prurient interest on the part of these watchers.

They closed around her in a circle; man, woman, man, woman, hands linked. They started chanting in a language she didn't know.

Zayn picked up the obsidian dagger and laid it over her old scar. Nyssa closed her eyes and tried to think about how she was going to have a long life with Abrial that would—for some odd reason—involve vacations in Hawaii and perhaps a puppy.

She didn't feel much of what Zayn did, and didn't watch any of it. Abrial was again in her mind, supplying her with the foreign words she needed to finish the ritual. Though he didn't flinch or gasp, she suspected that he was feeling much of the pain for her.

She sensed Thomas touching them with unintentional empathy, and understood that he had also once carried another's heart. Though it had been painful to cut it out, he seemed to say, his life after had been immeasurably better.

Then it was done. The weight disappeared from her body.

Zayn healed the incision in her chest without sutures. He was good. There was no pain, even after Abrial retreated from her mind. All Nyssa felt was exhaustion . . . and a sort of emptiness. There was no heart, and there was no Abrial.

The others were still there, both beautiful and terrifying in their alien bodies and nearly identical expressions of concern. They gathered around the operating table, looking at her with a mix of fear and anxiety written clearly on their faces. Only Abrial remained completely expressionless, and he set the stone vessel containing Qasim's heart on the surgical cart beside her. The lip of the vessel was covered in black ichor.

"It's time," he said. "Do we keep the heart or destroy it?"

Nyssa hesitated for a moment. She knew her answer would not be popular, and she was too tired to fight if they opposed her, but she tried anyway.

"Keep it," she said at last, looking into Abrial's eyes

and willing him to understand. "We may need it to find my mother."

The others exchanged swift glances, but Abrial never looked away from her.

"I don't intend to give it to him," she told them, guessing their thoughts. "But it's my only bargaining chip, and he'll know if I destroy it."

"Destroying it would probably kill him instantly," Jack pointed out. The death fey was healing fast, but he would have scars from his battle with the goblins. Those scars were her fault.

No, Abrial answered, immediately reentering her mind. *You were the victim here, and no one blames you for this war. Don't let guilt influence you now. Make a decision you can live with.*

"We could be rid of him and track your mother on our own. Every resource we have would be turned to the task. We would find her, Nyssa. I swear that we would," Jack was saying.

She turned her head to look at the death fey. His silver eyes were beautiful but worried. "It would probably kill him instantly," she echoed. "But maybe not. And if he doesn't die immediately, I can't risk him taking revenge on my mother if he has her somewhere."

"So, we wait," Abrial said, picking up the jarred heart and carrying it over to a niche that appeared in the wall. He said a soft word and the stone sealed shut, closing the heart into an undetectable crypt.

"We wait," Nyssa agreed, closing her eyes and surrendering to healing sleep. She hoped the sea salt Cyra was spreading around her stone bed would keep the bad dreams away.

Later she would think about the implications of

what they had just done, and face all the new questions of what her life would be like now that she was free of her father's blight. Would she see ghosts anymore? Could she still visit The Yesterdays? Would she begin aging like a human? And, above all, was the child she was carrying adversely affected by its short exposure to Qasim's heart.

Child? The thought nearly startled her awake.

"Rest." Abrial kissed her eyes and then her lips. She listened to his breathing, absorbing the fact that they were really alive and, for the moment, safe.

"Yes, we're safe. We'll deal with all these matters tomorrow," Abrial said.

We. That word reassured her.

Nyssa slept.

Chapter Twenty-two

Nyssa pulled her head out of the toilet and glared at Abrial.

"This is all *your* fault."

"Still not feeling well?" he asked sympathetically.

"No—and why the hell not? I thought getting rid of that heart was going to fix me up."

"It isn't the heart that is making you sick. I'm afraid that it's a different magic at work. You'll be fine in another week or two."

"Black magic," she muttered. Being sick annoyed her. She was a firm self-disciplinarian. Her stomach should not be beyond her control.

"Sometimes the magic seems black—when it wants something from us," Abrial said, sitting down beside her on a rocky ledge. Under other circumstances, Nyssa would have admired the bathroom at Cadalach. Instead of porcelain, all the fixtures were made of luminous stone. However, even the prettiest of rock palled when you had your head stuffed in it for any period of time.

"What does the magic want from us?" she asked. "It can have my stomach. I've decided that I don't want it back after all."

He spread his hands. "It wants us to mate, to carry on the species, to keep it company so it won't be alone and weak. Your stomach is irrelevant."

Nyssa blinked, taken aback by his frank words though she should have been used to them. "The magic wants . . ." She trailed off.

"It does. It mated Jack and Io and all the others this way."

"I see. And how do you feel about that?" She held her tongue after her question, and didn't try to lead him into saying what she desperately wanted to hear. The temptation was strong though.

"I feel a bit manipulated but also rather glad."

"Glad?"

"Perhaps relieved would be a better word. I didn't think it would ever happen. Not for me."

Nyssa thought about this. A part of her wanted to jump up and do pirouettes of joy, because perhaps this meant that he loved her too. But that was her own love for Abrial talking. And she knew that strong emotion made one incautious and forgetful of hard-learned lessons—which was probably by design, because people would only fall in love once without this amnesia. Abrial being manipulated into loving her wasn't good enough.

In fact, he hadn't mentioned love at all. She sighed. Time to back things up a few steps.

"Abrial, I . . . I'm half hobgoblin. Think what that could mean." Nyssa spread her hands. "Think about what might happen to our children. We have to consider these things sensibly. We can't just obey blindly, no matter what the magic wants."

"Your *father* is a hobgoblin," he corrected. "But there is little or none of him in you. Don't hesitate for this reason. Anyway, I think we both know that it's a bit late to worry about that. Our child is a fact."

Nyssa colored. "I was hoping you didn't know about that and I was only hallucinating."

"I'm sorry, but it isn't a dream. You are pregnant."

Nyssa looked into the eyes of a being who was older than Christ and suddenly felt frail. She wasn't young, wasn't merely human, wasn't weak. Yet she felt vulnerable in a way she never had before.

She lowered her eyes again, not wanting him to see the fear there.

"Maybe so . . . though I don't see how you could know this," she answered. "But if I am, I don't want you to stay with me for that reason."

Abrial shook his head, amused at the idea she could hide this from him. Or maybe amused by her romantic thoughts that he should be there simply because he loved her.

But all he said was: "Fey morning sickness is easy to spot even if you don't have a mind-side seat like I do."

"I may not be able to talk to ghosts anymore," she warned him.

"That doesn't exactly break my heart."

"What if I can't time travel anymore either?"

He shrugged. "I don't think that will be a problem, but if it is, we'll deal with it."

"What if removing my father's heart changes everything? What if I start aging like a human? I'll be old and wrinkled in practically no time."

271

"Don't exaggerate. You have at least fifty more good years in that body."

Seeking refuge in anger, she glared at Abrial again. "You are sucking at that comfort thing again," she told him.

He smiled a little as he tucked back a strand of her hair, but then he sobered. "Listen to me: None of these things matter. The only thing that should keep you away from this relationship is if you don't love me."

He waited—expressionless, patient—for her to answer.

"Love you?" Nyssa looked him full in his dark, unhuman eyes. Stars shone there, a universe vast and deep. That had frightened her once, but not anymore. For her, there was nothing more beautiful in the universe. She fell into him, opening herself to the midnight that waited there. There were no promises there. But she surprised herself by saying simply: "Of course I love you. How could I not?"

"And I care for you," the master of understatement replied. "And believe me, this isn't a recent event. I was fascinated with you long before magic took a hand. So stop worrying." Nyssa snorted. "Well, if we're agreed about these facts, then we are all set and good to go." His posture relaxed a degree or two, but he still didn't reach for her.

"Just like that?" she asked in consternation, wondering why he didn't kiss her or at least offer her a hug. Maybe he was afraid that she'd be sick all over him. Personally, she thought he deserved it for being so unromantic. What sort of unfeeling person made a declaration of *caring* while the object of his affections had declared her love? And while she was feeling so vilely ill?

"Yes, just like that. It isn't complicated. Unless you'd like to rethink your stand on weddings. I think I'd look wonderful in a tux, and you are one of the few women who actually look good in pure white— not that I'm a stickler for tradition. You'd also look stunning in blood red."

Nyssa shook her head, half in bewilderment and half in denial. *A wedding?* The mind boggled. She couldn't get married. She didn't even know how to think about getting married. It had never been part of her plans, never an option. Monsters didn't marry.

"I'm not rethinking anything until we find my mother. Anyway, what happened to your concerns about unwanted mental intimacy? Aren't you afraid that it will just get worse the longer we're together, and you'll never have a moment's privacy again?"

"My largest concerns are gone. I know the limits of our ability to read each other. We can set boundaries. You'll learn how to manage it in time." He added: "Strange to think that it's thanks to the goblins that this intimacy is a fact. I don't suppose we should send them a thank-you note, though."

"I don't suppose," Nyssa agreed faintly.

"And we'll go find your mother. Today, if you feel up to it."

"You are very full of decision this morning." Nyssa winced when the words came out in a plaintive tone. Abrial seemed to bring this trait out in her.

"Well, the matter is a simple one, yes? You want to find your mother. I want a wedding. I don't think discovering her whereabouts will be that difficult. I suspect she's in hiding somewhere nearby, just keeping a low profile. She may not know that you are alive. Who can guess what Qasim or the goblins told her about your fate?"

"Then how do we find her?" Nyssa asked. "How do we get her to come out of hiding so we can spot her?" *Before the goblins or Qasim do.*

"She'll have to be coaxed. Fortunately, as it happens, we know someone who can help with this."

"We do?" Nyssa blinked and then shook her head slowly. "You mean your uncle Farrar. You want to send the Pied Piper after my mother?"

"It's right up his alley—and he loves you. He loves all women. They're his favorite thing to hunt."

"I bet." Nyssa's brow furrowed. "Mother would hate that—being enchanted."

"I wouldn't blame her. But it would be effective. And fast. You two would find her in the dreamlands, and I'd go and bring her home."

Home.

"I like fast," Nyssa admitted. Then another wave of nausea washed through her stomach. She said crossly: "Now go away. Apparently I'm not done with my power struggle with our child—and I don't want an audience."

"Son," Abrial said casually. "He's a boy."

Nyssa clapped her hands over her ears. "Don't tell me anything else! I don't want to know. Give me a while to get used to the idea, okay?"

Abrial smiled slightly and got to his feet.

"I'll bring you something light to eat. I can probably help you get it down if you don't mind a little mind control."

"You do, and you'll clean it up," she muttered, turning back to the stone toilet. "Things go down, but they'll come right back up again the moment my attention wanders."

"It'll be over soon," he said with cheerful heartlessness.

"You aren't going to kiss me good-bye?" she asked as he got up and headed for the door.

"No." Abrial grinned. "I can read you very well—even when I'm not in your mind."

"And?" She glared at him.

"You'd bite me. I'll wait until you feel better. Then we can have make-up sex."

Chapter Twenty-three

Nyssa soon discovered that losing Qasim's heart didn't mean a loss of her psychic abilities. She had no trouble locating Abrial's uncle or convincing Farrar to help her find her mother.

Nyssa's reunion with her mother was a tearful one, but the weeping was all joy and relief. With Farrar there as bodyguard, Nyssa was able to stay with her mother in thought until Abrial arrived at the Farallon Islands just off the California coast. He and Zayn got Bysshe loaded into the helicopter without any particular fuss and headed back for Cadalach. The whole operation took less than eight hours.

Once reunited in the flesh, there were a few more tears and then several hours of catching up. Bysshe approved of her potential son-in-law, and threw her weight behind the idea of a wedding.

Later, after they shared a meal, Bysshe talked about her time as a goblin prisoner and told the others what she had learned from a frightened King Carbon and Qasim. The news was disturbing.

She was concerned when she heard of their plan to destroy Qasim's heart now that she had been found, and she argued against it. "Lobineau is capable of raising the other hobgoblins. He's found most of them already."

"All the more reason to do away with Qasim," Jack argued back.

"But don't you see?" Bysshe asked. "Qasim is the only one who can control them if Lobineau succeeds. Assuming Lobineau's plan is actually to raise the others."

This observation was met with silence. The room didn't actually drop in temperature, but everyone felt a chill.

"But why would Lobineau do that? He's the master of New Orleans now. What else can he want?" Abrial asked.

"I don't *know* that Lobineau actually wants to raise them," Bysshe looked at him. Her eyes were a dead match for her daughter's, and though it shouldn't have mattered, Abrial found himself moved to belief by the sincerity he saw there. She answered slowly: "No one said anything definite, but I have the feeling that he isn't acting alone. Qasim particularly feels that there is someone behind him, manipulating him."

Jack nodded. "It makes sense. Lobineau has changed sides more times. . . . His career is all cross and double-cross until he's more snarled than the laces on those high-tops you're wearing."

Roman looked at his shoes, to which Jack had pointed. They were rather hurriedly tied. "I had the feeling that someone was guiding Carbon's goblins after he died as well," he agreed. "Those lutins should have given up when their hive master died."

"Yes, but who is controlling them?" Nyssa asked. "Or what?"

"Another master vampire? Could there be a second one we don't know about?" Roman asked, earning him an alarmed look from his wife.

"I guess that remains to be seen." Jack exhaled and sat back in his chair. "In the meantime, we have a wedding to plan."

"A wedding? Now just a minute," Nyssa began, not ready to let go of the subject of some masterful evil in favor of talking about something that made her even more uncomfortable.

"Don't argue, sweetie," Bysshe interrupted. "I always dreamed of the day you would marry. And I don't want my grandchildren born in sin."

"Born in sin? Give me a break." Nyssa started to say something else but then caught her mother's pained eyes. She thought of all the shame and fear Bysshe must have felt, both at the rape by a hobgoblin, and also at being an unwed mother. Times had changed in the last couple of centuries, but Bysshe had been living in another world, and her sensibilities hadn't caught up with the rest of mankind.

Nyssa looked from Bysshe to Abrial, and realized that her lover also truly wanted the formal promise represented by a wedding. Having a succubus for a mother probably hadn't given him the best example of female consistency.

But it bothered her that Abrial hadn't said anything about being in love with her. Maybe the romantics had it wrong. Maybe love wasn't something that had to come before marriage, but . . .

"I would be happy to sew your wedding dress," Chloe spoke up softly. "And Clarissa could be your flower girl. She could carry a basket of rose petals. You'd like that, wouldn't you, sweetie?"

Nyssa looked at the toddler in Chloe's arms. Clarissa was half-troll and the ugliest child she had ever run across; but Chloe didn't see that. And the baby's big black eyes were Nyssa's undoing. She couldn't smother the excitement she saw there.

"Okay." Nyssa threw up her hands. "Let's have a wedding."

"Excellent." Jack got to his feet and lifted his goblet in a toast. "To the bride and groom."

"To the bride and groom," everyone repeated.

"And I shall be honored to give the bride away," Jack added.

"Just make it a night wedding," Nyssa requested. "I don't feel so well in the mornings these days."

"Oh, dear . . . have you tried ginger ale and soda crackers?" Chloe asked, and then the other women started offering suggestions and assurances that the nausea wouldn't last long. Nyssa's mother was especially concerned, and had a long list of instructions for her daughter. No one was surprised to hear about the pregnancy.

"Hey, it isn't that bad," Nyssa finally protested, feeling embarrassed at all the sudden coddling. In desperation, she added: "Really, we need to be thinking about wedding plans. If I'm going to have a wedding dress, I want to fit into it before I look like a blimp."

Abrial's hand settled in the small of her back. A

gentle heat spread through her as he rubbed the bare skin beneath her sweater.

Thank you, Nyssa. You've made everyone very happy.

She smiled up at him, shaking her head ruefully.

I'm insane. And you still owe me a new pair of shoes.

They'll be my wedding gift, Abrial promised.

That night, when they were finally alone, Abrial and Nyssa were allowed the long-delayed kiss their betrothal deserved.

The kiss, which left Nyssa drugged with pleasure and also longing, led to other things. Abrial's understanding of her body, and encouragement of her own explorations of his very male anatomy, intensified the force of the passion that seemed to be always lurking right beneath the surface of both their thoughts and skins.

It was only hours later, after their ardor had spent itself, that they found time to talk. Abrial settled his wings over her, using them as a blanket, and then they spoke of the day's revelations.

"I know what you're thinking, but a honeymoon in Hawaii would be wiser," Abrial said when she began working her way up to suggesting that they visit New Orleans. He then dropped a kiss on her forehead. His hand slid up the curve of her waist and paused near her breast.

"Don't try to distract me. It won't work." Abrial's hand moved to her stomach and then slipped lower. Her abdominals contracted involuntarily. "Okay . . . but it won't work for long."

"It seemed to work long enough last time."

"You've turned into a greedy monster," she scolded.

"Very greedy," he agreed, and then kissed the mouth he found so delectable.

Nyssa tried again later. This time, she had slightly more success in drawing Abrial into conversation. But though he was willing to talk, he was adamant that she not risk herself and their child in a search for Lobineau's puppet-master.

"Roman and Lyris know the area well. Zayn is good at this sort of work too, and he can leave now that your mother is here to take over his duties as healer." Abrial looked down at her, his hair tickling her breasts. "They don't have to worry about Qasim trying to kidnap them. You can't have forgotten about him, have you? Believe me, he hasn't forgotten about you. It isn't just the heart he needs back, but also your forgiveness. He won't rest until he has both."

"But—"

Abrial laid a hand on her belly. "Wouldn't you give it to him, if he threatened the life of our child?"

Nyssa sighed. "But I feel so useless."

"Don't. You have become a very good spy. Now that we are at Cadalach and know what sorts of defenses to construct, we should be able to turn you loose on the metaphysical plane to do what you will. Knowledge is key in this situation. It's what will keep our operatives alive. This war with the goblins has only just begun."

"Are you going to go with Roman and Lyris?" she asked, her voice and eyes unhappy.

"If I have to." His expression and tone were also sober. "But, like you, my gifts lie in other realities. I shall be a soldier in this coming fight, but it may not be in the physical world that I'll serve."

Nyssa nodded, and then she rolled onto her side, burying her face in Abrial's chest. "You're right. Forget about New Orleans. Let's go to Hawaii. I want a long honeymoon."

"All right. But first you need to sleep and get your strength back." Nyssa's sudden yawn underscored his point.

"Okay, but you aren't to sneak off and talk war without me."

"Don't worry. You'd know if I did. It's one of the side effects of our intimacy."

"Just don't forget it."

"I couldn't, even if I wanted to."

Chapter Twenty-four

The wedding was held in the garden of Cadalach. Nyssa could not have envisioned a more wonderful place. The garden's amazing plants were obviously alive, yet somehow none belonged to any reality she had ever been in—at least not while awake. Reality was about the human "*now*": that fleeting moment of brief mortal time. These gardens were timeless, seasonless; they belonged to the world of the fey Yesterdays, though they were situated in a cavern in the Nevada desert.

Nyssa walked through the garden, her bodily senses dazed. For the eyes and nose there were a series of cascading terraces, each covered in a waterfall of brilliant blossoms, flowers of inhumanly beautiful shades and more beautiful fragrances. It was all somehow familiar, yet not one flower was something she could identify. It seemed as though she were dreamwalking someplace beyond the human world.

The garden didn't only offer joy in what could be seen and smelled. It held pleasures for the ears as well: a soft sound of a phantom birdsong, a faint humming that rose up from the azure-tinged water of the gentle stream that meandered through the cave. There was also a tender breeze that moved, sometimes dusting the guests with a flurry of faded petals.

Jack gave the bride away. Roman officiated—an idea that gave Nyssa pause when she first heard it, but turned out to work well—and Thomas stood up with Abrial as best man. Io was Nyssa's maid of honor.

Clarissa did indeed play flower girl, and looked fairly adorable in her ridiculous pink dress. Jack and Io's son, Mathias, served as ring bearer, though he was less delighted than Clarissa at being drafted into the proceedings. The other children were too young to do much more than crawl, so they merely looked on with Lyris, Zayn, and Cyra, probably feeling relieved that they weren't wearing silly pink dresses or tiny tuxes.

Are you prepared to meet your fate? Abrial asked, eyes reaching for her from across the room, recalling Nyssa to the ceremony.

She nodded, looking up at her husband-to-be and smiling at his serious face.

And you?

Definitely.

"You look beautiful," Abrial whispered, as Jack passed Nyssa's hand from his own into Abrial's keeping.

Clarissa hurled a handful of rose petals at them, getting most on Mathias. She was obviously and thoroughly enjoying her job. Mathias looked like he wanted to chuck the small pillow bearing the rings back at the child, but a stern look from his parents kept him from succumbing to the impulse.

"I don't know about the dress," Nyssa whispered to Abrial. She smoothed a hand down the peach and strawberry chiffon confection, sewn over as it was with icy crystals that captured and broke the sunlight into rainbow segments that shimmered around her, adding more colors to the already magnificent garden. "The shoes are awesome, though. I just hope no one notices they're red."

Abrial shook his head. "The shoes make the outfit," he assured her. Then they both turned to face Roman.

The pooka had gone all out for the occasion, decking his magnificent body in some royal velvet robes that Thomas had collected while under the influence of the dragon that had inhabited his body. No human king had ever looked more grand.

Thinking of the dragon, Nyssa looked about quickly, making sure the creature hadn't made a late surprise appearance. She was grateful for the creature's help with the goblins but wasn't especially interested in having him attend her wedding. It was unnerving enough to know that Farrar was watching the event.

The Piper was watching through Bysshe's eyes. Nyssa's mother had volunteered to play psychic hostess to Abrial's uncle, and through the concentrated power of the gathering at Cadalach, they were able to make this happen. But one vaguely threatening or unsettling presence was enough for Nyssa.

The power in the room was actually much greater than she had expected. And it seemed to be growing at a phenomenal rate. The room was shimmering with it.

Nyssa blinked twice and then turned to scan the garden chamber, half expecting to see that more guests had arrived and were lending their thoughts to the effort. But there was nothing, not even shadow.

What is it? Abrial asked, looking over at her.

I don't . . . A familiar sickness crept over her. She said urgently: *It feels like Qasim. But different. Stronger.*

Different how?

The air around her began to quiver violently.

Could he still find me even without the heart? she began to ask, only to feel herself sucked away, torn loose from Abrial's mind and ripped from her own body.

A black vortex filled with some sort of an evil ghostly presence rushed her toward The Yesterdays. She and the malignant ghost slammed through the dead glades and traveled deep into the black forest.

And suddenly she was there, in that dark place of shadows where her darkest nightmares had been born, facing the author of her terrible dreams.

A woman, beautiful and yet appalling, was standing at the edge of the dead wood. She wore a dress woven out of cobwebs and starless nights, which didn't quite conceal her body.

"So, you got it out," the deep, dry voice whispered, issuing from the black lips that split her perfect, pale face. "But even now it isn't too late. You still *have* the heart."

"Yes." Nyssa was compelled to answer, the words forced out of her by this dark creature. She had to swallow hard not to vomit.

"Then I can still make use of it."

"Only if she brings it to you," Qasim said, stepping out of the shadows beside the dark woman. "And, my dear Mabigon, I really don't think that is likely."

The dead queen flinched.

"Qasim, you are here? But how?" she demanded of the hobgoblin. "This place is closed to the living."

"I'm much stronger now. I can do many, many unexpected things. Thanks to my clever child, I am able to travel to exotic places and see amazing sights that I never could see before," the hobgoblin answered pleasantly, turning eyes from his former lover to his daughter.

Recalling how he had spoken to the goblins right before killing them, Nyssa began to shiver.

Abrial! she called, trying to find a way out of the oppressive darkness. *Find me!*

There came no answer.

"Then make her give you the heart!" Mabigon said.

"But I can't," Qasim answered. "Recall the terms of my sentence. The heart must be given freely—and you won't do that, will you, child?" he asked, addressing Nyssa directly. "Not now that you have your mother."

Still under compulsion, Nyssa answered: "No, I won't."

"But *I* can compel her," the dark queen said, taking a step in Nyssa's direction. "I can rip the secret of your heart's location right out of her mind. I can even rip out her soul."

"But you won't," Abrial said, suddenly joining them. His fangs and claws were out, and he radiated menace.

Nothing on earth or in The Yesterdays had ever looked so good to Nyssa.

The dark queen hesitated for a moment, but then she smiled coldly.

"My Executioner, you're here too—and you've changed. Gotten bigger. But have you forgotten your oath?" she asked. "It was a little more binding than the usual 'til death do us part. You can't harm me. Not ever."

"True," Abrial said, taking Nyssa's hand. He filled her mind with heat and love, and while he did not attack Mabigon, he gave Nyssa the ability to drive the dark queen out herself.

Behind him, around him, Nyssa could feel the collective will of all their friends at Cadalach lending their strength to Abrial who fought to free her from the dead queen's grasp.

"Then you had best step aside," Mabigon said.

"I can't harm you," Abrial repeated. Then he added, "But *he* can."

"He?" Mabigon asked blankly.

Abrial looked at Qasim. They nodded to each other politely.

Mabigon laughed once at this suggestion, but there was suddenly more fear than derision in her voice.

"Very true," Qasim agreed. He asked of the air, "But shall I interfere?"

"I think you will," Abrial answered. "After all, if she takes the heart, she owns it. Do you really want Mabigon to have that kind of power over you again? I don't think age or death have improved her any."

"My love! Don't listen." The queen's dry voice tried to be beseeching. "He just wants to keep the heart for himself. You know the fey will use you if they can."

"Perhaps. But he has a very telling point," Qasim

admitted. He was still pleasant, still half-smiling. "I really don't think that I can trust you, my love."

"But how will you get your heart if not through me? You must have it!" she protested. "You'll fade without a heart. Even now you are weakening."

"True. Very true. But it needn't be my own, you know." Qasim's gaze turned back to his former lover and pinned her. "Any strong, magical heart will do—for a while."

Nyssa couldn't see his expression, but Mabigon blanched at whatever appeared in of her father's eyes.

Time for us to go, Abrial said in her mind. Then, aloud: "I think we'll be going. We have a wedding to attend, and we don't want to be rude to our guests."

Nyssa said nothing, concentrating all her will on finding the path of escape.

"Bon chance," Qasim answered, not looking away from the dark queen, whose lips had curled back in snarl. He added: "Only until we meet again, of course."

"Of course."

And then Nyssa found the thread of light that led back through the plane of dreams to Cadalach, and she and Abrial were flying, heading again toward the luminosity and the peaceful magic of that place.

She could finally sense her body again, and realized they had made it to safety. Abrial had picked her up in his arms, sheltering her as best he could.

"Glad you could rejoin us," Jack said. His voice was calm but strained. His face matched his tone.

"Me, too. Do you mind getting on with this ceremony? Anything that can strengthen our bond would be useful," Abrial said, returning Nyssa to her feet.

He kept an arm around her waist. "I don't think anyone else will try to join us, but just in case . . ." He had resumed his normal form and, other than appearing a bit waxen, he looked unruffled. Nyssa wasn't sure that she could say the same. She felt cold and drained.

A white-faced Roman cleared his throat and began the wedding ceremony. His clothing may have been whimsical, but his words were not. The ritual power he evoked crept around the bridal couple, surrounding them with strength and light.

"Most blessed of my brothers and sisters of the rainbow wherein the ancient magick dwells, draw near and witness the miracle. Life is again returned to our people, and through this love reconciliation with nature may begin." Roman's voice was beautiful and clear, and his words touched something tender inside Nyssa. For the first time, she began to believe that this formal wedding actually served a valid purpose.

Abrial squeezed her hand.

Roman continued, "May grace pour over the union and amply warm our brother and sister as they journey into a new life, and may the joy and hope that they have given to us be returned to their bosoms seven-fold." From the others, there came a soft murmuring hum in answer. Nyssa didn't know the words, and wished that she understood them.

I'll teach you, Abrial promised.

"We gather here to acknowledge this act of divine kindness, and to give our own humble blessings to this miracle—this revival of our flesh and blood, this renewal of hope that such unions bring. Through the

Goddess's grace, our people shall live still. The Goddess be with you always."

"And also with you."

"Let us have the rings." Mathias reluctantly surrendered his pillow.

"I am a forger of metals," Roman intoned, looking at Abrial and then Nyssa. "With my own hands, I made these rings. As I marry metal to metal, so do I forge the bands of marriage between this man and this woman who have plighted their troth before witnesses. . . . Abrial, give your bride her ring and your promise of eternal love."

Abrial accepted the simple gold band from Roman and slid it over Nyssa's finger. Legend had it that the ring finger had a vein in it that ran right from the hand to the heart. She believed that now. As the ring surrounded her finger, she could feel her love for Abrial strengthening in her heart.

"Nyssa, take now this ring and give it to your husband, along with your promise of eternal love."

Abrial's eyes closed for a moment as the ring was slipped into place. Nyssa wanted to lean over and kiss him, and to tell him of her feelings. But she realized it wasn't necessary for them to touch. He felt it all.

Roman waited until Abrial's eyes opened and then said: "And so it is done. All health and blessings upon you. May the seeds of this act of divine charity find fertile ground and bring prosperity to you in abundance. This, we wish for you both." Roman broke into a smile. "Go now and receive the blessings of your friends and family, and may the strength of your union shine forth as a beacon for all our people."

Abrial leaned over and brushed his lips against Nyssa's, drawing a cheer from the small assembly. A shower of vibrant petals from overheard filled the air with color and perfume, and the luminous blue waters of the tiny stream began to dance.

"It's done," Abrial said, joy in his voice. "You are mine for always."

Nyssa looked into his black eyes, filled with heaven's bright lights and also great love.

"For always," she promised.

They turned slowly and walked happily into the arms of their family and friends. The people of Cadalach did not share blood or even history, but they shared will, and a bond of experience that would not be broken—not even by death. There was danger ahead, but there would be life too, and in that moment, Nyssa and Abrial were certain that the light would triumph over the dark.

LIKE DARK
FAIRY TALES?

Then turn the page for
a special sneak preview
of LISA CACH'S

Come
to Me

Available September 2004!

Prologue

1423, Maramures, Northern Transylvania

Naked and full of mischief, Samira crept onto the bed of the ruling prince of Maramures. She paid no heed to the wench who slept beside him, and crawled over the snoring girl as if she did not exist.

The prince, Dragosh, mumbled and twitched in his sleep, as if trying to dislodge a bug from his face. Samira tilted her head, her long blood-red hair slithering over her bare shoulders, her black leathery wings fluttering once to keep her balanced as she peered into the face of her victim.

This was one of the many moments she enjoyed as a dream demon: perching on the bedcovers, gazing at a sleeping man's face, and savoring the power she held over him. He had no idea what was about to happen, the poor fool.

Prince Dragosh had a thick scar across his cheek, and deep creases etched into his square forehead: creases from a lifetime of strife, she guessed. Or maybe he was prone to indigestion. Stomach troubles, she had found, had a peculiarly strong effect on the tempers of humans. Sometimes she thought they cared more about eating than they did about having sex.

Silly creatures.

The prince's lips were thin, his skin weatherroughened, his nose a much-broken fist in the center of his broad face. Being a ruling prince probably meant he didn't have any trouble luring beautiful women into his bed, though.

Samira glanced at the young woman who was sleeping next to Dragosh, and on whose stomach Samira daintily knelt. Drool dribbled from the corner of the wench's parted lips, and a thin film of slime coated her exposed teeth. Samira shuddered, and moved her wing away from the girl's gaping maw. If this was the best that Maramures had to offer in the way of nubile young beauties, Dragosh had Samira's sympathy.

She turned her attention back to the nymphdeprived prince. A fanning of lines spread from the corner of each of his eyes, speaking of hours spent squinting into the sunlight, surveying the field of battle and happily counting the bodies of the slain. Or perhaps the lines spoke of kindness and humor. One never knew.

Dragosh was a strong ruler, she guessed. Fair. Hard. Which meant a lot of people probably hated him. Such was the perversity of humanity.

Samira looked back over her shoulder at her friend Theron, standing by the door to the prince's chamber. He was an incubus, a male dream demon who existed only to give dreams of sex to mortal women. Samira was a succubus, and gave such dreams to men. They were both demons of the Night World, winged beings who gave sexual fantasies—and sexual nightmares—to dreaming mortals.

The fantasies were fun, and the nightmares even more so. Samira's nightmares were a punishment to men who had behaved badly: men who ogled women's breasts while talking to them; who made rude remarks about the size and lumpiness of their wife's buttocks; who thought foreplay was for sissies; who passed gas in bed. The list of tiresome male failings was endless, and Samira's inventiveness legendary amongst the succubi. She was a virtuoso of female vengeance.

Dragosh, however, had done nothing wrong recently that called for a sharp slap on his nose, unless Samira counted finishing first when he'd made love to the wench, and then falling asleep on top of her. A crime, yes, but so common among men as to go without remark. No, Theron had asked her to deliver this nightmare to Dragosh as a favor to him, to fulfill his end of an outrageous bargain he had made with a human named Vlad.

Some would say that it had been a bargain made with the devil. And Theron wasn't the devil. Delivering this nightmare meant breaking half a dozen rules of the Night World, but the stakes of the bargain were high enough that Samira was willing to help Theron.

It was just another nightmare, after all. How much harm could it do? Dragosh had probably done *something* to deserve it. No man was innocent. She ought to punish them all just as a matter of course.

Theron nodded for her to proceed. Samira climbed

atop Dragosh's barrel chest, squatting weightless upon his rising and falling ribcage. Anticipation tingled through her, as it always did at the beginning of a dream delivery. The prince's latent sexual energy was feeding her powers and rousing an echo of his own hungers within her ethereal body. She had no physical desires of her own, and only felt lust when she reflected it back from a man.

She reached out and touched Dragosh's brow.

A jumble of images and emotions washed through her. Faces of men: worry; anger; distrust. The face of a young girl, tawny-haired: love; protectiveness. The vicious chaos of battle, Turkish armies in their foreign garb, with blood-stained spears and swords: fury; fear; bloodlust; determination. Peasant farmers in their tunics, bent in the fields: approval; paternal concern. The greatest enemy of Dragosh's family, the black-haired Bogdan of Moldavia: distrust; grudging respect; anxiety.

These were the echoes of the prince's thoughts, the impressions of his days, the bits and pieces of his history.

Again, and even more strongly, Samira sensed the tawny-haired girl. She knew already, from Theron, that she was Dragosh's youngest sister, Lucia, a miracle child born when their mother had been the astonishing age of forty-five. Samira sensed Lucia's purity in Dragosh's mind. Innocence. A deep love and pride in Dragosh, that this fragile angel amongst mortals should be his responsibility to protect and cherish, and to keep untouched by the foul, lewd hand of man.

Samira continued to invade Dragosh's mind like smoke through a house, discovering the paths of his emotions and the images that touched them off. From those inner emotions and images she began to weave the requested nightmare: Dragosh's beloved sister, the innocent, tawny-haired Lucia, was standing on a table in the great hall of the despised Prince Bogdan of Moldavia. She wore only a thin sleeping shift.

Dragosh gurgled in surprise and distress.

Bogdan's five sons sat around the table. Samira didn't know what they looked like, so she made the barbarian princes black-haired and dark-eyed like their father, and dressed them in the colors of Moldavia with the silhouette of a wolf on the shoulder. The wolf, the symbol of the ancient Dacian race from which they claimed descent, and which had inhabited Moldavian lands for millennia, present long before the Romans had come to stake their claim fifteen hundred years ago; and present after those Romans, their empire crumbling, had retreated to their homeland.

The young princes drank and thumped their goblets on the wooden table around Lucia, their lustful gazes centered on Dragosh's innocent, untouched, pure-minded sister.

Samira made Lucia quiver at being the center of such crude male appraisal. She shivered in the cold, her nipples hardening, the points visible through the thin linen of her garment. She tried to cover herself with her arms, but the movement caused her shift to fall off her shoulder. Her hair draped against her cheek as she bent her head forward, leaving the back of her neck exposed.

There was something vulnerable and deeply sexual about her pose on the table. Dragosh sensed it, and flinched away. He tried not to look directly at Lucia, her blatant sexuality touching on a deep taboo within him. She was his *sister*. His little sister. As far as he was concerned, she was a blank doll beneath her clothes. She did not have the body parts of a normal woman, and certainly none of the desires.

Samira watched Dragosh's reaction with amusement. He was bothered that it was his Moldavian enemies who surrounded Lucia, but even more disturbed by seeing his innocent sister in a sexual situation.

It was supposed to be the Moldavians who were the focus of the nightmare, but Samira was suddenly inspired by Dragosh's reaction to watching his sister. She decided to throw in a little extra torture for him, via Lucia herself. This could be fun.

One of the Moldavian princes grabbed hold of Lucia's hem, pulling on it from behind so that her breasts and the curve of her belly stood out clearly, as well as the smooth muscle of her thigh, and the shadowed valley in between. Samira made the dream-Lucia toss her tawny lioness's hair back, a salacious glint in her eye, a hungry grin forming on her soft lips. She thrust out her chest, giving the Moldavian men a better view of her breasts.

A soft cry of distress escaped from deep within Dragosh's throat. He tried to lunge for the table and snatch his sister away, but he was held helplessly in place by Samira. "Lucia! What are you doing?" he cried.

His sister winked at him, and then cast a come hither look to one of the more handsome of Bogdan's sons. She slowly licked her lips.

Dragosh gasped, his body going tense. "No, no, no,

no!" he scolded, and loudly clapped his hands together, as if startling a cat away from a bowl of cream.

Lucia gave as much heed as would a hungry feline.

The Moldavian prince pulled again on Lucia's hem, harder, and she dropped to her knees, grinning. The other Moldavian in front of her offered up his goblet, his eyes lightening to the golden tone of a wolf's. She refused the goblet, laughing, shaking her head, but he grabbed her by the hair and tilted her head back, pressing the goblet to her lips.

"Drink it, little cat!" the Moldavian ordered.

"Drink! Drink! Drink!" his brothers growled, their sharp teeth shining, the thud of their own goblets on the table a drumbeat that matched the beating of Dragosh's frantic heart.

"They're filthy beasts, Lucia!" Dragosh shouted, and fumbled at his side for the sword that wasn't there. "Don't let them touch you!"

Lucia pulled her mouth away from the edge of the goblet. She was smiling wickedly, her eyes shining. "They rut like beasts, too! They're animals, and hung like—"

Dragosh gave an unmanly shriek. "You stop that! You're a good girl! You don't know anything about men!"

"Hung like *bulls*."

"Lucia!" He gulped for air.

"And they have tongues like *dogs*."

"Tongues?" Dragosh asked, startled, momentarily confused. "What of their tongues?" His eyes were wild and fearful as he awaited her reply.

"They lick me, lick me, lick—"

Dragosh moaned in horror, squirmed and twisted, then shook himself all over. "Wicked child!"

"I'm wicked, and I *like* it. Just like I like their huge—"

Dragosh yelped, and tried to lunge again for his lecherous sister, trying to snatch her off the table as if doing so could somehow turn her back into a good girl. Samira held him helpless, leaving him only the power of his voice. "Lucia! You don't like being touched! You're a virgin!"

"Where am I virgin? They've been *everywhere!*" she shouted in glee. Then she laughed, throwing back her head. The Moldavian prince poured the drink in, and as she swallowed in great gulps, one of the princes behind her pressed his palm to her buttocks, then slid his long fingers into the dark, damp place between her thighs, her thin shift the only barrier between his hand and her flesh. Lucia arched her back in pleasure.

Dragosh slapped his hands up over his eyes, unable to watch. This was his sister—his sister!—engaging in sexual acts. Samira forced his hands down, and he yowled in protest, squeezing his eyes shut, shaking his head in denial.

The Moldavian prince holding Lucia's hair tossed the goblet aside and lowered his head to her breast, his wet mouth sucking hard at her nipple through the cloth, making animal noises of greed. Lucia moaned and rolled her head, her thighs parting in invitation.

Lucia's head turned to the side and she opened her eyes, meeting the gaze of her mortified brother. "You gave me to them, and now I'm their whore," she said. "Thank you, Brother, for I have sinned!"

"Noooooo!" Dragosh cried in his sleep, thrashing

at the bedclothes, the sound of his cry echoing in the dark, cold room where he slept. The wench beside him snorted and half-woke.

"They're *wolves*," Lucia said to her brother, her eyes glowing, the pupils turning into vertical slashes, like those of a cat. "Dacian wolves. We're cats and dogs, and oh! how we snarl and fight!"

In the Waking World, Dragosh cried out again. His body tried to rise, but he was paralyzed by the bonds of sleep, and by Samira holding him in dream thrall. The wench beside him stirred and opened her eyes, blinking half-asleep at the dark room, then with eyes still full of dreams she made out the winged shape of Samira perched atop Dragosh. The wench shrieked as if the gates of Hell had opened before her.

The wench's shriek let Dragosh break the bonds of sleep. His eyes flew open and he screamed, sitting up in bed, the covers falling off his shaking body. The dream shattered, the images falling away into the night, their shards leaving deep gouges on Dragosh's soul.

Samira fluttered off Dragosh, hovering in the air. For a moment he looked directly at her, the fog of dreams that still lingered in his mind letting him sense her presence, or perhaps even see a beat of black wing or a brief glow of blue eyes. The wench in his bed was babbling in terror, but Dragosh ignored her.

Dragosh stumbled to his feet, his pale body ghostly in the moonlight, his bare feet as bony and white as a skeleton's against the stone floor. He ran to the door, his long gray hair wild about his head. He passed within inches of Theron, who watched in surprise as the haunted man went by.

Dragosh pulled the door open, startling the men on guard outside. He ignored their queries, running naked down the shadowed corridor, his flabby buttocks quivering with each slap of his feet upon the floor. His men followed in confused pursuit.

Theron and Samira followed. "What did you *do* to him?" Theron asked.

Samira shrugged, amazed herself at the dramatic effect of the nightmare.

Dragosh came to another guarded door, that he pushed open without ceremony, stopping in the threshold. His breathing was labored and rough, catching on sobs, and he stood and stared with the eyes of a madman into the darkness within.

Samira looked in the doorway over his shoulder, and with her perfect night vision made out the slumbering form of a young woman; a girl, really, no more perhaps than fourteen human years. The brown-and-honey tangle of hair on the pillow told her that this was Lucia.

After a long moment Dragosh's breathing quieted, as he gradually realized it had all been a dream, and his sister remained as yet untouched by the bestial hands of his enemies.

In Dragosh's heart, though, Samira knew that his sister was no longer innocent. He now believed the wickedness of Eve to be a seed within her, awaiting the chance to sprout and grow.

Although the dream had been nothing more than a made-up story, it had touched him deeply enough that he would take it as a warning from the heavens. There would be no convincing Dragosh that Lucia would remain chaste, if given the least chance to do

306

otherwise. He was certain that a nymphomaniac lurked inside her, awaiting the chance to break free and rut with beasts and Moldavians.

The aging prince turned away from the doorway, and with glazed, sightless eyes walked slowly back down the corridor toward his own room. His movements were stiff, as if he were made of wood, and the dry skin of his soles rasped against the stone floor as he shuffled along. He moved as if something within him had broken on this night.

A whisper of human regret pierced Samira where her heart should have been. Dragosh's love for his sister, restrained and conditional as it had been, had yet formed the purest part of his soul. It had been as if Lucia were the chalice that held what remained of his own innocence, and his own belief in what was good and right.

Every time he looked at Lucia now, he would see the wolf-like sons of Bogdan lapping at her breasts, and her ecstatic acceptance of their touch. Innocent though Lucia yet remained in reality, in her brother's eyes she was tainted.

Samira wondered what frightful changes might happen in Dragosh himself, now that she had destroyed the one pure place in his heart.

She was surprised by her own concern, her own sudden sense of guilt. It wasn't her way to feel such things. Then again, neither was it her way to break the rules of the Night World.

"Go," Theron said, interrupting Samira's thoughts.

She looked up at him, a question burning inside her. Was Theron's bargain worth the cost they had just made Dragosh pay?

Theron touched her hair, his long, strong fingers combing through a silken red lock, and then he let his hand rest heavily on her bare shoulder. He had never touched her before. She felt his sexual power coursing through his hand, setting off involuntary responses in her own body that were echoes of the responses he had roused in thousands of sleeping women through the centuries. "You did as I asked, and I thank you. Now go." His hand tightened. "This shall not be spoken of beyond you and me. Promise me that."

She shivered, aware of what Nyx, the Queen of the Night, might do were she to discover this deed they had done, and all the rules they had broken. When Samira nodded her agreement to be silent, he released her. Her shoulder stung where he had touched her, seared by the unexpected power in his hand, even as her sex throbbed in the shadow of stolen mortal desire.

She was eager to be away from both Theron and the scene of this misdeed, as if by escaping both she could forget it had ever happened; forget that she had spoiled the protective love of a brother for his innocent sister; forget that she had driven him half-mad, and seared images into his memory that he would never be able to forget. She began to slip away into the plane of the Night World, but before she was gone she glanced back, once.

Theron stood on the threshold of Lucia's doorway, his glowing eyes gazing intently upon the sleeping, innocent princess of Northern Transylvania.

Chapter One

Six years later

Samira flew above the earth, its landscape a shifting vision in black and grays, formed by the minds of dreaming mortal men. Villages, forests, and mountains rippled and changed like a world glimpsed beneath the waves of the sea, occasionally glowing with a pale wash of color as someone dreamt a particularly vivid scene about that spot. Beneath her, a pack of wolves loped across an open hillside toward a flock of sheep, then disappeared into nothingness as a dreamer banished them. A farmhouse changed shape and grew extra rooms; a river turned shallow and changed course. The tableaus faded as quickly as they appeared, sometimes lasting no longer than a moment.

Samira paid them scant heed, her senses searching out something else. It wasn't long before she found it: the trail of a man with unfulfilled desires. Finding such a trail was like stepping into a flowing creek of lust, or hearing a distant sound of entrancing, erotic music; it was a thrum, a vibration in the night that belonged to a single sleeping man, and that she as a succubus could not help but follow back to its source. Her body hummed in response, a faint tingling pleasure vibrating through her, luring her toward this drowsing male who needed release in the form of a sex dream. This was the main work of a succubus: giving sexual release to sleeping men through their dreams.

She had no existence apart from her work. No solid body on the plane of mortals, and no lover in the Night World. No home or close family, no talents or skills beyond weaving dreams. Up until six years ago, it had suited her perfectly.

Lately, though, a bleak and depressive mood would sometimes steal over her. She would wonder—absurdly!—whether she was nothing more than a shadow of the mortals she visited; a poor imitation, making up stories for their entertainment, and pretending to herself that those stories were real. As if, somehow, telling stories could be the equivalent of living a true and mortal life.

As if a mortal life were something worth living! She was not like Theron, who wanted such a thing. Humans lived but a flashing moment, the space between birth and death no more than the duration of a sigh, and that sigh filled with mud, cold, fleas, disease, and great puddles of bodily fluids that Samira shuddered even to think about. Humans were cruel and greedy and violent, and not half so beautiful as the creatures of Night. What did a mortal life hold,

310

that could compare to existence in the Night World? It was foolish of her to feel even a moment of envy for mortal creatures. And she didn't. Not for a moment!

She pushed such wonderings aside, and set herself in the invisible current of male lust, pursuing it through the shadows of the Night World toward its source.

Who would it be this time? she wondered, trying to distract herself from her own pointless thoughts. An adolescent boy, with far more sexual energy than opportunity to release it? Maybe a long-married man with a brood of children and an exhausted wife. Or perhaps it was a shepherd alone in the hills, far from his maiden fair.

Making up stories about sleeping men was about the only thing that still kept her interested in her work. Ever since that night she'd given the nightmare to Dragosh, nothing had been the same for her. She was no longer a virtuoso of vengeance. She'd lost her taste for the delivery of nightmares.

She pushed this thought aside as well, trying as she always did to ignore it. What could she do about the past, anyway? Nothing. And what could she do about who she was now? She was a succubus. She could be nothing else. There was no escape from the Night World, for either her or for Theron.

Better to chase intriguing rivers of male lust through the night, than to wish for the impossible. She didn't even know exactly what impossible thing it was that she wished for, other than that it be different from what she was now.

Change. A different life. A different world. A different *her*.

You're just bored, she told herself. *You'll snap out of it in a couple hundred years.*

A sense of something strange, something amiss, interrupted her thoughts, making her slow in her absentminded pursuit of the sexual thrum. She hovered where she was for a long moment, the forest of dream trees beneath her shifting from full leaf, to winter bare, to autumn yellows and oranges as dreamers dreamt scenes within it. The sky above filled with dark gray clouds, as thick as wool, and then parted again to let through streamers of moonlight and a twinkle of distant stars.

A frown between her garnet brows, Samira tried to figure out what was wrong, what had caught her attention. There was a flavor to the sexual thrum she pursued, almost a scent, that was out of the ordinary. Unique.

She bit her lip. "Unique" could mean "dangerous."

But "unique" also meant it was different, and therefore it piqued her curiosity.

After three millennia of exploring the sexual minds of men, she had seen it all. She hadn't come across anything truly new in the sexual mind of a man for at least 500 years. The fantasies were always the same, year after year, culture after culture:

Making love to a wife's best friend or her sister, or to the big-breasted woman who once passed him in the street. Being ravished by an eager young wench, who can only be satisfied by *his* impressive manroot. Two women at once, pleasuring each other and the man with equal passion. Thrashing bare bottoms with a switch. Being thrashed in return, while wearing the wife's favorite chemise.

Well, that last one wasn't so common, but more so than most mortal women probably knew.

She was overdue for finding something new. Her own dream creativity had been suffering these past few years, and she needed inspiration. She was repeating herself too much, and often being so lazy as to give a man satisfaction with nothing more than a dream hand job.

She was becoming a disgrace to the succubi.

The only time she felt her old enthusiasm rising up was when she came across a sleeping man who was deeply in love, and needed nothing more than a dream of holding his beloved close in his arms and making love to her tenderly. For that, she still took time and care, and would feel within her a shimmering of emotion that she could not name.

Was it envy? A longing for something similar? She was not supposed to have a heart of her own, or human desires for things like love. In truth, she didn't understand love, except when it came as an intense sexual yearning. *That* she understood, and could feel as she reflected it back to a man. Something inside her whispered that love might be more than that, though. It might hold treasures of which she was utterly unaware, and which she could never know.

It made her want to weep, if only she were capable of it. Succubi had no tears, nor a heart to break.

But maybe, after so many centuries of playing in the minds of mortals, she had become infected by their emotions. Maybe part of her was turning slightly human. Humanity might be contagious, like the plague.

She wasn't sure if that was an encouraging thought, or a repulsive one.

What she did know for sure was that something interesting, like this tantalizing, unique thrum of male desire she was following, should not be passed by for so paltry a reason as fear. She would follow it and see where it led. How dangerous could it really be?

The thrum of desire from the unknown man was beginning to attract other succubi, who approached like wolves to a fresh kill. One, a blonde, approached too close to the stream of desire, and Samira bared her teeth, hissing, asserting her ownership. The blonde bared her teeth back, hissing in return, but then gave way, flapping off into the darkness, tossing her hair back over her shoulders with a pout and a glare.

Samira made a face at her, feeling disappointed. The coward. A territorial bat-fight would have been fun.

Samira turned her attention back to the thrum. The scent was growing stronger now. She must be nearing its source.

The warning sounded yet again in her mind, chasing a shiver down her spine. Something truly wasn't right about this thrum. Something wasn't natural. Three millennia of experience were telling her to slow down, to be cautious.

Curiosity and the deliciously strong desire of the sleeping man lured her forward, regardless. Common sense fled, and she happily waved it good-bye. Boring old common sense. What use had she for it?

She slipped out of the charcoal landscape of the Night World and emerged into the nighttime landscape of mortal men. The plane of the Waking World, they of the night called it. The hills and forest beneath her were the same as a moment before, only now they did not waver or shift, and their washed-out colors were from true night, not the influence of dreams. Everything was "real," everything was solid, and now she herself was the one who was not, and she could not be seen by waking eyes.

The land flattened out beneath her, and the trees gave way to fields and pasture. She flew low over the roofs of a village, and then on to the low, swampy, reed-clogged bank at the edge of a lake.

A fragile wooden walkway led from the bank out across the dark water to an island. She flew over the narrow walkway out toward the island, noting the missing boards and places where the rail had fallen into the black water.

As she approached the island, she made out the thick walls of a ruined fortified monastery, originally built for protection from invading Tartars and Turks. What was left of the brutal low outer walls were punctuated by two remaining stubby towers, guarded by a single dozing sentry.

Inside the crumbling fortress knelt a half-fallen stone church, its surviving walls blackened by long-extinguished flames. A massive square spire rose from one end, miraculously still standing, tall and strong. The spire dwarfed the outer protecting walls, thrusting upwards like a spear, its roof a tall tapering pyramid covered in red tile, the peak stabbing the night sky like a bloody blade that had pierced the belly of the moon.

A flickering yellow light glowed from the narrow windows in a room at the top of the high tower. It was from those windows that the river of desire flowed. A shiver of anticipation ran through Samira, the last vestiges of rational thought flickering and dying under the pull of the unknown man's desire.

Samira flew up toward the windows, and then alit on a sill, her hands clinging to the stonework. She crouched for a moment in the embrasure, peering inside at the square, dimly-lit chamber, and the man who slept therein.

When nothing threatening appeared, she folded her wings back and inched through the opening, scrabbling along like the demon she was. She dropped to the floor, landing soundlessly and with only the faintest sense of the rough-hewn wood floor beneath her bare feet. She could have passed straight through the wall itself if she had so desired, but such passages through solid matter were painful and tiring for succubi.

Red coals burned in a large iron brazier set on a tripod, and was the only source of heat in the room. Red velvet draperies half-concealed a wood-framed bed in one corner, its linens and furs disarranged and tumbling to the floor. Above her, beams held iron brackets where once had hung the bells of the tower.

A massive table dominated the room, covered in sheets of parchment and leather-bound books, some open, some shut, all of them cracked and stained with age. A candle guttered in its wax-coated holder, casting flickering light onto the books and the bare stone walls, and onto the single occupant of the room.

A dark-haired man slept with his arm sprawled across one of the open books on the table, his face resting on his white sleeve, his black hair concealing all but a pale triangle of forehead from her view. His other arm was drawn up close to his body, resting atop his thighs under the table.

It was from him that the river of latent desire was coming. This close, the desire was so strong that she could feel it coming into her as if through the pores of her skin, setting every inch of her alive with his tingling, unquenched lusts. She stood still, soaking it in, helpless for a moment to do otherwise. She'd never felt anything like this, the man's unsatisfied desires coursing through her body with the sweetness of honey, pooling in her loins with a hungry anticipation of things to come.

For the first time in all her thousands of years, she was vaguely aware of the danger of falling captive to the lusts of a man. It had always been easy for her to weave her dreams and fly away, never losing control, never being tempted to stay.

Such thoughts of control were far from her, now. Almost any thought at all was beyond her.

She tread silently across the room, sidestepping piles of books, and small tables loaded with vials, bowls, and jars of colored powders. Her gaze flicked over them, almost wondering what this man had been doing, but her mind was drifting in and out of a welter of caution and sexual excitement, and she could make no sense of the things.

She came around behind the sleeping man, noting the strong line of his back beneath his simple white tunic, and the broad line of his shoulders. His long legs, clad in heavy black hose, were sprawled beneath the table. He was seated on a bench, his body canted to the side in slumber.

Samira stepped lightly up onto the bench and squatted on her haunches next to him. His latent desire was coming off in waves, pulsing through her, her entire body vibrating in echoing response. It was so strong, she almost imagined that her body rippled with its pulse.

She reached out her hand toward him. It was shaking, and the sight startled her out of her passion for a moment, making her laugh nervously. *Midnight sun! You'd think I'd done this before*, she said to herself. *It's only a man. A sleeping man.*

She shifted from foot to foot, her bare breasts pressed against her thighs as she squatted beside him. She fluttered her wings once, nervous, making a rustling leathery sound. She wanted to touch him so badly, the desire was making her weak and uncoordinated.

She reached out again.

And again stopped, her fingertips a mere breath away from his pale forehead. She *should* be squatting on his chest, to have the best control over him. Impossible, given his position at the table. Clinging to his back would be a fair substitute, though.

She looked at the broad expanse, and quivered at the thought. She wanted to lay her breasts against him, to wrap her legs around his waist and to feel the total strength of his yearnings through every inch of her naked body. She wanted to melt into him, she wanted to become part of him, she wanted—

Her own eagerness stopped her, scaring her in its strength. What was happening to her? An hysterical fright climbed its way up her throat, and she felt on the verge of either wild laughter or a shriek.

Do it! she urged herself. *Touch him!*

No, there is danger . . . a softer voice within her said. *Think, Samira, something is not right . . .*

Without moving from her place on the bench, she closed the distance between her fingertips and his forehead.

Energy cracked through her with the force of lightning, slamming into her and blasting her away from him, her hearing deafened by a thunderclap of power even as her mind and senses reeled with a burst of images and emotions, blinding her to the room around her.

Instinct had her fluttering blindly into the safety of the air, images of battle and blood and ghastly violent horrors swimming before her eyes. She bumped against a spike protruding from a beam, the iron making her yowl in pain and sending her tumbling again through the air. When she came up against a wooden rafter she clung tightly to it as the images and emotions from the man washed through her: Fury. Despair. Utter, soul-destroying loneliness.

Her hearing began to clear, and through the ringing in her ears she made out a whimpering from deep in her throat, and from down below the sounds of the man, awake now and as scared as she was.

"Who's there?" he asked harshly, his deep voice bouncing off the stones of the walls. "I know you're here. Come out!"

The images of bloody mayhem faded from Samira's eyes, like the afterimage left from staring too long at the full moon. She blinked, and made out the man standing ten feet below her, turning round and round, staring into the shadows in search of the intruder.

Samira climbed on top of the rafter, taking careful note of where the iron spikes and brackets were placed on the beam. She lay atop the beam, a safe distance from the iron, and watched over the edge.

The man moved toward the heavy trap door near the end of the bed, his step betraying a limp. His left leg was plainly weakened, and she saw now that his left arm was held closer to his side than his right.

He unbarred the trap door and jerked it open, staring into the darkness below, his muscles tense. It was a long moment before he slowly shut the door again and slid the bar back into place. He turned round and looked carefully around the room.

Then he looked up.

Samira quickly hid her face behind the beam on which she lay.

He can't see you, you foolish creature! she reminded herself. Nevertheless, it was a moment more before she mustered the courage to look again.

He was squinting up into the darkness, but not directly at her. It gave her her first chance to see his face, his shoulder-length black hair now falling away from his features.

His brows were dark and devilish, with points at the center of their arches. A short, dark v-shaped beard covered his chin and upper lip, framing a masculine, sensuous mouth. Her gaze focused on the subtle lines and arches of those lips, and it was a long moment before she noticed the other remarkable feature of his face: a splash of webbed pink that started below his left eye and then poured down the side of his cheek, broadening to the width of a spread hand along his neck and then disappearing into his tunic.

She recognized the mark as a burn scar. In three millennia of being a succubus, she'd seen everything a human body had to offer, as well as a thousand vividly-imagined things it *did not*. Scars were nothing new, although one like this was unusual.

His gaze was still searching the darkness. She turned her own head and looked behind her, and saw that the roof of the tower stretched for another thirty feet above her, narrowing to a single point at the peak. To mortal eyes, anything at all could be lurking in that vast, dark space.

"I am Nicolae. Who are you?" he asked the shadows.

She caught her breath, surprised beyond words. He was trying to talk to her? *No one* ever tried to talk to her. In three millennia, no human. Not one.

"Show yourself. I know you're here. I can feel you." His voice was still edged with the harshness of fear, but he was gaining confidence, even his stance becoming stronger. He had his legs braced apart, his arms crossed over his chest.

She suddenly realized that she could no longer feel that unnaturally strong desire coming off him. His latent sexuality, yes, she could still feel that, could feel it pulling deliciously at her very core, but not to the exaggerated, frightening degree of before.

What had changed? Was it only his waking?

And how could he sense her presence?

"Or instead of asking *who* you are, perhaps I should ask *what* you are?" he asked, a brow lifting.

"I am not a *what*," Samira muttered, indignant, and then clamped her lips shut. It was stupid of her to make a sound.

But he gave no indication that he had heard her. He stared into the darkness above him for several seconds more, then lowered his head and shook it, as if dismissing his fancies. He rubbed the back of his neck, and limped slowly back to the table spread with books. He stared at the open book upon which he had been sleeping.

Samira hesitated, afraid he was bluffing, but then as the minutes went by and he continued to do nothing but stare at the book, she gathered the shreds of her courage and spread her wings, sliding off the beam. With a few gentle flaps she slowly coasted down to the floor, landing lightly on her feet at the opposite side of the table from him.

Nicolae lifted his face, a frown between his dark brows. Samira froze, fear blooming full force within her. She tensed, ready for flight. His gaze searched the area around where she stood, but again, he seemed to see nothing. She saw that his eyes were a warm, clear brown flecked with yellow, the iris rimmed by a darker brown that was almost black.

She stepped closer to the table, nervously watching his face for reaction and seeing none. She fought against her trembling fear and dared herself to test the limits of what he could sense. She leaned her hips against the edge of the wood.

No reaction.

She made herself bend forward, until her own face was inches from his, and she could almost imagine the faint feel of his breath against her skin. The puzzled look came back into his eyes, even as they failed to focus on her.

"Are you still here?" he whispered.

She blinked in astonishment.

He continued to stare blindly through her. "If you're here, please tell me. Show me, somehow."

She pressed her cheek to his, just enough so that the surface of hers made the lightest of contact with his. It was not a true touch of solid matter to solid matter, but he might feel the faint tingling of it.

He jerked his head back, startled, plainly having felt *something*, and it not having been to his liking. "What are you?" he demanded, the harshness back in his voice.

Something small suddenly broke inside her at the question, for it was as if he were interrogating a loathsome beast he'd found hiding under his bed. She was a *thing* to him. The sadness that had plagued her for six years welled up once again, and again she wanted to weep like a human, with tears to relieve the ache inside her.

For what was she? A defiler of a brother's love. A soulless creature with no heart, and no future other than to look from her lonely vantage into the loves and lusts of others, doomed always to pretend to live, and never to feel or grow or change.

She fought against the despairing thoughts, her pride begging her not to admit them even to herself. "I'm your every dream come true," she said aloud instead, fighting to believe her own words.

This man Nicolae was no better than her, she told herself. He had no one to love him, and he loved no one in return. He needed a *creature* like her, whether he knew it or not. He needed to be taken by her in his dreams, again and again, until he was drugged with pleasure and woke every morning with the echoes of bliss still in his blood, and the horrors of war pushed far to the back of his mind. Then he wouldn't need to ask her what she was. He would know, and be grateful.

Nicolae's gaze suddenly dropped, and she dropped her own to see where he was looking. It was the book upon which he had been sleeping. The open pages were covered in dense black writing, and in the middle of one was a drawing: a naked female with spread black wings. Before she could make sense of what that might mean, Nicolae touched the page with his fingertips, and suddenly Samira felt a powerful jolt of his sexual desire, the same as had drawn her to him in the first place.

"Good Christ!" he gasped.

Samira looked quickly at his face, and found her gaze met by his own wide-eyed one, his face gone pale and frozen as he stared at her. She jerked back, a small shriek escaping from her lips as she realized he could see her.

"What *are* you?" he asked again, his voice hoarse and fearful this time.

She backed away from the table, with his eyes following her every move. Fear coursed through her, chills washing over her skin in waves. He wasn't supposed to be able to see her, not while fully awake. This should not be happening. It *could* not be.

"Succubus," he said, the word as much a statement as a question.

She gathered what remained of her courage, and lifted her chin. Could he hear her, as well? "Samira!" she said, throwing out her name in frightened defiance. She would not be a *thing*. She had a name. She tossed her head, her crimson hair moving aside to reveal her full breasts.

His gaze dipped to them, and she felt the force of his desires pulse higher. In a desperate bid for control, she reached up and rolled one of her pink nipples between thumb and forefinger. His lips parted, and he stared at her moving fingers as if in a trance.

"Samira," she said again, firmly this time. She was an individual, not just another demon. Even as the force of his desire ran through her, bringing every inch of her to involuntary, tingling arousal, it was her name on his lips that she wanted most.

"Samira," he said, granting her wish as if he'd felt her demand.

She sucked in a breath, going as motionless as he was, her nipple in mid-roll. He'd heard her.

Good gods of the night, he'd heard her.

Nicolae lay his weak hand on the book and lifted the strong one, reaching across the table as if to touch her, almost as if he had no choice in the matter, feeling as drawn to make contact with her as she was to him. "Samira."

She swayed toward his outstretched hand, and took one step toward him, drawn by her name spoken so irresistibly in his deep, mortal voice.

He saw her. He knew her name. He spoke to her.

His fingertips were inches from her skin. If she took one more step, he'd be able to reach her. She remembered what had happened last time.

"You can't," she said on a weak breath, even as she could not stop herself from taking that final step toward him.

And again, the lightning bolt of energy blasted her

away from him, his emotions and memories storming again through her mind. She tumbled, hitting up against the stone wall and falling half through it before she could stop herself. She crawled back out of the dull ache of solid matter, her vision clearing to see Nicolae sprawled on the floor.

She whimpered deep in her throat. Was he dead? The river of energy had again been cut off.

She launched herself from the wall and with one awkward beat of her wings landed beside him, her whole body shaking with weakness and shock. She squatted down and peered at Nicolae's face, then at his chest. There was a slow rise and fall of breathing. Inside herself, she felt a faint beat. It was an echo of his own heartbeat, she realized in wonder. She had never felt such a thing before, from any man. Was it that lightning jolt of energy that had done it?

His heart might not beat much longer, if he received another jolt such as that, though, she realized. A sense of shamed responsibility for his injury washed through her. She hadn't wanted to hurt him; had only wanted to touch him.

She fluttered up into the air, hovering in the center of the room, not knowing what to do next. Stay or go? Fear, shame, and an unnamed longing—for what? for his attention?—did battle within her.

She should make up for what she'd done to him. It would be cruel to have him wake up feeling frightened and sore. The least she could do was give him a pleasant memory to take into his waking hours.

She floated down to the floor, and then gingerly touched his hand. Nothing unusual happened, and she gave a small sigh of relief. As she'd thought, there was no lightning bolt of energy between them without the magical book.

She crawled atop his chest and squatted, her bare feet planted neatly upon his sternum, her body rising and falling with his breathing, as if she were in a boat upon the ocean.

He was a handsome man, even unconscious. His lashes were heavy and dark, and a widow's peak of black hair dipped its spade into his pale forehead. He looked as if he had been physically powerful not long ago, but also as if he had been ill. It struck her as queerly sad, that such beauty as he possessed should spend itself on so frail and impermanent a being as a human.

She wasn't here to lament his eventual decline and death, though. She was here to give the man a moment of celestial pleasure.

She curled her toes in anticipation, reached out, and touched his brow.

Resource List

The Rites of Odin by Ed Fitch

A Dictionary of Ghost Lore by Peter Haining

Cornish Faeries by Robert Hunt

The World Guide to Gnomes, Fairies, Elves and Other Little People by Thomas Keightly

Ireland by Richard Lovett

Oicheanta Si (Faery Nights) by Michael mac Liammoir

The Ghost Book by Alsadair Alpine MacGregor

Spirits, Fairies, Leprechauns and Goblins by Carol Rose

Glossary, Place & Cast List

Abrial (from *Still Life*): "the Executioner"; night demon, killer for the Unseelie Court

Ahriman: Abrial's father

Az: Abrial's aunt

Bysshe: healer for the Seelie Court; Nyssa's missing mother

Cadalach: *tomnafurach; shian;* home of the Fey Parliament, located in Nevada

Chloe (from *Traveler*): sister to leader of Detroit chapter of H.U.G.; mother of a half-troll child

Clarissa (from *Traveler*): Chloe's half-troll daughter

Cyra Delphin (from *Outsiders*): half selkie, half kloka (a powerful conjurer)

Farrar: Pied Piper of Hamelin, Abrial's uncle

Father Lobineau (from *The Courier*): goblin; religious leader; current hive master of New Orleans

fey: any of the magical beings that have corporeal form, including all faeries, elves, and pixies

Fornix (from *Outsiders*): a general in the United States Army

goblins: also known as lutins; six-armed, greedy and odoriferous bipeds

Gofimbel: ancient king of goblins

Hille Bingels (from *Traveler*): current leader of the Detroit hive

hobgoblins: super-goblins—meaner, faster, and smellier

Horroban (from *Traveler*): late goblin king of Detroit

Humana Vox: goblin; second-in-command of L.A.'s King Carbon; televangelist

H.U.G.: Humans Under Ground, a movement founded by humans in 1973 to protest and work against magic and all things magickal

Innis: Lyris and Roman's infant son

Io Cyphre (from *Traveler*): half siren; wife of Jack Frost

Jack Frost (from *Traveler*): death fey and leader of the faerie folk of Cadalach

King Carbon: goblin; L.A. hive master

King Quede (from *The Courier*): late hive master of New Orleans, and master vampire

kloka: a conjurer elf that can cause visions for the masses; an illusionist

Lilith (from *Outsiders*): former hive master of Sin City

Lyris Damsel (from *The Courier*): half sylph

Mabigon: late queen of the Unseelie Court

Mathias: Jack and Io's two-year-old son

Meriel: Thomas and Cyra's infant daughter

Nyssa Laszlo (from *Still Life*): dreamwalker, ghost-talker

peri: a faerie of extreme beauty, a creature made mostly of light

pooka: a mischievous animal spirit, often takes the form of a river horse

Qasim (from *Still Life*): imprisoned leader of the hobgoblins

Quede (from *The Courier*): master vampire; goblin; king of the New Orleans Hive; killed by Roman

Roman Hautecoeur (from *The Courier*): pooka; wounded destroyer of King Quede

seelie: faeries belonging to the realm of light

selkie: one of a seal people who can shed their skin and assume human form on land

shian: a faerie mound

siren: a creature able to seduce with voice or glance

sylph: an animal fey; a hunter; often assumes the form of a raptor or fox

Thomas Marrowbone (from *Outsiders*): part jinn, part wizard, part peri, part dragon, all computer hacker

tomnafurach: another name for a shian

trolls: goblin thugs; stupid, slow, and vicious

Unseelie: faeries belonging to the darkness

Zayn (from *Traveler*): a healer, former member of Humans Under Ground

Important Dates in Fey History

10 BC — Abrial is born

14 AD — Abrial becomes executioner for the Unseelie Court

212 AD — the fey retreat to the underground begins

1367 AD — Gofimbel, Dragon Slayer, becomes first goblin king in Europe, uniting the warring hives

1692 AD — Qasim is born

1778-1792 AD — at the death of Gofimbel, the European Goblin Wars resume

1793 AD — The human expulsion of the goblins from Europe begins

1805 AD — Qasim, hobgoblin leader, is imprisoned by Mabigon

1806 AD — the other hobgoblins are imprisoned or executed

1973 AD — Humans Under Ground is formed

1991 AD — The Great Drought kills off almost all pure-blood fey

2001 AD — Jack & Io kill Horroban, cripple the Detroit hive; find Cadalach, new home of the fey resistance; establish Fey Parliament

2002 AD — Thomas & Cyra destroy the Sin City hive

2003 AD — Roman kills Quede, master vampire and head of the New Orleans hive

2004 — Lilith & Fornix are destroyed; Qasim, the leader of the hobgoblins, escapes

Author's Note

Hello—and good-bye for now—from The Wildside. *Still Life* is the last of the series for 2004. Other projects beckon (coax, demand, screech loudly), so I'll be taking a brief break from chronicling the antics of the Lutin Empire and moving on to new things. Don't worry, we'll be back soon.

Because many of you asked to know more about previous stories' characters—and especially their children—it was an easy decision to reunite them all for the great goblin battle that Nyssa and Abrial face in this book. Truly, I don't know how my hero and heroine would have survived without their friends' help when the showdown came.

The characters in this story are quirky, and it's my sincere hope that many of you will sympathize with their foibles—especially my heroine's shoe fixation. That trait is slightly autobiographical, though my own passion is less for Prada than for the wonderful fantasy shoes designed by Sergio for Spanish Leather. My favorite of his creations is a pair of burnt-red heels draped with gold chains. I feel like a gypsy dancer every time I put them on. . . . Sigh.

Abrial is another matter. I haven't a clue where he came from. I'd like to claim he was the man of my dreams, but I've never met anyone like him, not in this world or in the one of sleep. Hopefully you are as intrigued by him as I am.

I need to say some thanks to the people who contributed to the birth of this series. First and foremost, thanks must go to my husband for saying *why not goblins?* when I was hesitating about writing the first book. I also owe a huge debt of gratitude to Christine Feehan, who has been behind the series from the very first. She was there, a gentle ramrod, whenever I thought about quitting. Of course, I have to show appreciation to my editor and publisher for taking a chance on these books. Dorchester has the corner on the paranormal market, but even for them, this was going a long way out on a limb. Thank you, Chris and everyone.

Lastly, I want to say thanks to all the readers who have enjoyed and supported the series. You are wonderful! As always, I would love to hear from you. You can reach me through my website at www.melaniejackson.com, or at P. O. Box 574, Sonora, CA 95370-0574. If you feel the need to keep an eye on the goblins between books, they can be found at www.lutinempire.com. You can also reach any of my characters at this domain. Just write to their name—for example, Jack@lutinempire.com—and they will probably receive your e-mail. Though with the goblins, you just never know.

Blessings upon you,
Melanie

OUTSIDERS
MELANIE JACKSON

Cyra Delphin never felt quite right in her skin. As a child, her parents made her hide her gifts. What others are afraid to acknowledge—the modern world's seedy underbelly, its Wildside ruled by dark magic and goblins—doesn't simply go away. And when that darkness comes to call, Cyra seeks sanctuary in the Nevada desert.

She finds Thomas Marrowbone. Beneath his tormented shell lurks something powerful and inhuman, but also something primal and erotic. Cyra recognizes it, and for love she follows the enigmatic loner into the depths of Hell. The journey tests both their bodies and hearts . . . but their quest's success promises salvation and a happiness Cyra has never known.

TRAVELER
MELANIE JACKSON

Evil forces are on the rise, and Io is part of a secret association dedicated to stopping them. Lutins are replacing society's bigwigs—no one is safe. The only solution is to travel beneath the Motor City into the hordes thronging Goblin Town, rendezvous with Jack Frost and uncover the plot.

The quest will force Io through labyrinths of vice and challenge every aspect of her incomplete training. And if enemies aren't enough, her ally will imperil her heart. Jack Frost is much more than a simple sorceror: He rules the realms of love and death. Yet in Jack's hands, a little death could be a very, very good thing.

NIGHT VISITOR

MELANIE JACKSON

All self-respecting Scots know of the massacre and of the brave piper who gave his life so that some of its defenders might live. But few see his face in their sleep, his sad gray eyes touching their souls, his warm hands caressing them like a lover's. And Tafaline is willing to wager that none have heard his sweet voice. But he was slain so long ago. How is it possible that he now haunts her dreams? Are they true, those fairy tales that claim a woman of MacLeod blood can save a man from even death? Is it true that when she touched his bones, she bound herself to his soul? Yes, it is Malcolm "the piper" who calls to her insistently, across the winds of night and time . . . and looking into her heart, Taffy knows there is naught to do but go to him.

__52423-6 $6.99 US/$8.99 CAN

DOMINION
MELANIE JACKSON

When the Great One gifts Domitien with love, it is not simply
for a lifetime. Yet in his first incarnation, his wife and unborn
child are murdered, and Dom swears never again to feel such
pain. When Death comes, he goes willingly. The Creator
sends him back to Earth, to learn love in another body. Yet life
after life, Dom refuses. Whatever body she wears, he vows to
have his true love back. He will explain why her dreams are
haunted by glimpses of his face, aching remembrances of his
lips. He will protect her from the enemy he failed to destroy so
many years before. And he will chase her through the ages to
do so. This time, their love will rule.

THE SELKIE
MELANIE JACKSON

While the war to end all wars has changed the face of Europe, some things stay the same; the tempestuous Scottish coast remains a place of unquenchable magic and mystery. Sequestered at Fintry Castle by the whim of her mistress, Hexy Garrow spares seven tears for her past—all of which are swallowed by the waves.

By joining the water, those tears complete a ritual, and that ritual summons a prince. He is a man of myth whose eyes hold the dark secrets of the sea, and whose silken touch is the caress of the tide. His very nature goes against all Hexy has ever believed, but his love is everything she's ever desired.